LITTLE
DEADLY
SECRETS

LITTLE DEADLY SECRETS

a novel

PAMELA CRANE

wm

WILLIAM MORROW
An Imprint of HarperCollinsPublishers

LITTLE DEADLY SECRETS. Copyright © 2020 by Pamela Crane. All rights reserved. Printed in the United States of America. No part of this book may be used or reproduced in any manner whatsoever without written permission except in the case of brief quotations embodied in critical articles and reviews. For information, address HarperCollins Publishers, 195 Broadway, New York, NY 10007.

HarperCollins books may be purchased for educational, business, or sales promotional use. For information, please email the Special Markets Department at SPsales@harpercollins.com.

Originally published as *One Perfect Morning* in Great Britain in 2020 by HarperCollins Publishers.

FIRST U.S. EDITION

Library of Congress Cataloging-in-Publication Data has been applied for.

ISBN 978-0-06-298491-3

20 21 22 23 24 LSC 10 9 8 7 6 5 4 3 2 1

To the friends who have stood beside me, you are the light to my darkness. Keep shining.

Chapter 1

It was a strange, unexpected thought as I glanced over at the man I had married, wondering how the ugliest of hearts could be wrapped in the most beautiful skin. The down comforter was tucked up under his chin, hiding his lithe body that required no effort whatsoever to maintain. Sometimes I joked that I despised him for it—eating anything he wanted without gaining an inch on his waistline. If I even *looked* at dessert, I gained two pounds. Sometimes I wasn't joking when I said I hated him.

It wasn't that I *hated* him, not exactly. Years of togetherness had given me so much, but now he had taken too much. For so long I had just followed him blindly, until he led us both off the ledge. I needed to find my way back, and I couldn't do that with him anymore.

1

For years he had been my rock . . . tied to my ankles.

"I'm sorry," I whispered, and I meant it.

Once upon a time we had loved each other deeply. It showed in the way he carried me over the threshold when we first bought this house. Or when we took our first vacation together to Asheville, North Carolina, where we toured the Biltmore House and oohed and aahed over the thousands of tulips blooming in the gardens. Or the first time we made love, on a bed of rose petals as he sucked the tender spot on my neck and caressed my thigh longingly. Those memories had been so pure and good. But now only painful memories remained. Like chess pieces, the bad had knocked all the good off the board.

All I could remember right now was the way he hurt me. The way he betrayed me. The way he lied.

A moonbeam cast a silvery stripe across the bed. He slept soundly beneath covers that were charcoal like the sky, unaware of me standing over him, and I regretted what I was about to do. I wondered if he had any unspoken regrets. I had a mouthful of them. I had spent the best years of my life loving this human being more than anything else, deeply and passionately with a forbidden desire I couldn't quench. Only now did I realize it had never been love, but obsession—an obsession with stability, with security. I needed him, but he had never needed me back.

We had been wrong from the beginning, I knew this, but I let him consume me regardless. Nothing could stop me, not even myself. Not even all the red flags.

The mystery of love—yes, it had enthralled me, and now here we were, lost in its unanswerable riddle. I still couldn't figure it out, why I had ever loved a monster. Some days he felt like a warm rain, but recently he had become a torrent sweeping me out to a stormy sea, drowning me.

Now here I stood over him, wrapped in Sunday morning nostalgia, watching him sleeping in the Ethan Allen four-poster bed we shared, controlling my breath as I whispered my good-byes. I reminisced about the idyllic weekends of long ago. Pure heaven. The scent of French roast coffee wafting to our bedroom, the humming stillness of the house, two lovers pretzeled together beneath mulberry silk sheets, our bodies sweat-glazed from creative and energetic sex.

Now that was laughable, really. His touch burned me, his lips disgusted me. Not because of time's toll on our bodies— gravity works extra hard after age forty, you know. It wasn't that. It was the slow rot of who he used to be. Once upon a time, we cuddled like two toothbrushes in a cup, the length of our bodies resting on one another. I wished I could reach that man today, right now, but I knew he was long gone.

I thought about the apology flowers he had just bought me, how his face lit up as he handed them to me. How I tenderly placed them in a vase, admiring his thoughtfulness for a moment. That moment had dried up with the crisp petals currently scattered along the coffee table. Wilted, dead flowers—they were my marriage's final curtain call, but they weren't enough. Not to save us. Not to save *him*.

"Remember when we first got married and lived in that tiny apartment in the basement of Cat Lady's house?" The whispered question was more for myself than for him. I didn't want to risk waking him. I shook the memory loose.

Cat Lady was the nickname we gave the white-haired

woman who rented out her basement to us. We could never remember her actual name—it was Slavic, with too many syllables for our all-American tongues to pronounce—but she had at least a dozen cats that we counted the only time she let us into the first floor of the house. The ammonia stench took our breath away; it was a wonder the waterfalls of cat piss didn't leak through the floorboards into the ceiling of our apartment below. Life had been so full of adventure and hope back then.

"We used to snuggle up on that ratty old sofa we found on the curb, talking about our plans for the future." I smiled at the memory. Reaching out a finger, I touched his stubbly cheek and recoiled in distaste.

I would never forget when the mouse came crawling out of the sofa cushion and darted across my leg. I was pretty sure the whole neighborhood heard me scream. The most baffling part about it was how the mouse had managed to slip by a dozen cats. I chuckled softly, then wiped a tear that dripped down my cheek.

The Simple Days, I called them. Back then, when life made sense and I knew who I was, where I was going. These days I aimlessly trudged through the mire of one moment to the next.

I couldn't resurrect the Simple Days, though, could I? They were too far gone. Some things just aren't meant to last, no matter how many stars we naïvely wish upon.

My eyes traveled down his sleeping body—his brawny arms hugging his pillow like it was an illicit lover, his long legs sprawling under the covers. Asleep, his face looked so sweet and boyish, incapable of uttering a harsh word or criticism. Of course, I knew that was only an illusion. In the mad rush of days filled with housekeeping and packing school lunches and folding laundry and prepping dinner, I rarely saw the softer side of him anymore. We rarely saw each other at all.

The barking of the next-door neighbor's dog prodded me with sudden urgency. Before long the street would erupt in the commotion of families rushing off to church or Sunday breakfast. I needed to make this quick, get it over with before I talked myself out of it. Or before he woke up. It was time.

There's no better time than the present, my mother often said. Even when it didn't relate to anything pertinent, she loved using that tired old cliché. I was still wearing yesterday's clothes, hadn't bothered to slip into pajamas when I snuck back in this morning. Pajamas wouldn't fit with the story I had already planned out. I could feel daybreak approaching. While early risers all across my suburban neighborhood held steaming mugs of coffee, I held the knife I'd slid out of the butcher block minutes ago. My hand trembled as I lifted the blade and sucked in a steadying breath.

Lightly moving the covers aside, I took one last long, lingering look at the man I was about to kill. The man I had sworn to love and cherish until death do us part. And yet I had kept my vow, hadn't I? On the count of three I would forever alter my future—giving myself the freedom I needed, the sole choice I had never been given to control my own life.

One.

Two.

Three.

I pressed the blade lengthways against his throat. I closed my eyes and turned my head. His flesh resisted. But not for long. While across the neighborhood wives kissed their husbands good morning, I planted Death's kiss on mine.

Chapter 2

NINE DAYS AGO

When you put three best friends from college in a room together, you're asking for trouble. And trouble was exactly what Robin Thompson, Mackenzie Fischer, and Lily Santoro had found.

The rain hadn't stopped since last night, spreading a dreary gray haze across the morning sky. It was typical Western Pennsylvania spring weather, making sunshine and blue skies a rare event. Robin, Mackenzie, and Lily sat thigh to thigh in the living room where tiny smudged handprints "decorated" the antique white walls. Lily, who had no fondness for children, often sardonically compared them to the ones on the walls of the creepy abandoned house in the climax of *The Blair Witch Project*. That flick had freaked

7

them all out when they'd gone to see it together back in 1999. It had cured them of the desire to ever go on a camping trip together.

Robin reached for her favorite teal mug, grabbing empty space instead. "Has anyone seen my coffee?"

It wasn't her fault she was so forgetful. It came hand in hand with having young kids. Like forgetting the load of wet laundry still in the washing machine, now turning mildewy. Or the milk you accidentally placed in the cupboard and the cereal box you put in the fridge. Or the cup of lukewarm coffee you never got around to drinking after you misplaced it for the umpteenth time.

Lily laughed while Mackenzie empathized.

"It's probably in your bathroom," Mackenzie said. "That's always where I find mine."

Lily shook her head. "*Allora*, when you have kids, do they suck your brains out? You both are perpetually losing shit . . . mostly your minds."

"It's true. Kids do that to you. But they're worth it." Robin kissed the sleeping baby she held against her breast. Nestled in Robin's arms was her youngest, Collette, an eight-month-old bundle of cuteness and colic. Robin couldn't remember the last time she'd enjoyed a full night's sleep.

"Did you know that the average mother doesn't sleep soundly for the first six years of her child's life?" Robin pondered aloud.

"That means you haven't slept in"—Mackenzie paused, mentally calculating the math—"eighteen years, Robin. And you still have six years to go. Girl, you're overdue for a nap!"

"And that is why I'll never have kids. Too much work and not enough sleep makes Lily a dull girl." Lily stood up from the soft leather sofa stained with breast milk and an unknown sticky substance. She hoped it was just juice. A pile of Cheerios had collected where she had been sitting. As she shuffled past Robin, their knees bumped and Lily gripped the coffee table with one hand to steady herself. "*Che schifo*, Robin! Don't you ever clean? *Puah!*" Lily squinted with disgust as she examined something gooey on her fingers.

"Is that Italian for you offering to do it?" Robin lobbed the question back at her.

"If I knew it'd stay clean, I would."

But that was the nature of motherhood. Dirty and selfless. Unsung heroism as they tended to real life in the background while their husbands wore scrubs and suits to work, building their careers while the mothers built their homes.

The women wore fake smiles, hiding their secrets like they did every day. On their own they were bitterness, submission, and obsession. Together they were loyal, inspired, and fierce. But there were some things out there that could break the strongest of bonds. And that something had found them today.

"Are we still on for dinner Sunday night?" Mackenzie asked. "The kids always have a blast at your dinner parties."

Robin nodded, rocking back and forth in her seat as Collette fussed herself awake. "Of course. Grant's even cooking on the grill. He told me it's *a meal that will change our lives*, whatever that means."

The three women laughed at the great pride Grant took in his grilling techniques, unaware of just how right he was. That night would forever change their lives, splitting their world open and letting the ruthless reality pour out.

1999, PIZZA JOE'S, BEAVER FALLS, PENNSYLVANIA

If you were a teenage girl in the 1990s, you couldn't escape the girl band sensation the Spice Girls. Maybe you even danced to their pop music, emulated their glam fashion, or fantasized about being them. The Spice Girls had distinct personas; it goes without saying every girl had her favorite. The year was 1999, in a small Western Pennsylvania town hugging the outskirts of Pittsburgh, where three best friends in college formed their own girl group, the Spicier Girls. Except they weren't exceptionally musical or gifted at synchronized dancing.

Lily was the natural-born leader, the hand-talking Italian, the rebel, the creator. She spoke life into action, and it obeyed. Everyone submitted to Lily because she was a power you didn't question, and a force you trusted.

Robin was the planner, the organized one, the goody-goody, the glue. Her brilliance was not just in her sharp mind, but in the way she dotingly tended to people like flowers. Gently, lovingly, as if each one would wither and die without her magic touch. And in some cases they did.

And then there was Mackenzie, the sheltered Southern belle of the ball, except she had forgotten her worth long ago. She was the victim who didn't know she could be the victor. She was always there, the supporting actress in her own life, applauding everyone's achievements but her own.

They were simply three friends brought together by fate, who lived to be loved by one another, sealed with a pact to stay friends for life . . . a pact that would test their bond for decades to come. They were there for one another through the laughter and tears, and they were there when everything shattered.

"What do you think life will be like after we graduate college?" Robin's gaze trailed from Lily to Mackenzie, then to the cute server she'd been flirting with for the past twenty minutes while they waited for their large pizza, extra cheese. Mackenzie claimed that pepperoni would make her nauseous; Lily thought she was a hypochondriac.

"Well, if you're Mac, you'll marry the first guy who asks you." Lily coughed the name *Owen*. "Then pop out two-point-four kids, overextend yourself in a mortgage you can't afford, and live blissfully ignorant in your suburban soccer-mom existence." Lily nudged Mackenzie's side, her lips lifted in a playful smile.

"Hey, what's that supposed to mean?" Mackenzie whined, propping her elbows on the black-and-white-checkered tablecloth. Her ponytail swung back and forth, brushing her narrow shoulders. With her blond hair and blue eyes people often mistook her for a cheerleader, and Mackenzie always huffily corrected them that she was a book nerd. "Don't be a hater just because I know who I am and what I want, and Owen happens to be the perfect guy for me."

"*Per favore*, perfectly narcissistic and controlling, you

mean," Lily scoffed. "You've known him for like a minute and you're already planning a future with him."

"Whatever. It's not like I'm marrying him. We're just seeing where things go."

"Lily's right, Mac," Robin interjected. "We're only sophomores in college—take a few different guys out for a test run before you settle down."

Mackenzie rolled her eyes, then followed Robin's stare. "Speaking of cruising for guys, you gonna ask Cute Waiter Guy out, Robin?"

"I don't need to. He'll do the asking, I'll do the accepting."

"Wow, you sure are confident," Mackenzie grumbled.

"She should be," Lily retorted. "And you should be too, Mac. Hell, we all should be confident. We're young, we're hot, we're amazing. And we don't need men to be happy, *capisce*?" Lily aimed the question at Mackenzie, who shrugged it off.

"What about you, Lil—what do *you* think life will be like after college?" Robin asked.

"We've only just begun *this*. I still have two years left before I need to figure out life after college." Lily had always lived moment by moment, a trait that Robin yearned for and Mackenzie loathed.

"Have you even picked a major yet? You need to start figuring things out, Lil, because before you know it, we'll be out in the real world." Mackenzie, always the realist.

Lily thoughtfully sipped Dr. Pepper from her extra-large Styrofoam cup and sighed. "I want to do something adventurous. With lots of travel. But I don't ever want to lose touch with you girls. I want us to grow old together."

Mackenzie rested her hand on Lily's. "Me too, Lil. You

guys are my best friends. I'm so glad we got stuck together as dormmates. Let's never lose touch, okay?"

"Promise," Robin said, adding her hand to the pile.

"Girl power and forever friends. We'll be like the Spice Girls—only spicier." Lily winked.

"The Spicier Girls?" Mackenzie parroted with a contagious laugh.

"That's right, we're the Spicier Girls. I'll be Adventure Spice, Robin can be Homemaker Spice, and Mackenzie's Dr. Spice."

"Dr. Spice?" Mackenzie raised a skeptical flaxen eyebrow.

"Because you're super smart and majoring in science," Lily explained. "Together we'll rule the world."

The girls giggled as Cute Waiter Guy carried the pizza to their booth and slid it onto the table.

"My friend thinks you're cute"—Lily adjusted the name tag on his uniform for a better look—"Geoffrey F. You should ask her out." Lily pointed to Robin, whose cheeks flushed with embarrassment.

The boy flashed a cocksure smirk. "I don't need to ask. I just take."

Lily glared up at him with shrewd eyes almost the color of coal. "Then you can *just take* your ass elsewhere. No one messes with the Spicier Girls." Lily flung an arm around Mackenzie while Robin hid her blushing face behind her hands and auburn bangs.

As he left, Robin peeked between her fingers. "God, you're embarrassing. I can do my own asking out, thankyouverymuch. Why do I put up with you?"

"Because you luuuurve me." Lily beamed at her two best

friends, the sisters she never had but had always wished for. "We gotta stick together, right, girls? You know I'll always have your backs."

"And we've always got yours. Until death do us part." Mackenzie pulled the trio into a group hug, arms linked, foreheads touching, as they burst into self-deprecating chuckles.

"Oh, that reminds me," Mackenzie said, producing three colorful cords from her pocket. "I made these friendship bracelets—one for each of us." She passed the macramé charms out, and each girl fastened the delicate metal clip.

Robin traced the threads with one finger. "Fits perfect. And it's gorgeous. Thanks, Mac. You're a creative genius."

Typically, she deflected the compliment with a wallflower's diffidence. "I've got an idea. Everyone repeat after me." Mackenzie bounced in her seat, a happy dance, as poetry effortlessly flowed from her lips:

"With this bracelet I do vow
To these two girls forever bound.
Through life and love, through thick and thin
Until that day when death will win."

That night was the beginning of an era. The inauguration of a lifelong sisterhood, of shared dreams and tears and secrets and lies that would one day unravel their friendship to its core.

Chapter 3

Mackenzie

Melting skin. Charred flesh. Heat ripping through my cells, crisping the side of my wilting face. The fire blazed around me, imprisoning me as flames climbed the kitchen walls, blocking my escape. I wanted to scream, but my voice fell mute. Then I heard her calling me, her silhouette visible on the other side of my fiery prison:

"Mackenzie."

I couldn't answer her. I choked on the thick smoke.

"Mackenzie!"

Except it wasn't her. And it wasn't back then. It was now, and it was Owen calling me.

"Babe, you're burning the gravy," he said.

I blinked myself back into my own kitchen, where I stood in front of the gas stove, eyes transfixed on the blue flame licking the pot. I turned off the burner and stirred the bubbling sauce. Outside the patter of rain tapped on the glass.

"Sorry . . . I must have been in a daze."

"You look exhausted. Long day, huh?"

I nodded numbly, the vision still so clear, so alive in my mind. Over the years, I could never truly lay the memory to rest, no matter how hard I tried. A therapist once told me as long as I continued to harbor bitterness over the accident, I'd never move past it. But who could blame me? She had not only disfigured my face, but also marred my entire life. And somehow she was still my closest friend.

Despite the pact, bitterness over a distant mistake I had never forgiven festered in me like a cancer. Over time it began rotting the only good left in me. No matter how much time passed, the resentment rattled inside my heart.

After dinner was served, Owen talked about work while Aria caught me up on school and her weekend plans. I asked all the right questions and laughed at the right times, never uttering a word about my *daymare*, because it was upsetting to Owen, and God forbid my past trauma upset him. So instead I started writing about it in my journal of horrors. It didn't matter anymore, though. Tonight I would shed my Owen-pleasing shell, initiating my revolution.

But like all revolutions, there would be bloodshed. For once, it wouldn't be my own.

I am a people pleaser. And I fail at it miserably. The

problem with people pleasers is that in their attempt to please everyone, they please no one. Least of all themselves.

Take tonight, for instance. It unfolded in the way that all people pleasing unfolds—where I'm always the loser. It was a role I had adapted to well over the years. But now I was determined to win, even at the cost of lying, of creating a secret that my husband would never forgive. I didn't care about his forgiveness anymore. Tonight my people pleasing was put on hold as I put my plan in motion.

"How do you like the roast, shugga pie?" I asked, stabbing a slice of beef with my fork and rolling it in thick gravy. I grinned, knowing how Owen hated the countrified way I said *sugar* as my Southern drawl slipped out here and there. I'd spent a lifetime burying it, but apparently not deep enough. One's roots had a way of worming to the surface.

Ironically, he loved Southern cooking, just not Southern talking. He couldn't get enough of my fried chicken, but God forbid I slip up when *warshing* the clothes or *fixin'* to make supper. According to him and his stringent Western Pennsylvanian upbringing, Southerners sounded stupid and illiterate . . . not that a dialect had anything to do with one's ability to read or write. But I never dared challenge him on this, because a good wife never should. Especially one who was about to lie to his face and leave his life a crumbled heap of rubble.

"It's delicious, Mac." Owen was a meat and potatoes kind of guy, and I hoped dinner would be the perfect bribe. "Tender and juicy, just how I like it."

Owen winked at me from across the handcrafted oak table that we paid too much for but was worth every penny, and

I chuckled while Aria groaned next to me. "Ew, Dad. Seriously, extra cringey."

Ah, the teen angst. Everything parents did was either mortifying or smothering or neglectful. We could never win. But I suppose it was the plight of every parent with a fifteen-year-old daughter.

Owen glared at Aria. "You should appreciate that your parents are still together and in love. Most marriages don't last as long as ours has."

When he turned his attention back to me, he flashed that same charming grin that had won me over more than twenty years ago, brimming with boyish mischief mixed with desire. *Blondes have more fun,* he had told me, *which is what first drew me to you.* Despite his many faults, he knew how to win me over again and again. With Owen, all it took was a smile. With me, all it took was a lie Owen wanted to believe.

"It's true, Aria," I said. "I'm so lucky to have a man like your dad to keep the marriage thriving." The words tasted bitter, but I pasted on the same adoration I did every night over dinner.

"It's just that I'm trying to eat and imagining you guys . . . ugh, never mind. I'm happy if you guys are happy."

"Oh, Aria, one day I hope you experience what love like this feels like. One day far in the future, though. Not anytime soon, ya hear?"

I squeezed her hand, and she laughed with a shake of her head. "Don't worry, Mom. I'm not at risk of falling in love anytime soon. The boys in my class are either self-absorbed jerks or clueless nerds. Definitely not my type."

"Good girl. Stay away from the boy drama. It's nothing

but heartache at your age." I stabbed a cooked carrot with my fork, saluted Aria, and popped it in my mouth.

Sure, we had our battles over curfew and chores, but Aria had always been my miracle, in more ways than one. My miracle child after I found out I had polycystic ovarian syndrome; my miracle angel because of how perfect she was. While other teenagers rebelled, my Aria remained *my* Aria. My devoted sidekick, shopping companion, pedicure lover, partner in crime. I could never figure out what exactly I had done *right* to end up with a teenager who enjoyed my company and laughed at my jokes and watched romantic comedies with me on Saturday nights, but I didn't question it often. Maybe it was Owen's divisive nature that nudged us closer. Or maybe it was her genetic code that made her a mommy-pleasing mini-me. My petite blond-haired, blue-eyed duplicate. Whatever it was, it worked for us and I loved her for it.

"Are you coming to Lily's with me tonight to work out?" I asked her.

Owen darted his eyes at Aria, then at me. "What's this about Lily?"

I chewed my last bite of meat, silently configuring the words in my brain. I hadn't anticipated his sudden interest in my workout schedule with my best friend. This wouldn't do—not at all. I had too much planned for this evening, and I couldn't risk his interference.

"Mind if Aria and I head over to the gym to meet Lily? Lily invited me to work out with her on Friday nights—plus it's free training so I can get in shape." The word *free* usually won him over, unless it involved golf, in which case no cost was too high. "I'm still trying to lose the weight I gained over

Christmas." Sure, the holidays had been five months ago, but it took ten times longer to lose weight than it did to gain it. I pinched the flab around my waist, a nervous reflex.

"No, not tonight. I'd prefer you stay home, Mackenzie. It's not like those exercises are going to help; you never stick to them anyway."

"That's the whole point, Owen. I'm trying to stick to it this time. I really want to lose the weight, feel good about my body." It was so like Owen, to refuse such a simple request in his need for control. This was why I lied. This was why I kept secrets. This was why I came up with the plan. But I didn't feel like fighting tonight. I needed everything to go smoothly—as smoothly as it could go when plotting your husband's demise.

He laughed, and I shrunk at the scornful undercurrent. "Hon, I love you, but nothing you do is going to turn back the clock. Not those age-defying creams you junk up the bathroom with. Not all those useless exercise gadgets you pick up at Costco. You aren't nineteen anymore, *shugga pie*. Just accept the way you look and learn to love it. *I* have."

I knew what his thinly veiled reference really signified. I touched the scar on my face and thought of *her*. The skin felt rough and rubbery, a shiny wrinkled patch that ran up my neck along my cheek. I knew I wasn't any beauty queen, but at least I could cover my disfigurement up when I styled my hair a certain way.

"Why do you have to be so cruel?"

"Oh, stop being so self-conscious. I married you looking like that, didn't I? You know I love you no matter what you look like."

But I didn't know that. If it wasn't my body that he found lacking, then it was the way I talked, or my cooking, or my housekeeping, or my childrearing. Maybe other women would be grateful if their husbands didn't care if they let themselves go, but for once I wanted control over my own damn weight. Control over anything, really, but my own workout regimen seemed like the only option within reach.

"I already told Lily I'd meet her, so I have to go." I dropped my cloth napkin on the table and rose from my chair, taking my plate with me. Beneath the smear of meat juices, the cherry blossom pattern peeked out from the white background of the dish. I remember picking the pattern out, with Owen hovering over my shoulder. I had initially wanted a turquoise dinnerware set—something bright and bold, the way I wanted to feel on the inside. *Too blinding,* Owen had scoffed. *Let's go with something more subdued.* We came home with sixteen settings of pale pink cherry blossom that afternoon. And I had hated it ever since.

Aria had stayed silent during our tiff, but I could sense her seething. She followed me to the kitchen with her plate and deposited it in the sink.

"Mom, mind if I skip and catch up on some reading? I've almost finished *Doctor Sleep*. We'll work out together some other time," she said. She gave me a quick peck on the cheek, adding, "By the way, Mom, I think you're beautiful."

I needed that. God, how I needed that!

As I placed my dirty dishes in the sink, Owen's footsteps padded behind me. His arm draped across me, pulling my back against his chest. His breath tickled my ear as his lips kissed my earlobe.

21

"C'mon, it's raining and miserable out. Stay home and watch a movie with me," Owen whined. "Besides, it's not safe for a woman to be out after dark alone. Not every husband loves spending time with his wife as much as I love spending time with you, Mac. You should be grateful."

"I am grateful, I just . . . I need time out of the house. Being here all day, every day, well . . . sometimes I need to get out. Be with friends." See that? I had slipped a truth in with the lie. He didn't know I had spent the morning gossiping with the girls, and I wouldn't tell him either.

"Mac, you're acting awfully strange tonight. What's going on?"

Cold apprehension snaked up my neck. Did he know what I was up to?

"Nothing's going on. I'm just worn slap out. And, you know, my usual anxiety that I'm trying to work on—remember? I can't fix it if I don't face it. Please don't fight me on this."

Another defective thing about me was my social anxiety. I had self-diagnosed when looking up the symptoms on WebMD one day. It had started off innocuously at first, right after I'd given birth to Aria. Breaking out in a cold sweat when I went grocery shopping alone. Pulse racing when heading to Mommy and Me activities. Hives spreading across my neck when talking to the bank teller.

As dread of leaving the house weighted my feet down, I nursed the anxiety to life by quitting Mommy and Me and isolating myself from everyone. That's when my friends took notice and begged me to get help. *You need to get out and have some fun,* Lily had scolded me in her protective Italian mamma way. *If you don't take control of your life, you're going to crack,* Robin had warned. Boy, were they right. After all, it wasn't normal to break out in hives when talking to people, was it? Days before a planned outing, I would stress and worry myself into a migraine, until I lost every part of my life outside my four walls.

Who had I become? Certainly not the aspiring free-spirited traveler I remember from college. The girl who ate authentic pad thai in Thailand, rode horses on a beach in Puerto Rico, and helped build an orphanage in Mexico. That girl was dead, buried, forgotten. But I was bringing her back to life, even if it killed me . . . or preferably, Owen.

"I don't want to fight either." Owen pouted. "But you can take one night off to spend with me. I have something special planned for tonight."

"Oh really? Why do I have a feeling you just suddenly came up with these *special plans*?"

"Come on, babe. I do everything for you. This house—it's for you. The cars—for you. Why can't you give back just a little?"

"Seriously, Owen? You don't think I give back?"

"Of course you do. I just want you here tonight, with me."

Grabbing me around the waist, Owen lifted me up, propping me on the cultured marble counter. I straddled his waist with my legs and he cupped my chin with his palm.

"I promise I'll make it worth your while. You stay home with me to watch any movie you want, and I'll give you a full-body massage tonight. Happy ending for you included." He whispered the words in my ear, and I almost couldn't resist.

Damn it. My biggest weakness—a massage. But my plans . . . I couldn't put them off any longer. I needed to set things in motion while I still had the nerve to finish what I started.

"Please don't," I begged. "I promised Lily."

"Then break your promise." If only he knew how many promises I had already broken. His lips kissed a trail down my neck—the side that hadn't been marred by fire—dashing the angry red splotches of anxiety away. "Imagine my hands rubbing all that stress away."

It did sound amazing. And it had been ages since I'd last gotten a massage. Besides, there was no way he was letting me out tonight, so I might as well get something out of it.

"Fine. But it better be a five-star backrub—or else."

"Anything for my girl."

My ass!

Two hours later, after Owen whined his way into watching what *he* wanted, a sci-fi action movie filled with soulless CGI, rather than the uplifting romantic comedy I'd picked out on Netflix, the selfish bastard snored beside me in bed while I pulled out a book to read. *Pretty Ugly Lies*, a nifty psychological thriller about a psycho wife plotting to murder her no-good husband. *Ha, maybe I'll get some tips,* I joked to myself. He'd reneged on my promised massage too. It didn't matter, though. Tomorrow was another day, another chance. And then, for the first time in my life, I could stop the lies and deceit. But as it turns out with most people pleasers, that was just another lie—the worst kind. A lie to myself.

Chapter 4

Robin

Nine Days Ago

My husband was going to kill me if I didn't get around to it first. Even if I did take my own life, I'd need to make sure it didn't look like a suicide. Life insurance policies didn't pay out for suicide. By tomorrow I would be front-page news on the *Monroeville Times Express*: HUSBAND MURDERS WIFE OVER $40,000 CREDIT CARD DEBT. Even if Grant didn't kill me, he'd divorce me. I couldn't let him find out, not until I figured out a way to pay it off.

Folding the paper credit card statement back into thirds, I tucked it into the envelope, ripped it in half, and tossed it in the garbage, shoving it under a slimy chicken foam tray for good measure. Eliminate the evidence, then deal with the debt. I had no idea how, and I wish I'd considered that sooner—particularly before a 21 percent interest rate hit. *Why not enjoy it now when you can pay for it later?* That had become my mantra in my quest to live uninhibited, and it was catching up with me. I'd lived in an organized, efficient box for so long. I had wanted out, I had wanted freedom, I had wanted to be like Lily. And now all I wanted was to return to my safe, square box.

Debt was a persistent stalker.

In the living room Grant's cell phone silently buzzed against an antique oak end table. I often wondered why he kept it on silent, what he was hiding, but I never asked. He was the perfect spouse—reliable provider, adoring father, attentive husband. I had no reason to be suspicious of his vibrating phone or calls taken out on the back porch. But a wife couldn't help but wonder. After all, I had my own secrets, so maybe he had his.

A moment later the vibration stopped and his deep voice rumbled throughout the first floor. I was hiding a mountain of debt; Grant was hiding his calls. I guess we all had our hidden skeletons. Though mine seemed to be piling up lately.

As I shut the garbage can lid, Grant strode into the kitchen, pecking me on the cheek. "Babe, I'm heading out now."

"Out? Now? It's almost eight o'clock at night and raining pretty bad. Plus, it's Friday. I thought we were going to spend the evening together?" I hoped the disappointment tinting the question would guilt him into staying home. We were long overdue for a night together. Cold sheets had created a rift between us that only hot sex could bridge; certainly he felt it too.

"Sorry, I forgot it was poker night with the guys. You know I can't miss it or I'll never hear the end of it. We'll do something tomorrow."

I groaned. "Grant, you were out of town for that medical conference thing all last week, and this week you've been working late every night. I need some time with you. I miss you."

"I miss you too, but we've got a flu outbreak, honey. I can't help it that my schedule's crazy right now. Patients need me; I can't turn sick kids away."

"I'm not asking you to skip work. I'm asking you to skip poker night."

"Robin, I can't. I've already missed the last couple times. Can't you wait up for me? I won't be home late."

"You know things never work out when we try to plan time together. For once Willow and Ryan are both at friends' houses tonight, Lucas is in bed, and I finally got Collette nursed, diaper changed, and she's settled down. We've got at least a couple hours of uninterrupted time together." I grabbed his hand and kissed his fingers.

His sigh was weighty as he released my hand. "Honey, as tempting as that sounds . . ."

"I'll do anything you want tonight—*anything*." My words were laced with desire as I unbuttoned his top button, then another, tickling his chest with my fingertip. I could be persistent when I wanted to. "I know what you like . . ."

I brushed my lips against the patch of exposed skin, then licked it and smiled up at him.

"Please. It's been so long, Grant." Too long. Months long. We needed this. Our marriage needed it.

"You're killing me," he said, pulling me in for a kiss.

"Is that a yes?" I said between panting breaths and urgent fondling.

His hands gripped me hard, almost too hard as if I'd flitter away. It had been days since we'd had more than a passing peck on the cheek. His crazy work schedule, four demanding children, a nursing infant—it had taken a toll on our love life and right now, more than anything, I wanted to make up for it.

My core ached for my husband, and as his hands slid up my back, lifting my shirt with his warm palms, I knew he wanted me too. I remembered the last time we'd made love: a rare night of passion that ended abruptly when Lucas wandered into our bedroom, scared that Mommy was being attacked by a monster. That monster was Daddy.

Unbuckling Grant's belt, I pulled him toward the bedroom with my hand gripping his open waistband. I could feel his swelling erection against my probing finger-tips. As he tore my shirt up and over my head, his lips searching my neck, my pulse jumping under his tongue, I felt the rush of adolescent newness, the rush of passion, the rush of . . . Collette's cries.

Everything came to an abrupt stop. Collette's whimper echoed from the baby monitor.

"Oh, come on!" I grumbled into Grant's chest.

"Well, that ends that. As usual."

He was pissed, and I couldn't blame him. Hell, I needed it just as much as he did.

"Please don't leave. She'll go back to sleep," I assured him. But he was already rebuttoning his shirt. I was losing him—and not just tonight. The distance between us was growing into a wide chasm.

"Honey, we both know you're going to spend the next hour soothing her. Then another hour getting her back to sleep. By then I'll be home. Let's take a rain check."

"I don't want a rain check. I want tonight—with you."

Collette's shrieks on the monitor intensified. He gestured at the frantically blinking red light.

"Robin, her majesty is summoning you. I'll see you later."

I grabbed his wrist, forced him to look me in the eye.

"Grant, is our marriage dying?" It was too big a question as my husband was running out the door, but I needed to know. His mouth opened, closed, opened in a tentative sequence. I waited for him to crack the safe and say what I needed to hear.

"Of course not. I promise you, we're okay. How about this: Ryan can watch the others and we'll go out tomorrow. How's a nice dinner at the Wooden Nickel Restaurant sound? I'll order pizza from Della Sala's for the kids; you know how they love those square slices." He sealed the evening's fate with a step away from me. "In fact, treat yourself to a new dress. Oh, which reminds me, you need to call the credit card company. Something's wrong—they declined a charge I tried to make, which shouldn't be possible. Can you look into it?"

A chill prickled my skin. "Sure, I'll sort it out."

"I love you, babe, but I gotta run." He tossed the words behind him as he closed the front door, leaving me stunned in his brisk wake. My husband, *the pediatrician,* didn't even offer to look in on his own child. Unreal.

On my way to deal with Collette, I popped in the bathroom to grab a migraine pill. The headaches had grown more frequent as Collette's colic kept me up all hours of the night. There, on the vanity, was the teal mug Willow had made me when she was six years old, a third full of cold coffee that I'd been missing since this morning. I felt just as empty inside as that cup.

If only Grant knew I had already bought myself a new dress for tonight—a whole wardrobe, in fact, the last time he ditched me for *the guys*—maybe he'd have thought twice about leaving.

Chapter 5

Lily

Nine Days Ago

Friends are the flowers you pick to beautify your life. But eventually they lose their vibrancy and begin to smell like *cacca*.

I could have slapped Mackenzie through the phone, but I decided to go easy on her. As easy as a fuming Italian woman could be. I had lost my patience.

"You've got to be friggin' kidding me with this *merda*, Mac. Stop letting Owen control you. *Basta basta!*" I yelled into the phone. It was the same old, same old with her—always committing, always canceling. An exhausting wheel I was tired of being run over with. Once again she had canceled our workout, but more than that, she had canceled on *the plan*.

"Language, Lily. And stop with the Italian. I have no idea what you're saying." Mackenzie always sounded so defeated that it physically hurt me to hear her speak.

"Enough is enough—that's all I'm trying to say." I paced the living room to work the rage out of my system. It was a wonder I had any carpet left. "You've got to stand up for yourself. Do what's best for you, not that asshole husband of yours."

"Please. No need to swear at me just because I bailed on our workout." Mackenzie's unruffled acceptance of her miserable life irritated me even more than the cancelation. A little righteous anger would have been nice.

I picked up an empty plate from the coffee table and carried it to the kitchen. "I'll fuckin' swear if I want to. You're pissing me off. I have a right to be upset when I clear my evening for you, clear my damn life for you, and you screw me over . . . again. You realize you have zero credibility as a friend, right?" I dropped the dish into the sink.

Mackenzie sighed over the line. I hoped the weight of guilt suffocated her enough to shed the doormat act.

"I'm sorry, Lil, but it's complicated."

"What about the plan? Did you decide to just skip it?" We'd been planning it for weeks. The bank account was set up, money transferred, every detail figured out—even Aria wouldn't miss a beat. If Mac bailed now, she'd never find the nerve to follow through again.

"No, I'm still going to do it. Just not tonight. It's not the right time."

"Every day is the right time to leave an abusive spouse, Mac. Think about Aria. It's not good for her to watch her mamma die a slow death. But it's your life, not mine. Do what you want."

"Are you mad at me?" She sounded shocked, but she shouldn't be, because I had made my feelings about their union clear from the first moment I met Owen more than twenty years ago.

I'd never forget how he used her to pass English 101 for the first four months they knew each other. She was his passing grade; he was her feel-good crutch. I couldn't blame her for falling too hard and too fast, though. Especially not after what happened to her in the fire. But I knew the truth—Owen used her insecurity against her. He was a jerk back then, and an even bigger jerk now. People don't change their stripes, and my friend was living proof of this. No matter how many times she vowed to escape him, she never followed through.

"No, I'm not mad at you. I just want better for you and you keep chickening out." Having lost my motivation, I headed into the bedroom to change out of my workout clothes. I deserved a Friday off to binge-watch *Stranger Things* and indulge in a bag of Doritos.

"It's not as easy as you think it is. We have a child together, Lily. For you, cutting Tony loose had no aftermath. For me, I'm setting Aria's life on fire. Please at least try to understand my position."

"I am trying to sympathize." I stepped out of my bike shorts. "It's just . . . sometimes I think you're afraid to leave him because you don't think you can do better."

"Can I really? You think I can just hit the bar and pick up guys like you do? You try wearing my face for a day and see how confident you are when people gawk at you in public, or kids run away in fear. It's not easy, let me tell you."

"*Va bene*, I get it. I'll be here when you need me. Now go be a good little lapdog and tend to your overbearing master. I guess I'll talk to you later." I spat the words.

"Are you *sure* you're not mad at me? Because it sure as hell sounds like it."

"No, I promise." Maybe I was a little mad at her as I stomped into a pair of sweatpants.

"I love you, Lil. I'm really sorry. I just couldn't deal with a fight tonight."

"I know, just go. I'll get over it." I always did.

I hung up the phone, hating how she let Owen dictate her every move. We were living in 2020, for God's sake, not the 1950s when women were expected to be mealymouthed possessions that kept the house spotless and didn't bitch about being perennially barefoot and pregnant. Why she purposefully chose a life of servitude was a puzzle I'd never piece together. I would rather be forty, single, and childless than be prisoner to my spouse—and I was . . . single, childless, and loving it, that is.

Maybe *loving it* was a bit much. A slight exaggeration. The dating game was played out, and I'd grown bored with my empty evenings in my empty apartment with my empty love life. Yeah, I'd had my share of one-night stands. I'd done the walk of shame, tottering home and leaving my dignity behind. Can I help it if guys find me irresistible? And I admit, I was drawn to the bad boys, the swaggering hunks that knew how to find my G-spot, but weren't good for anything else. Mostly bums looking for a sugar mamma that I ditched after I'd used them for what I wanted: a good screw. And, if I'm being honest with myself, to dull the pain of a life less-loved.

Did I want to find a wonderful man who would treat me right and give me the white-picket-fence life every woman—no matter how hardened—secretly wanted? Sure. But I had already done that and lost him. Maybe singlehood was my fate. Yep, that was me. A whiz with money, a loser with love.

Except for the one man I couldn't have. The only man who made me laugh from my belly, who made my skin tingle when he brushed against it, who gave me hot dreams that I wanted to slip into forever. I couldn't tell anyone about my feelings for him, though. He was my little secret, and I was his. Together we were a dangerous explosive.

It wasn't as if we had done anything but flirt . . . so far. But we toyed with the idea of more. Foreplay at its finest. His fingertips grazing my neck. My lips brushing against his ear. His hands lightly exploring the curves of my ass. He wanted sex; I wanted a love story. I was tired of being the girl who didn't get the guy. It always ended before it began, but my resolve was growing weary. Especially tonight. I needed an outlet—anything to distract me from thoughts of him.

I considered heading down to the South Side to see if any live music was playing, but I didn't feel like putting on my face. It was daunting, going through the whole makeup routine and picking out just the right outfit that said *available but not slutty*. Then sweating my ass off on the dance floor amid a crowd of twentysomethings fifteen years my junior while they scowled at me like I didn't belong. None of it sounded like fun tonight.

I headed back to the kitchen, thirsty for alcohol but not wanting to throw off my diet completely. Chips and a health shake—a perfect combo for a rainy night in. Throwing a handful of kale and blueberries in a blender, I added a banana, Greek yogurt, and almond milk, then watched the concoction swirl into a delicious pale blue. I poured the liquid into a glass and *boom*—dinner served. Maybe avoiding glutens, eating antioxidant-rich food, and working out obsessively weren't a guaranteed recipe for eternal youth. But I was damn proud of my toned body—it was the only thing that made being single and forty endurable.

I sipped the blended shake between mouthfuls of chips, sitting at my cluttered kitchen table while scrolling through my Facebook newsfeed. If only Tony could see me now. Ah, the one that got away. My only real true love who *got me*. There was no act with him. No vow of submissive silence like wallflower Mackenzie, or playing the perfect housewife like Robin. I backed up my bark with a helluva bite. A proud woman who stood on her own two feet, lived by her own rules. And was shamelessly confident. Why hide who I was when it got me what I wanted?

Don't get me wrong; I'm not self-obsessed or more vain than any other woman on the planet. But I knew I was a catch, and self-assurance was key at my age. You didn't dispel lonely nights or find your bliss by moping around at home or worrying if you were pretty enough to keep your husband faithful. Confidence is what I gave my clients—women who needed to discover their beauty and embrace it, enjoy it, flaunt it. My job was as satisfying as sex . . . or at least a close second. Fitness, nutrition, balance—they were what I taught, what I lived.

Except my balance had been recently upended by a man. Of course it had to be the wrong man. The wrongest man.

I closed Facebook and checked my email. One message, which I would have ignored except for the subject line: *Legal Action Forthcoming*.

Dear Ms. Santoro,

Because you have ignored my requests for a full refund, I will be pursuing legal action against you and your company, Workout Wonder. This is your last chance to settle out of court.

Sincerely,

Irving

Asshole Irving at it again, this time threatening legal action. The only sincere thing about him was his tenacity to make life a living hell for me. He was the thorn in my side after he'd been using my services for months, then suddenly decided he wanted a full refund. No explanation why. Sorry, but I don't negotiate with thugs. I filed the email away to deal with later.

As I scrolled through my spam folder, the phone beeped with a text. A blocked number. I read it, confused by the wording:

I'm coming for you.

It sounded too cryptic to be the only person who would covertly text me. I decided to call him and find out, mostly because I needed a distraction from Asshole Irving and his empty threats.

"Hello, gorgeous," he whispered after he picked up. His voice had a way of dispelling all my worries. "How'd you know I wanted to hear your voice?"

"Because I'm stalking you," I said after swallowing a mouthful of chips.

"How romantic. I'll let you know when it stops being cute and starts getting creepy."

I enjoyed our repartee more than I should have. We were two live wires that created a volatile spark.

"Did you just text me?"

"No, why?" His voice was raspy and secretive.

"I'm guessing you're not alone. Is she in the room?" I asked, instantly regretting the call. The last thing I wanted was to get him in trouble with the missus. I actually cared about his family, unlike the other married men I fooled around with.

The phone crackled with his movement and the background noise dimmed. "Not anymore. What's up?"

"I'm bored. I got stood up by Mackenzie. You able to hang out tonight?" I reached into the empty chips bag, surprised I had eaten them all in one sitting. Apparently I was in a self-destructive mood.

"I could be. What's in it for me?"

"That depends on what you want from me." I was playing coy, and he knew it.

"How about you buy the first round of drinks and we'll go from there?"

"That doesn't sound so bad." But I was wrong. It was so very, very bad.

After a few minutes of flirty banter he told me he'd meet me in thirty minutes at our usual place, his voice thick and throaty and sexy as hell. An outfit change and half an hour later I walked into James Street Tavern, as obscure a meeting place as one could get in the suburbs of Monroeville, Pennsylvania, and saw him leaning over a pool table, his ass hugged in denim. I approached from behind, then slipped into his periphery as he nibbled on his lower lip in concentration for the shot.

I picked up his abandoned bottle of beer perched on the corner of the pool table and took a swig. "Hey, there. Don't let me distract you," I teased, wiggling up against him.

"Oh, you always distract me, Lily. How about you help me with this shot?" He winked. I laughed. Our chemistry sizzled.

Gently grabbing my wrist, he tugged me closer, nesting my body in front of his. He guided me into position to take over the shot while he took over my self-control.

With the pool stick slipped into my palms, I leaned over with an exaggerated butt thrust, aiming the cue ball at a cluster of balls in the corner. I didn't care about the shot as I felt his hot body against mine. The only balls I thought about at this moment were pressed against my rear.

"You're going to miss it if you don't aim right," he whispered in my ear.

"I'm sure you *always* hit your mark." I licked my lips, fully knowing what I was doing. Taunting him. Teasing him. And yet my hands were bound. He was off-limits.

The line was still intact, dull but existent. I could assure myself it was just harmless flirting up to this point. But once we crossed that thinning border between innocent and guilty, there was no going back. After that, I couldn't forgive myself. Life would shift and shatter into unrecognizable pieces. I'd never be able to glue the shards back together. We could never be, him and I. Not because he was married with a mortgage. Not even because he had kids.

But because he was my best friend's husband.

Chapter 6

Mackenzie

Trapped between Lily and Robin on an overpriced sofa that Robin scoffed at but really loved, I fingered the friendship bracelet on my wrist, frayed, discolored, rather shabby. Over twenty years later I still upheld this youthfully naïve heart-bond, devoted to our friendship and growing old together, regardless of how far Time swept us apart. Our vow made us family; our shared lives mingled our blood.

It hadn't always been easy keeping the promise while juggling kids and competing work schedules and lacrosse practice and baseball tournaments and PTA meetings. But once a month we sliced out some time together when Robin and Grant hosted a dinner party where the women could gossip over half-empty glasses of Moscato, the men could talk Steelers draft picks over Iron City Beer, and the kids could retreat to the basement game room to binge on chips and *pop*—the native Pittsburgher's word for *soda*. Proving you could take the Southerner out of the South but not the South out of the Southerner, I insisted on calling all soft drinks cokes, and for some reason it cracked everybody up whenever I'd ask for a *Co-Cola*.

As much as life and jobs and kids and petty fights wedged us apart, we always returned to find our place in the fold.

"Moooommy!" a child's voice cried from the kitchen. This same small voice had just finished crying about his juice spilling on the carpet—where he was forbidden from drinking juice—after wailing about breaking the lamp he shouldn't have been throwing a ball at. "Willow won't share the cookies with me!"

"You've got to be friggin' kidding me. He never stops," Robin mumbled, frustration and exhaustion sharpening her words. "Mommy's coming, Lucas!"

Robin rose from her seat, leaving me and Lily alone with our wine and appetizers.

"She makes parenthood look like a nightmare," Lily said, draining half a glass of wine in one swig. It was an unfair observation, because any child looked like a nightmare to Lily. "Maybe I should start hosting our get-togethers—except no kids allowed."

"Oh, Lil, it's not as hellish as it looks. You might be surprised how fun kids can be. Aria's my world. I couldn't imagine life without her."

Collette crawled along the floor, gripping Lily's socked toe in her chubby fingers.

"She wants you to hold her." I reached down and tickled the eight-month-old at Lily's feet.

Lily winced and waved away what she saw as a drooling rug rat. I saw cooing perfection. "No thanks. You know I'm not a baby person. I'm always worried I'll drop her."

"What is wrong with you?" I shook my head at Lily and picked up Collette. "How can you see this cute little ball of fat rolls and turn down a chance to hold her?"

"All she does is slobber and fuss and poop. I don't get the appeal."

"It's the heart explosion that you're missing. When you have a baby, Lil, there's nothing like it—the sheer force of love filling and breaking and mending your heart all at once. It's life-altering how much you can feel for one tiny little human."

"Sounds exhausting," Lily said.

"Sounds like you have baby fever," Robin interjected as she breathlessly trotted into the living room, dropping onto the sofa. She squeezed my knee and grinned.

"Unfortunately that ship has sailed, but I'll relish being Auntie Mac to this widdle cutie. Pretty as a Georgia peach, you are." I planted kisses along Collette's forehead, cheeks, and neck as she giggled and squirmed. I longed for it again, that baby stage.

"Anytime you want to babysit, she's all yours."

On one auburn top-grain leather sofa I sat between Robin and Lily, thigh to thigh, shoulder to shoulder, not a sliver of daylight between us. (I often said we were a three-headed critter with one heart, which made Lily gag.) On the opposite matching sofa were Grant and Owen, an empty down-blend cushion gaping between them. Grant's legs stretched out under the handcrafted petrified wood coffee table, and one elbow casually rested on the rolled arm of the sofa, fingers rubbing the brass nailhead trim, while the other hand animatedly gestured as he talked about sports that I didn't follow. Owen, sipping lager from a chilled pilsner glass, wore a bored expression that said *kill me now*.

"Did Lucas go downstairs like I told him to?" Robin asked the room, glancing over her shoulder. "I hope he's not annoying Aria to no end with his toy dinosaur collection."

At age five, Lucas was a budding paleontologist, whose yen for anything dinosaurian put the similarly obsessed boy in *Jurassic Park* to shame. He could talk your ear off for hours, rattling off facts without taking a breath. The precocious kid was like a walking, talking kindergartener-sized Wikipedia.

"Don't worry, Aria adores him. I'm sure she doesn't mind humoring him," I assured her.

"I think I saw Fizz dragging Willow upstairs," Grant said. Lucas had earned the nickname Fizz as a baby during his first sip of Sprite at a dinner outing together. The fizz from the carbonation gave him the most shocked expression as soda trickled out of one nostril, sending our entire table and waitstaff into hysterics. It stuck right then and there—Fizz. "I heard him mention something about finding his velociraptor."

Lucas's footsteps rumbled above us, followed by Willow's loud warning to stay out of her room.

"Any moment now I'll be refereeing whatever argument those two are going to get into." Robin glanced at the ceiling. Willow's threats were growing impatient and loud.

"Congratulations, you'll have your first teenage girl in a

couple months." I patted Robin's shoulder with a welcome-to-the-club shrug.

Robin returned a weary glare.

"It's not so bad. They can get mouthy, but Willow's a sweet girl." Although Aria rarely got mouthy, and when she did, it was aimed at her father.

"You can't talk, Mac. You got it easy with Aria. She's the perfect teen. With the psychotic girls Willow's been hanging out with from her lacrosse team, I'm scared she'll become a serial killer. You should hear the hazing these kids do to one another. Twelve years old and throwing water balloons with pebbles in them at the new girls. Then dousing them in syrup and making them roll in feathers. It's barbaric!"

Maybe Willow wasn't as sweet as I thought.

"What? No, I'm sure Willow's not doing that stuff," Lily interjected.

"She says it's not her, but that's what she's surrounded by. I wish they could stay innocent like this forever." Robin brushed her finger against Collette's cheek, then handed me a plush toy, which I rattled in front of her. Her chubby hand gripped it then waved it wildly. I inhaled the scent of baby powder as I repositioned her on my lap.

"Willow is a strong-willed girl who can stand up to peer pressure. She knows who she is—and she's not like them." At least I hoped not.

An earsplitting screech bounced down the stairwell from Willow's room, and Robin rolled her eyes. "Tell that to the junior Annie Wilkes upstairs."

Grant laughed at the Kathy Bates *Misery* reference. "You

want me to intervene?" he offered. It was the first time he'd dealt with the kids all evening.

"No, they need to learn to work it out on their own." Robin exhaled, her fatigue evident in the sagging eyes that her concealer couldn't camouflage.

"Anyone need anything while I run to the kitchen?" Grant stood up and smoothed the wrinkles from his Calvin Klein flat-front khakis. He looked every part the sophisticated pediatrician, even in his casual wear.

Lily gulped the last of her wine, casually delivered an unlady-like burp, and lifted her empty glass. "I could use a refill."

While Lily trailed after Grant toward the kitchen, Owen, Robin, and I sat alone, with only Collette's babbling poking holes in the stifling silence. With her eyes fixed on Owen, Robin primly crossed her legs and folded her hands on her lap. She was searching for something to say; I could always tell when Robin stiffened like that.

"How was Friday night's poker game, Owen?" Robin asked.

"What poker game?" Owen's face was a blank slate.

"I thought the guys had a poker game. Grant went. You didn't go?"

"I didn't hear about it. I guess I wasn't invited." Owen's nonchalance showed just how little he cared about such things. Time with *the guys* had always been more an obligation than a pleasure. If Owen had his way, we'd be living in the boonies on acres of sprawling land and not another house in sight. *Buddies* were for needy pussies, as far as he was concerned. But humoring me was part of the marital package, so he attended the trite events that I dragged him to and maintained the status quo with obligatory poker games and suffered through *boring* dinners like this one.

"Oh. Well, I'll let Grant know next time not to forget you." Robin reached for her wineglass, bumping mine with her knuckle. The crystal tipped and broke on the coffee table, sending wine across the table and onto Robin's lap. "Eff my life!"

As Robin jumped up in a fluster, I grabbed a napkin and tossed it on the rosy puddle. "No big deal, Robin. It's cleaned up. Sit down and relax."

But Robin could never relax. I understood, always living on the edge with Owen. As Robin rushed to the bathroom, I sensed something darker going on beyond her usual worry. She was hiding something behind this dinner theater that she was an actress in. Everything felt fake tonight. I knew this because I was faking too, playing my role in the happy family performance. When Robin returned with her lips stuck in a grim line, Collette was already done with me, reaching for her mamma.

"So did you hear about that college coach who was caught diddlin' his cheerleaders?" As an unapologetic devotee of supermarket tabloids, I sought to distract my best friend the only way I knew how.

"Can we not talk about perverts and cheaters?" Robin cast a glare at the kitchen toward Grant's wake. "Men are selfish pigs. What else is there to say? They take what they want, no matter who they hurt."

Apparently Robin had a lot to say, but I knew this wasn't about a national scandal. A bigger question nagged me: was a scandal happening right in Robin's own home?

Chapter 7

Lily

Sunday Evening

Today was the day my life began and Robin's ended.

Grant stood on one side of the kitchen island while I lingered on the other, reaching for the wine bottle.

"Santoro, you're such a lush." Grant wagged his finger at me as I topped off my third glass of wine for the evening. I'd always liked how he referred to me by my last name. It felt so empowering, somehow. Like I was one of the guys.

That was my *first* mistake, believing I was innocent. Because women held the power too. I just hadn't harnessed it yet.

"I think you like me a little tipsy."

"Why do you think that?" His hazel eyes bore into me, singeing me with their intensity as he crept along the counter toward me. Even separated by space and granite, I felt his heat.

"Because I know what you want, and you can't have it. You're thinking maybe if I'm drunk I'll lose my head. Do something foolish. Typical guy." I cocked my head, daring him to prove me wrong.

"Typical guy, huh? What exactly is it that you think I want?"

"To get in my pants," I said as I headed into the walk-in pantry where food items were lined in neat rows—snacks, canned goods, various pastas, spices. Robin's obsessiveness knew no bounds. Grant followed behind me, pausing in front of the canned soup section.

"That's pretty presumptuous of you."

"So you don't find me attractive?"

"I didn't say that."

"And you don't want me?"

"I didn't say that either."

"Well, then it stands to reason that everything you're *not* saying says everything I need to know."

Grant shook his head, his lips turning up in an irresistible grin that I wanted to kiss. I couldn't. I shouldn't. Not in his own home—Robin's home. With her sitting a few paces away in the living room.

His hand rested on my shoulder, his thumb brushing against my neck. "You've lost me."

The tension between us sizzled as his fingertip lingered too long. One small step forward. I lifted my chin. He was a forbidden gasp away. I felt more than saw him lean down slightly, the air between us thick and heavy. I arched into him, my eyes closing, as if I could magic us into another world where this was okay. Where I wasn't betraying my best friend, seducing her husband, wrecking a family.

Swept up in selfish desire, I let it happen. Egged it on, even. Teased and invited and welcomed Grant's passionate lips on mine. I wanted the intrusion.

It was a greedy kiss, as if it could never be enough. Grant's agile tongue tasted spicy; I fantasized about putting it to good use in certain other places. He grabbed my ass, drawing me against the bulge in his uptight, old-man khakis. He wasn't my usual type. Too clean-cut, Mr. Preppy. Not a rebel like Tony, tattoos snaking over his skin in tribal glory, ripped jeans, and a Korn T-shirt his standard uniform. And yet I was recklessly attracted to Grant. Maybe I wanted to find out if he was a bad boy wearing choirboy clothes.

I slid my hands through his thick hair, the dark brown waves mingling between my fingers. I pulled back breathlessly, alarmed by a sudden sensation of being watched. I turned, catching a glimpse of a blond phantom disappearing around the doorframe.

"*Merda*. Did you see that?"

Grant glanced back at the pantry door where my eyes were locked. "No. Why? Was someone there?" His voice cracked.

"I think it was Willow."

"Did she see us?" he said angrily, and roughly pushed me away.

"I don't know, Grant! I'm not even sure it was her. It could have been Mackenzie or Aria, for all I know."

"Should I go talk to Willow?" Grant pressed.

"She's your kid, not mine. I have no idea what to do. Maybe she didn't see anything. I mean, what would you even say?"

Grant stalked into the kitchen, pacing feverishly. I followed. "All right, I'll see if she acts weird at bedtime," he said. "Maybe I can explain it if she saw us."

And maybe he couldn't. Willow was twelve years old, not a little child who'd believe it was normal for her dad to be groping and locking lips with a woman who wasn't her mom.

"Just don't say anything," he added, waving his hands at me. "I can't let Robin find out . . . not like this."

That was my *second* mistake—believing this secret could stay hidden.

This was bad. Marriage-destroying, friendship-crushing, end-of-the-world bad.

Chapter 8

Aria

As long as Aria Fischer had known him, Ryan Thompson had always been a combo genuine science/science-fiction geek. One wall of the basement game room in his parents' house paid homage to three sci-fi flicks from the 1950s. A vintage poster of *The War of the Worlds*, a bona fide classic, hung between repro lobby cards for two kitschy B-movie favorites, *Flight to Mars* and *Killers from Space*. *Mystery Science Theater 3000*, which celebrated and skewered exactly that kind of show, flickered on the big-screen TV in the corner. With his goofy grin and curly cap of hair—not to mention his social awkwardness—*nerd* was too charitable a word to describe Ryan, in most circumstances. But tonight, thanks to the wine Aria had generously sampled—her teenage *eff you* to the pedestal her parents had put her on— she didn't mind the nerdiness so much. In fact, she had always found Ryan to be kind of cute, and this feeling grew on her as their conversation smoothly flowed like the forbidden alcohol down her throat.

Sitting cross-legged on the carpet, they leaned against the foot of the sofa, chuckling at the wisecracks of Joel Robinson, Tom Servo, and the MST3K gang as they watched *Women of the Prehistoric Planet*. The lacquered coffee table in front of them was littered with pale rings of condensation from their red Solo cups and a dust of snack crumbs from the mostly empty bowls of chips and cookies.

Ryan lifted the bottle of wine he'd snuck out of the wine cellar, offering it to Aria. "Want to finish this off?"

She knew she shouldn't. She had been pouring herself glass after glass to the point where she'd lost count. It was her first time drinking, but she already knew she was drunk. Too drunk to act like she wasn't.

She nodded anyway and offered him her half-full cup. "Sure."

As Ryan poured, Aria admired the ripple of his arm muscles, developed over years of playing Little League and high school baseball. His parents had made him play, insisting he couldn't spend all his time indoors poring over science journals, playing video games, and binging on old sci-fi movies. It had paid off. The more her eyes roved his body, the more she found to appreciate. Brains and brawn with a touch of sensitive in one attractive package. You didn't find that very often.

Her fingers played with the sleeve of his *Star Wars* T-shirt. "So you were saying there are plants in your backyard that can *kill* people?" Aria asked, her voice drunkenly loud. Somehow the topic had turned to plants—the villainous side of them, of which Ryan was apparently an expert. "Why do you have lethal plants in your yard?"

"Shh! You want our parents to hear us plotting their murder?" Ryan laughed tipsily and pressed his finger to her lips.

"Sorry," Aria said between giggles. "So you're a master horticulturist, huh?"

"No, not quite. Horticulture is the science of growing certain plants. Botany is the study of their properties."

"If for a moment I doubted your geekiness, that moment is gone, dude." Aria looked up at him, her vision hazy like smudged glass.

"What? I find botany to be interesting. Especially the mysteries of plants, like how a flower can cause a heart attack. But it's not like I'm harvesting poisonous plants. The foxglove I grow is actually pretty common in gardens. And it's only lethal if you eat a bunch of it."

"Well, I better never get on your bad side. Don't want you to poison me in my sleep."

"I wouldn't do it in your sleep, silly. I'd put it in your food or drink." He winked, but Aria felt her stomach knot. It was either the low rumble of his words or the alcohol churning in her gut about to make a second appearance.

"You're freaking me out, Ryan."

"I'd never poison you, Aria," Ryan said, his voice shifting to a brighter octave. "I like you too much to do that."

"You *like* me, huh? You're, like, three years older than me. Why would a senior ever be interested in a sophomore?"

"Because you're smart . . . and beautiful . . . and fun."

"And drunk," Aria added.

Ryan's eyes were all pupil, from booze or lust or both, Aria couldn't tell. She'd never kissed a boy, but she recognized his posture as that of a boy hoping to lock lips. A casual slant toward her, a subtle shift closer. Aria scooted back to insert space between them. Oddly charming nerd-jock or not, Aria didn't know if she was ready for her first kiss yet. Especially one she might not remember tomorrow.

"Where are you going? Are you scared of me?" Ryan asked. "I'm not going to bite, you know. Unless that's what you're into." He laughed, a not terribly attractive braying sound, and waited for her to join in. She didn't. "Uh, sorry, just a little joke. Besides, I know a girl like you would never go out with a guy like me."

"What do you mean?" Aria felt guilty but she wasn't sure why.

"You're popular and I'm not. Guys like me never get the girl."

"What are you talking about? You're an athlete. And a freakin' brainiac too. I thought that equaled instant popularity and chicks."

He *humphed*. "Well, that's a load of crap. Athlete doesn't necessarily mean popular. So I can hit a ball. Big deal. Girls like me if I have a good game, but off the field is a whole different . . . ballgame." He grinned, and Aria chuckled.

"I see what you did there," she said, playing along. "God, you are such a nerd!"

"So I've been told. A couple times tonight already." He shrugged. "No worries. I get it. I'm not your type. Let's just watch the show."

Face ruddy with embarrassment, he sat back and fixed his gaze on the movie. A lump settled in Aria's throat. She wanted to tell him what she really felt—that she liked him, *a lot*, but that she wasn't ready to be more than just friends. She wasn't even sure if she was allowed to date yet. So instead she rested her head on his shoulder in a wordless confession as the world wobbled under the spell of her last gulp of wine.

"I really like you, Aria. Even if only as friends. You're the best person I know." Ryan spoke to the empty air in front of him. His words were soft and dreamy sliding over her.

"I like you too, Ryan. Really—nerd and all." Tipping her face up to his, his lips were so close, his breath hot and moist. Any trace of nervousness had been snuffed out by the adrenaline coursing through her.

Then he leaned in, her heart beat harder, and he kissed her. The kiss didn't feel like she had anticipated. It was slippery wet. Her mind whirred. She didn't know what she should be doing with her mouth or hands or tongue. She didn't know if she should be doing any of this in the first place. As she glided into a soused fog, she vaguely realized they'd already gone past first base.

First base slipped to second base . . . then the room turned on its side as she laid down on the floor.

Chapter 9

Mackenzie

The tension between Robin and Grant was subtle but palpable. I first noticed the shift in the air when Grant returned from the kitchen carrying a plate of bacon-wrapped scallops, still sizzling from the grill. His face was flushed from leaning over the glowing coals or a few too many beers or maybe something else entirely.

"Where have you been?" Robin questioned.

As Grant set the serving platter down, he seemed jumpy at the sound of her brisk tone. I couldn't be the only one who noticed it, but Owen seemed oblivious and Lily was nowhere in sight.

"Making these, like you asked," he answered.

"Oh. Okay."

The mood tamed, though subsequent conversation felt curiously stilted.

"You okay, Robin?" I asked. If she wasn't, she wouldn't admit it. Not in front of Owen, at least. She'd never really taken to him, though I couldn't understand why. She claimed it was because he was possessive and controlling—the same two adjectives used again and again, but did anyone really know what they meant? My husband liked to spend time with me. Why make such a fuss about it? Why turn it into something so villainous? And yet sometimes it felt wrong to me too. One morning I'd wake up adoring him. Another morning I'd wake up abhorring him. It was marital Stockholm syndrome.

"Sure. I think I'm just getting tired. Wine does that to me." She grinned but I could tell it was fake.

"Maybe it's time we head home, huh, Owen?" I glanced at him, expecting a fervent yes. He'd been ready to leave the dinner party the moment he chewed his last bite of orange duck with au gratin potatoes and grilled asparagus. Privately he'd confided to me he thought dinner tasted like warmed-over shit. His sour mood alone was already giving me a headache, which wouldn't be enough of an excuse to avoid his drunken, grabby hands tonight.

"I'm ready when you are," he said, getting up with a little groan. "Dinner was superb, Robin," he added unctuously.

I knew it was bullshit. We all tasted the same overcooked meat and burned veggies.

"Glad you enjoyed it, Owen. You don't want to stay for

coffee or tea?" Robin held up a rose gold carafe that she'd just carried out with a cute matching sugar and cream set. Only Robin would place such importance on the presentation details for coffee.

"That sounds tempting, Rob," I said, "but we've got an early morning tomorrow—school and work and all. I'll go get Aria."

Thick wool carpet muted the sound of my footsteps as I descended into the basement where the stairs led into an open-floor game room. Wood paneling insulated the space, giving it a cozy warmth. As my feet hit the bottom step, I wasn't sure what I was looking at, but it couldn't be what my eyes were transmitting to my brain.

It just couldn't be.

My innocent daughter, sprawled out on the floor with Ryan thrusting away on top of her. His jeans hung below his bare butt. My baby's shirt was pulled up and her bra undone, exposing her budding breasts. She still had her underwear on, but just barely. She looked totally wasted.

"Aria?" I asked, my voice hardly audible.

They hadn't heard me.

"Aria!" My voice returned with force, startling Ryan upright. "Get the hell off of my daughter!" I screamed, crossing the room.

Ryan rolled off Aria, a genuine look of fear and panic in his eyes as he hurriedly pulled his pants up. "Mrs. Fischer, I—"

"Shut up! You're lucky I don't call the cops on your ass."

"Mom? What're you doin'?" Aria sat up, gazing around the room dazedly. Her eyes alighted on Ryan, who hung his head remorsefully. Looking down, she pulled her shirt across her exposed chest.

I couldn't bear to look at my little girl, or whatever she was now. I yanked an afghan off the back of the sofa and tossed it to her. She covered herself and began rearranging her clothes.

"Were you drinking?" I demanded.

"No . . ." she lied, giggling self-consciously.

"It's all my fault," Ryan pleaded. "Please don't blame Aria. I'm the one who got the wine out—"

I silenced him with a glare, then turned it on my daughter. "I can't believe you, Aria. Your father is going to tan your hide good and . . . I don't even know what he'll do. Ground you for life, if you're lucky." Then I aimed a shaking finger at Ryan. "And you, you piece of shit, never touch my daughter again or I'll set Owen on you. And I assure you, boy, once he's done with you, there won't be anything left to bury."

Hauling Aria up the stairs, her one arm limp around my neck, the other clinging to the railing, I wondered what exactly had happened. She was clearly too intoxicated to know what she was doing. Had Ryan plied Aria with alcohol, then taken advantage of her? Would Aria even remember anything tomorrow?

If I told Owen, God knows what he'd do to Ryan—nothing he didn't deserve, though. He'd want to kill the boy. Hell, I'd probably help him. But the last thing Aria needed was a circus erupting over this. Maybe she had consented, even though technically she wasn't over the age of consent. Though I couldn't wrap logic around that. As far as I knew,

Aria had never even kissed a boy. She certainly wouldn't indiscriminately sleep with one.

As I reached the top step, the growing headache sliced through my temples, as if my brains were tumbling around inside my skull. Too many jumbled thoughts. Too many scenarios to sort through. I just hoped my baby girl would still be my baby girl come morning.

Chapter 10

Lily

Two fifty-one. That was the time the clock displayed in blazing neon green. I had to be at work in five hours, an insomniac teaching clients about self-care. The drooping gray skin under my eyes sure as hell wouldn't be inspiring my clients' confidence if I didn't fall asleep soon.

It was almost three in the morning and my wide-awake brain was kicking my ass tonight. I stared at my bedroom ceiling where cracks meandered across the peeling paint, my thoughts blurry from the mixture of residual alcohol, guilt, and the painkillers I had just swallowed.

A twinge shocked my lower back where the bulging disk

had never quite healed from the car accident almost five years ago. The idiot was texting while driving, didn't see me stopped at a red light. Slammed into me going at least forty-five miles an hour.

Three months of disability.

Nine months of physical therapy.

One lost job.

Five years of pain-pill popping.

And here I was, permanently injured by one asshole's recklessness.

I closed my eyes, waiting for the drugs to send me far away to where my thoughts couldn't reach me. Although my body sunk into the mattress, relaxing to the lull of opioid bliss, my senses remained alert. Every sound remained sharp and in focus. The *drip, drip, drip* of the faucet that I'd requested the landlord fix half a dozen times. The whir of air blowing through the vent overhead. The scrape of furniture across the floor in the apartment above me.

Who moved furniture at three in the morning? Inconsiderate assholes, that's who.

More than the sounds were the sensations. A tickle of ant-like feet crawled up my arm. My lips tingled with the poison of Grant's kiss. I tensed as I imagined his hands cupping my butt cheeks, his tongue probing me eagerly.

My eyelids fluttered open. Banish the thoughts. Erase them, please. I sat up and stared out the window at the city lights peppering the horizon. Lit-up glass and metal peaks jutted into the Pittsburgh skyline, dots of light against an inky void. Streaks of red taillights added a dash of color, along with the neon reflection against the calm river water.

Any other night I would have appreciated the mesmerizing view. But not tonight.

The demons were haunting me, and I was too weak to fight back.

Why did I have to go and ruin everything? Why couldn't I bottle up my feelings and shove them way down deep, in the depths of my black soul where they belonged? I felt like I'd shredded a part of myself, torn it open to the point where it could never be salvaged.

Robin and I had been friends since college. She was my soul sister, a woman I would die for. But out of all the men on the planet, I had to pick her husband, the father of her children, to mess around with. What the hell was I thinking? That's just it; I wasn't thinking. Not about the devastation I would cause, or the betrayal, or the ruins I would exile us all to.

And yet why did his kiss still burn my lips? Why did I relive it over and over and over again, as if my life depended on it?

My tabby stretched his lean body along mine, burying his claws into my thigh before he casually slunk into a comfortable resting position. His green eyes watched me in that unnerving way cats had, as if I were a mouse he wanted to stalk, catch, and eat. Although I was mildly allergic to cats—especially mine, particularly when he chose to sleep *on* my face rather than next to it—I'd decided to keep him because on the lonely nights he kept my cold, empty bed warm and occupied. He was good company when I had none, which was most of the time—the exception being when I'd snag a boy toy, bang his brains out, and kick him to the curb. Stormy, my purring companion, was worth the puffy eyes and stuffed nose he gave me.

Of course Tony helped convince me to keep the one animal I was allergic to. Stormy was the last remnant of our soured marriage, so I put up with the clawed furniture and watery eyes so that I could cling to the good memories. And fantasize that Tony would come back someday—for both of us.

I'd named the cat Stormy the day Tony found him, a tiny month-old ball of gray fluff, the size of my palm. He'd been hiding under a bush in the middle of a summer downpour, with no mamma or siblings in sight. Tony had tried to catch him, but the kitten was skittish and quick like the lightning flashing above him. When a boom of thunder sent him into my arms, however, I carried him inside my "no pets allowed" apartment and it was love at first purr. I'd never gotten around to telling my landlord about him, and I had no plans to. I was an act first, ask for permission later kind of gal. It had worked for me . . . until now.

Until Grant.

It always kept coming back to Grant.

"Sorry, I gotta get up, boy."

Nudging Stormy to the side of the bed, I checked the clock. Three ten. Enough was enough. I rolled out of bed and padded to the bathroom where a little orange bottle promised me relief. I dropped one more pill into my hand and tossed it to the back of my throat, then gulped a mouthful of water from the faucet. I'd be wrecked for the next few hours, but at least it was better than this carousel of thoughts.

On my way back to the bedroom a flutter of paper in the hallway caught my attention. I picked up the folded paper, not recognizing it. I opened it, finding four simple blood-curdling words scribbled across the page:

Watch your back, bitch.

Merda! This wasn't the first passive-aggressive note I'd received from a woman, but my heart sank as I jumped to the conclusion it was from Robin. She must know. Was it Grant who confessed? Or Willow telling her what she saw? Whoever it was, I had to get ahead of it if there was any chance I could fix things. I knew mending the friendship would never be possible, but I could take all the blame, say I seduced Grant, at least save their marriage. Give their family a fighting chance.

Unless it wasn't Robin. It didn't look like her handwriting, but if it wasn't her, then who? I had no enemies of late . . . none that I knew of, at least.

Placing the note on my kitchen counter, I felt its hate, then the unfamiliar sting of tears. I tasted the foreign tang of mourning. I hadn't cried once since Tony left me, but suddenly my emotions and sadness and grief were alive and kicking.

I cried until I couldn't cry anymore. My eyes stung, my throat was sticky, my body ached from heaving sobs. I fell back into bed face-first, dulling the brightness of the street-light outside my window with my pillow. Maybe I could suffocate all the sorrow away.

As my bedroom faded into a black haze, I wondered how I would move forward from here. There was only one way to smother the worry and fear churning in my skull, one way to pull the plug on my life support: tell Robin everything, then watch helplessly as all of our lives imploded.

Chapter 11

Mackenzie

I've never feared death, even as a child. Instead, I fear life. Life is much more horrifying and soul-shredding and cruel than death could ever be. But this fear had never felt more real, more alive, than it did right now.

I sat silently in Aria's room as the dawn broke through her semi-closed window blinds. Watching her sleep took me back to a time when things were much simpler. I had thought her bedwetting days were the worst it could get. Night after night she'd wake up covered in pee soaking her pink horsey bedspread and Scooby-Doo pajamas. Every night, no matter what time I cut off drinks or how many times I made her pee in the potty before bed, the whole house would shudder awake as her cries drifted to my bedroom. And every night I'd change the reeking sheets and cuddle her back to sleep for another couple of hours until dawn.

This is the worst of it, I'd thought back then with sleep-deprived certainty. *It'll get easier as she gets older.*

And for a while, I was right. Up until age ten or so, when her desire for independence started showing. It was the little things at first: not wanting me to kiss her in front of friends; needing personal space. But she was still princesses and ponies and ballerinas—little girl dreams and little girl dramas. Everybody said she was the perfect teenager, the rare one who didn't turn into a rebellious hellion overnight. I often said it myself. But last night . . . last night she sullied that absurdly Pollyannaish image beyond repair. I wasn't experienced or sophisticated enough to handle this—whatever it was. It was mind-boggling, and there were no easy answers. Hell, I didn't even know the right questions.

I had married the only man I'd ever made love to. I'd gone through four years of high school and two years of college with my virginity intact. Maybe it was because I was a prude, or maybe it was because I wasn't given an option otherwise. The boys weren't exactly kicking down my door, and even if they did, Daddy would have chased them away with his shotgun. He really was that archaic stereotype, clinging to outmoded chivalric notions of virtue, and protecting his daughter at any cost.

How different things were now. How different my experiences were from Aria's. I'd imagined a parallel life for us; we were always so much alike, after all. We got along so well, shared the same interests. I'd always thought our relationship to be more like gal pals than mother and daughter—fluid and easy. Boy, was I wrong. I clearly had no idea who she was. In the face of my sleeping daughter, I could no longer recognize the little girl who sucked her thumb and fell asleep with a board book in her tiny, chubby hands.

"Honey," I whispered, not sure I should wake her, but too worried not to try. I sat next to her, in the crook of her bent knees. I swept her sweaty hair out of her face, pressing my palm to her cool forehead. "How you feeling, sweetie?"

Her eyelids fluttered open, then squinted back shut.

"My head hurts so bad. Can you get me some pain medicine?"

"Sure, honey. But we need to talk about last night."

She groaned, curling into the fetal position and holding her stomach.

"I think I'm going to be sick, Mom. Can we talk about it later?"

"I just want to make sure you're okay."

"I feel like I'm dying. Am I dying?" She opened her eyes and grimaced. I recognized that hungover plea for sweet death and smiled. I might have been a prude in high school, but I drank my share of hunch punch.

"No, honey, you're not dying. But that's not what I'm talking about. Are you okay after what happened with Ryan?"

"What are you talking about?" She looked up at me, puzzled.

"You know . . . you and Ryan . . ." *Please don't make me say it aloud.*

Her expression was blank, confused. "Ryan? Mom, my

brain hurts too much to try to figure out your hints. Just spit it out."

"You don't remember last night—what happened?"

"No. I don't even know what day it is. Do I have school today?"

I rubbed her back like I used to do when she was little. "Yes, it's Monday, but you already missed school. I'm trying to see if you recall the party at Robin and Grant's house last night. Nothing?"

"Oh, yeah, the party. I know Ryan and I shouldn't have been drinking, but I just wanted to try it. I had no idea I'd wake up feeling like this. Please don't tell me I did something mortifying in front of everyone . . ."

"You did get drunk, honey. And . . ." I stopped. I couldn't put words to the horror of seeing my daughter with Ryan on top of her. Her hollow eyes staring up at him, his hungry gaze locked on his prey. Because that's what she was, wasn't it? His conquest.

My fists tightened as I let the truth sink in, boiling my blood. I wanted to kill Ryan. A dozen ways to do it flashed through my mind. I shook the rage away. He was only a boy. He was Robin's *son*. I needed to remember that. He was practically family. I was there at his birth. I was at his baptism. I went to his Little League games and now to his high school ones.

Ryan was the kind of kid who visited his elderly next-door neighbor because he didn't want her to be lonely. The one who took Aria under his wing when she first started high school so that she wouldn't get lost finding her classes. He never struck me as a typical adolescent boy, but how well did I know him, *really*?

"Am I grounded?" Aria pressed her fingertips to her temples. "I won't even care if it means I can go back to sleep and make this headache stop."

"We can talk about this another time," I decided aloud. We would figure this out together, later. Maybe I was over-reacting.

"Sorry, Mom, but I don't feel so good—" Aria paused and looked at me pitifully. "I'm going to throw up." She bolted up, the bedsprings squealing as the quilt clung to her halfway across the floor. A moment later I heard the bathroom door slam shut as she heaved into the toilet.

I couldn't tell if she had any recollection of what happened other than drinking. Maybe the full memory would return to her, but what if it didn't? I didn't know what any of this meant. Should I tell her? Should I let her remain blissfully ignorant? It was uncharted territory that I had no idea how to navigate.

The truth felt like swallowing sand. All I knew was that I saw what I saw, I was the only person other than Ryan who knew what happened, and my sweet baby girl's innocence had been stolen.

Unless Aria wasn't so innocent. What if it hadn't been her first time? A teenage girl was bound to keep secrets. It wouldn't be the first time a mother discovered her daughter was living two different lives—one at school, one at home. What did I really know about my own child? Absolutely nothing. I only knew what she showed me, and last night I'd seen more than enough.

But that look on her face . . . the confusion and vacancy . . . it told me a story that I was afraid to read. A story that my daughter had no idea what had been done to her, and she couldn't stop the ending even if she tried. The ending would be the same no matter what I did—my daughter's soul would be broken.

Murderous rage bubbled up inside me. Maybe Daddy was right all along. Daddy said teenage boys were no good; that their brains were in their peckers and sex was all they thought about, the only thing they wanted. Well, I wanted to wrap my fingers around Ryan's scrawny throat and squeeze the life out of him. And if I couldn't follow through with killing the little shit, I knew someone who would.

Chapter 12

Robin

I felt the crack in my heart splitting deep. A physical pinch in my chest. It had been two days. Two excruciating, torturous days holding in this suspicion. I couldn't bury it any deeper, so I decided to unleash it on the one person I knew would listen and understand.

"Hope you don't mind a visitor, Mac." I stood on her front porch wearing Bermuda shorts, a V-neck T-shirt with PINK glittered across the front, and Collette on my hip. May in Pennsylvania was the perfect time of year, when the winter chill you thought would never end had finally thawed into balmy spring, but summer hadn't scorched the grass brown just yet. Purple and pink hyacinths sprang up along the sidewalk, their sweet fragrance hanging in the air like fresh linen on a clothesline.

"Hey, Robin. What are you doing here?" Mackenzie looked less than happy to see me and barely opened the door.

"I need someone to talk to. Are you busy?"

"Um, kind of."

Something wasn't right. Mac never turned me away. Ever. Bored housewife plus neglectful husband plus coffee plus baby kisses always equaled yes.

"Collette needs some Auntie Mac time." The bribe that never failed.

I'd never told Mac the truth, but I often wished she'd had Collette instead of me. Her heart ached for more kids; mine ached because of them. I'd been taking birth control religiously, but apparently I was the 1 percent statistic when Collette was conceived.

After Willow I had planned to be done. My boy and my girl. The perfect family foursome. Then came Lucas, a surprise that wasn't exactly welcomed, but not unwelcome either. Definitely done, Grant and I agreed. And then the birth control oops. Here comes Collette! I had finally enjoyed the luxury of a full night's sleep right before she was born, and Grant and I even made room for a couple of date nights each month. Now it was back to two hours of sleep each night and a head full of hair that was quickly turning gray.

"Well, okay. Come on in." She waved me in while her coffee sloshed precariously close to the mug's rim. She was still in her silk pajamas, her hair a disheveled mass of blond knots.

She pulled a few strands over the scarred side of her face. Even after all these years she still tried to hide it. It broke my heart that she dwelled on this one physical flaw when so much beauty lived inside her. It broke my heart even more that I was the reason she had to hide her face at all.

"Sorry I didn't call first." It was a formality, really. When you've been friends for more than twenty years and a crisis arises, you never need to call first. At least never until now.

"It's okay. I actually need to talk to you too."

"Uh-oh. Sounds serious. You sure you should be wearing jammies for this conversation?"

I laughed, but Mac didn't. Suddenly I felt awkward, like a stranger in her home.

"Coffee? Tea? Hard liquor?" Mac offered.

"Ha! After Sunday night I think I'll be laying off the alcohol for a while. Coffee sounds great. I'll serve myself; you sit." I passed Collette to her waiting arms and grabbed the same mug I always used—a gift I'd given her a few Christmases ago. I'd had it personalized with an old picture of me, Mackenzie, and Lily at a college dance. We were striking *Charlie's Angels* poses, fingers pointed like guns in different directions. Fresh-faced, hopeful, and uncorrupted . . . before we understood real life was messy and unscripted, and perfect hair, teeth, and bodies were only on TV.

"So, what's up?" Mackenzie asked, sitting at the breakfast table that she had refinished in a French country style—slick cocoa brown on top, contrasting white painted legs. She'd poured hours into making it perfect—sanding, staining, painting . . . it sounded grueling when it was easier to just click "purchase" on Wayfair. I couldn't help but feel a little jealous at her ingenuity and thriftiness, especially as I sat on a $40,000 mountain of debt that I had yet to tell Grant about.

"Been having a rough patch lately," I admitted with a shrug as I dropped into the chair across from her. "I think something's going on with Grant."

"Something like what?"

"I don't know exactly. I just . . . I think he's lying to me about something."

"What makes you think that?" Mackenzie, always the logical one. Always assuming the best about people. Sometimes it balanced my more skeptical nature, but right now it simply irritated me. For once I wanted her to side with me, not question me.

"On Friday night he told me he was playing poker with the guys, but I asked Owen about it at dinner on Sunday and he didn't have a clue what I was talking about. It just seemed so sudden—Grant hadn't mentioned the game, then suddenly he's running out the door. Maybe I'm being paranoid."

"He has other friends he plays poker with, right?"

It was a reasonable question, one a spouse should be able to answer. I should know who he hangs out with, who his friends are. And yet no one else came to mind.

"I honestly don't know. The only friends I've ever been aware of are Owen and Tony . . . and God knows where Tony is these days. It's not like Grant invites anyone else to our house for barbecues or has ever mentioned golfing with anyone from work. Don't you think, as his wife, I should know about his social life?"

"Well, yeah, sure. But have you ever asked him?"

"No. I didn't think I had to."

"Maybe he's got work buddies. It's probably guys he works with."

"Mac, he works primarily with young female nurses. So if he *is* making work buddies, we might have a problem."

"Just ask him and stop overthinking it."

Maybe I *was* overthinking it. Just because I shared every detail of my day with Grant—minus my secret compulsive shopping—and introduced him to every single one of my friends didn't mean it came naturally to him to do the same. All I needed to do was talk to him about it. Easy. Problem solved. And yet why did I dread that conversation?

"I guess you're right. I don't know why it's been bothering me so much."

Collette began fussing in Mac's arms, reaching for me. I tickled her bare feet, then lowered her to the floor where she flopped on her chubby legs. She gripped my index finger as she raised herself back to standing, one arm resting on the chair's edge for support.

"Well, I declare, is she walking already?"

"Close to it. She's taken a few steps. Haven't you, my sweetie-poo-pumpkin-head?" I kissed her round cheek as drool dribbled down her chin.

Collette released her grip and fell in a heap on the floor, arms and legs in vigorous motion as she scooted away under the table. I turned my attention back to Mackenzie, whose face was strangely ashen.

"You okay? You don't look so good."

"No, I'm not okay." Her tone was solemn. Mackenzie sipped her coffee, then looked at me like she had something to say. "I need to tell you something," she began, her voice cracking. She placed her mug on the table. Her eyes watered, and fear filled me.

"You can tell me anything. What's going on?"

"It's about Aria . . . and Ryan." She stopped, exhaled, then continued. "Something happened on Sunday night."

Aria and Ryan had been friends since birth. They were fixtures in each other's lives because of my friendship with Mac. Like brother and sister. "Something like what?"

Mackenzie glanced away, tears clinging to her eyelashes. Her gaze seemed glued to a simple square vase of fresh-cut hyacinths. She couldn't even look at me.

"Mackenzie, please talk to me. You're worrying me." I teetered between anger and terror.

Turning back to me, the muscles of her jaw tensed. "I caught them having sex in the basement."

Like a trapdoor beneath me swung open, I plummeted. "What?" I yelled. "Are you serious?"

She nodded wordlessly.

I didn't know what to say. I knew Ryan had become sexually active about a year ago when I found condoms in his underwear drawer. He had just turned seventeen, after all, and I figured it would happen sooner or later, no matter how much I preferred he wait. It was a short conversation, one that Grant took the lead on, that went something like this:

Grant: *Your mom found condoms in your room, Ryan. Are you thinking about having sex, son?*

Ryan: *You don't need to have this conversation with me, Dad. I'm already having sex. And yes, I'm being safe.*

Grant: *As long as you're being careful, we don't need to talk about it unless you want to.*

Ryan: *I will never want that conversation, Dad.*

Grant: *All righty.*

Ryan: *Okay.*

Grant: *Want to watch the Steelers game with me?*

Ryan: *If it will make this less awkward, yes.*

We never discussed girls or sex again after that, and I was perfectly happy leaving that topic in Grant's domain. Although I had secretly hoped he, as a doctor, might discreetly leave some pamphlets on venereal diseases and HIV on Ryan's nightstand, no, apparently that would be a violation of the rules of the Guy Club.

"I had no idea they even liked each other like that," I said. "Please tell me they at least used protection?" I asked at length.

Mackenzie glowered. "Shit, Robin, I didn't look to see whether or not he was wearing a rubber."

"It's a valid question—"

"You don't understand, Robin. Aria was trashed. Your son had his way with my little girl and . . ." She left the rest of the sentence hanging in thin air.

"Are you implying that Ryan *raped* Aria?" My breath left my lungs like I'd been sucker-punched.

"No, I'm not implying it. I'm stating it as fact. Aria has no recollection of what happened that night. None. No memory whatsoever. But Ryan clearly knew what he was doing."

"Mackenzie, that doesn't sound like Ryan at all. He would never do something like that—not unless Aria wanted it." Ryan was no predator. Not my straight-A, honor-roll son who babysat his siblings and helped me wash dishes every night. No, I knew my son and that wasn't him.

"No one ever thinks a rapist looks like one. It's not like they wear a sign or something."

"Did it cross your mind that maybe Ryan was trashed too—maybe they both were drinking and it was consensual?" I needed this to be true, because if my own son had done something so unforgivable . . . no, it was incomprehensible.

"I'm sure they were both drinking, but that doesn't change the fact that he went too far."

"*They*—they both went too far," I corrected. "She could have said no."

"You of all people know that's not always true." Mackenzie sighed, closing her eyes and shutting me out. "Look, I know Ryan's history, where he came from. You know, your big family secret, Robin. And like they say, the apple doesn't fall far from the tree . . ."

"You better stop right there." I stabbed at the air.

I hadn't thought about it in so long—the lie I had perpetuated for eighteen years, the lie I had told everyone, even myself, about my son. Only Mackenzie knew the truth, and that was due to a particularly vulnerable night of cocktails mixed with guilt shortly after it happened.

"That has nothing to do with this," I argued.

"Are you kidding? It has *everything* to do with this. You've been lying to everyone for years—lying to your own son about his father. And now you're surprised to find out Ryan is broken?"

Broken? She was speaking as if Ryan was a monster.

"Your son victimized my daughter, Robin. You need to

face that fact. And I think it has everything to do with your lies."

Victimized. Predator. Rape. No no no. That wasn't my son, the boy I raised. I knew Ryan. He loved botany and baseball and sci-fi and his friends. He was kind and considerate and cared about people. There was no way he was capable of hurting a girl he adored, who was like his own sister. Whatever Mackenzie thought she knew was wrong. I held my finger up, a warning. Her only warning.

"You better be very careful what you say next, Mackenzie. If you dare spread this shit about him, you will regret it. Aria could be lying. She could be feeling ashamed for getting caught and isn't being honest with you. I'm sure she knew what she was doing, and she's not that much younger than Ryan. If you think your fifteen-year-old daughter is Miss Purity, you've got a lot to learn about teenage girls."

Mackenzie's mouth dropped open. "Wow, way to take it to a whole new level, calling Aria a slut."

"You're basically accusing me of raising a rapist. What do you expect me to do?"

"I expect you to talk to your son. Tell him the truth about his father. Tell Grant the truth."

"And then what? Let you send my son to jail on trumped-up rape charges when your daughter could be the one lying? Aria could be sleeping around for all you know, and you'll let her tarnish my son's name, destroy his future, all because you don't want to accept who she is?"

Anger and accusations and hot estrogen bubbled around us. I couldn't understand why Mackenzie would go on the attack like this, without getting the facts first. But when I looked her square in the face, I knew why. She was still bitter.

"Is this because you never forgave me for what happened to you?"

"What?" Her palm flew to her cheek, covering the ripple of skin where the scar began. "No! This is about our kids, not about my damn looks. Not everything in life is about feeling pretty, Robin." The way she spat my name seemed to say otherwise.

"I think you're still harboring resentment. You never have gotten over it, so now you're taking it out on Ryan."

Mackenzie jumped up from her chair, knocking it over. She jabbed her finger toward the front door. "Get out. Don't talk to me in my own home like you know me. You know nothing!"

I rose, grabbing my diaper bag and Collette before heading for the door. How did the conversation get so twisted and gnarled? It took a lot of love to hate her like I did right now. But I owed her. I'd always owe her.

"Look, let's take a breather. I don't want this to come between us, Mac, but clearly we're both a little heated right now. I've got to pick Lucas up from school, but maybe once we cool down we can discuss this more rationally."

"I don't want to discuss this again. End of conversation."

"Then what do you want?"

Her eyes were unblinking like a porcelain doll's. "I want you to stay away from us."

Now standing at the doorway, I turned and glared at her. "You want to end more than two decades of friendship just like that?"

"Yeah, just like that."

I faced the front door, wanting to leave but unable to move. Fury clenched me in its fist. I couldn't stop the anger dripping from my lips. "Just because you were invisible in high school doesn't mean everyone else is—especially Aria."

"And just because you were a slut in high school doesn't mean everyone else is," Mackenzie shot right back.

So many lies haunted me from the past that if I turned around to face them, they would swallow me whole. Lies that only Mackenzie knew, secrets she had kept for me. I opened the door, ready to flee, but I couldn't forsake the one person who had held me together all these years—Mackenzie.

I glanced back at her, with her eyes blazing, mouth set crookedly, arms folded. How could our friendship mean so little to her? How could she throw it away over what was probably a misunderstanding?

We stood for a tense moment in a stare down. I didn't want to leave like this; we'd never fought before—not *really* fought—and I didn't know how to cross this divide. But I'd had enough of the unfounded accusations of someone who was supposed to be my closest friend. Mackenzie had always been the peacekeeper. I'd never seen this side of her.

"Please let's not end things like this," I said finally as the warm May air gushed past me. "Can we talk later, once we've both had time to process this?"

"Until you're willing to talk to your son about what he did, there's nothing to talk about. Either you talk to him, or I'll have Owen talk to him. And you know Owen doesn't handle things with words. The choice is yours."

I knew what Owen was capable of. Which meant there was no choice.

Chapter 13

Lily

We need to talk. The most dreaded words in the English language. They never segued into anything good.

We need to talk was the text Grant had sent me five minutes earlier, and the chill that caused the hairs on the back of my neck to stand up warned me it was about to get ugly. A million questions spiraled through my mind in a tornado of worry. Was it Willow who caught us in the pantry? Did Robin find out about the kiss? Was she going to come after me? What did this mean for our friendship—if one still existed?

A tremor pulsed through my hands as worst-case scenarios popped in and out of my head. I headed for the bathroom cupboard and pulled out my bottle of painkillers. Just one to ease my nerves, stem the panic rattling my bones. Maybe two. It was an emergency, after all.

Another *beep* from an incoming text as I swallowed. I walked back to the living room, my chest tightening with each forced breath.

Can I come over?

Well, that didn't make sense. If Robin had found out, Grant certainly wouldn't be flaunting it in her face by coming over. Unless he was coming to warn me. Oh God, was Robin going to kick my ass? I had earned the reputation of a scrapper. I'd gotten in plenty of knock-down, drag-out fracases with other girls when I was a kid. Hell, I'd even been in a couple of damn good catfights in bars as an adult. Somehow I couldn't picture a Goody-Two-shoes like Robin getting down and dirty like that. But if she thought for a moment I'd been boning her man, I knew her claws would come out. I'd rather have that than the mind games chicks tend to play. If only women could be more like men where they used fists to handle a dispute and it was over with, all forgiven with blood and knuckles.

I needed to know what was going on, so I typed a simple answer:

What's going on?

I'll tell you when I get there. On my way.

I paced through the next ten minutes while the drugs worked their magic until I heard a knock. I rushed to the door, preparing myself for the worst as I hurried him inside.

He was barely across the threshold when I blurted out, "Tell me what happened. I'm about to lose my fucking mind, Grant."

He rested one hand on each of my shoulders, then leaned down to hook my gaze on him. "Hey, calm down. There's no problem. I just wanted to see you."

I flicked his hands off my shoulders and backed away, fuming. "What the hell was that all about then, *idiota*? With all that cryptic shit you were texting I was about to go over there and start apologizing to her, begging her to kick my ass!"

Grant pulled me into a hug, his body a warming balm. "Hey, it's okay, Lil. Everything's fine."

"So Robin doesn't know about the kiss?"

"No. Why would you think that she did? Did she say something to you?"

"No, Grant, but your text was vague. Who says they need 'to talk'"—I air-quoted—"unless it's bad?"

"I guess I do." He chuckled, but I wasn't laughing. I was still coming down off my panic attack. I slumped into the sofa. My legs felt sleepy and my arms heavy as the living room rippled like it was underwater.

"What do we need to talk about?" I demanded. "And next time don't word it like that or I'll cut your friggin' balls off."

"Ouch." He cupped his balls; that made me grin. "Well, I wanted to talk about *us*."

I gave a derisive snort. "There is no us, Grant. What we did was a huge mistake, and one I don't want to make again. Willow might have seen us. And even if she didn't, I don't want to risk it again. Plus you're my best friend's husband, father of four, respected pediatrician . . . in the running for Man of the Year. Do you really want to throw all of that away?"

"Being with you doesn't mean I'm no longer a father or doctor, Lily. It's just that things between Robin and I have gotten . . . bad, lately."

"Bad how? Bad enough you don't want to be with her anymore?" Robin had never told me things were anything but perfect. She loved Grant, believed he loved her. She was happy, fulfilled. Everyone could see it in her adoring glances, outspoken praise, the way she orbited her existence around him.

Grant sat next to me and examined the wall behind me intently. I examined *him* intently. Where was this coming from? And who was telling the truth—Robin or Grant? Unless there were two different truths.

"I don't know what I want anymore, Lily. I want to feel something, anything. With Robin, it's been months since we've gone on a date or even had a private conversation without the kids crawling all over us. It's getting too hard."

"Marriage is hard, family is hard, no matter who it's with. If anyone knows that it's me. When Tony left, it destroyed me. I still haven't recovered from it and it's been months, because once you find the right person, you don't let go. You hold on with everything you've got."

"I'm tired of being the only one holding on, Lil. She let go a long time ago."

I wagged my finger in the air at him Italian style. "Not true. She's never let go; she's just got too much to hold on to right now, burdened with four kids and all their activities, managing a home, supporting you while you got your practice up and running, keeping your perfect lives in place. Give her time."

Grant raised a skeptical eyebrow. "Why are you defending her?"

"Because I love her, and I love you two together. You think I want to feel this way about you—lusting after my friend's man? Hell no! Robin is family to me, and she's the most amazing woman you'll ever find. We're both lucky to have her in our lives, so don't go screwing that up."

"I think we already did."

I shook my head, backing into the arm of the sofa. "No, it's not too late to fix it. I was lonely and you filled the hole in my heart. But it's over; we can pretend it never happened. So go back to your wife and woo the shit out of her, okay?"

I wanted Grant, but I wanted Robin more. Grant would be a fleeting mistake that washed in and out of my life. Robin was my rock, and if our friendship crumbled, I had nothing left to stand on but sinking sand. And yet as Grant shifted across the sofa toward me, he smelled so damn good right now . . .

My emotions were all over the place—desire, guilt, push, pull, push, pull.

"I've tried, God knows I've tried. We always end up getting interrupted with the kids, or Robin's too tired from the baby being up all night. There's always *something*."

I rolled my eyes. "Man up and masturbate like the rest of us. But don't throw your life away for an easy fuck. As your friend, I'm telling you that you have a good thing—a *great* thing—with Robin. Leaving her will kill her—and you. And your kids. You think about that before you go proposing to the next loose *puttana* you meet."

He chuckled and shook his head. "So now you're a *puttana*?"

"If the shoe fits . . ." I'd been called worse, and I didn't care. I knew who I was and where I came from, and I accepted myself, flaws and all. They gave me character, as Papa always told me. All that was left was figuring out where I was going.

"So your sage advice is I'm supposed to be resigned to misery?"

I groaned. This man was insufferable. "Don't you think you're acting a little melodramatic? It's Robin—she'd do anything for you."

"Anything? She doesn't touch me, Lil. We haven't had sex in over eight months! A man has needs . . . and at the rate I'm masturbating, I'll have carpal tunnel any day now!"

If my jaw hadn't been hinged to my face, it would have dropped into my lap at that number—eight months! If there was one thing Tony and I had never lacked, it was sexual chemistry. I knew how to keep my man satisfied, and let's just say it wasn't through my Italian cooking. As for masturbation, I knew how he felt. I could barely get through a week myself without paddling the ol' pink canoe.

"I'm so sorry, Grant. I had no idea it was that bad. Do you know why?"

"Like I said, the kids. Work. Extracurricular activities. You name it, it's coming between us. The second we get alone time, Collette wakes up screaming. The moment I try to get frisky with Robin in the shower, Lucas barges in wanting Daddy shower time. That damn baby is always attached to her boob like a friggin' milk vampire. I can't win. And I don't know if I want to keep working at it. We've grown apart. I hardly know her anymore. I don't think she knows me either. When you've been married as long as we have, things get . . . more than just tough. Sometimes you can't go back to what you had; it's easier to move forward into something new."

"Grant, we're not talking about a new pair of shoes here. We're talking about a marriage. Kids. A home. Family. You can't just throw that away because you want something new."

"I don't just want something new, Lily. I'm trying to tell you . . . I want you. I want you, Lily. I'm in love with you, and I don't know how to turn it off. You're all I think about, morning, noon, and night. You're everything I ever desired in a woman. Feisty. Passionate. Fun. Sexy. I hate that I feel this way, because I know it's wrong, but it's real. It's the realest thing I've felt in a long time. And I don't know what to do about it anymore."

This couldn't be happening. I wanted his attention, but not his heart. And yet here he was, pouring it out on the floor in front of me. I wanted to wade in it . . . but I couldn't. I shouldn't. Damn, the temptation was so strong.

"What do you think you should do about it?" My words were a whisper. I could feel the high of the drugs, of the pheromones surging through me. My control slipped through my fingers.

In one heartbeat his thigh was touching mine. His hand pulling mine. His fingers intertwining with mine. The room warped as my vision swayed under his spell.

"I know what I *want* to do about it."

"Tell me."

"No. I'll show you."

He leaned forward and kissed me, and I kissed him back. He lifted up my shirt, his tongue tickling my stomach and fingers unclasping my bra. His lips sought my nipple, found it, knew exactly what to do. I was lost in my desire with no way out.

Pulling my legs up under him, Grant climbed on top of me, tearing at the fabric that separated us. My legs instinctively circled his waist, drawing him into me. I wanted his flesh touching mine, his sweat soaking my skin, his weight pressing me. As we ripped each other's clothes off, a small voice in the back of my brain warned me to stop, saying we couldn't ever come back from this, that it would destroy everything and everyone I loved. The voice filled me up with warnings: *There is no return,* it said. *No return . . .*

And then I shut the little voice up.

Chapter 14

Mackenzie

I drove with the windows down, wind teasing my hair back to the 1980s, as I pulled into my lily-white suburban neighborhood. I unstuck a clump of blond strands from my lip gloss and admired the manicured lawns and power-walking moms. Owen and I had been house-hunting for months when we found it. Well, until Robin talked it up so much it was either stick an ice pick in my ears or drop in on the open house. She was right; it was perfect. Everything about the neighborhood, from the gated entry to the fenced-in playground to the lifeguarded community pool, felt safe and secure from drive-by shootings and home invasions and gangs roaming the inner-city streets.

How naïve I had been. Because shadowy horrors lurked among us in our glass houses. There was no escaping them, even among friends. Even among spouses.

The trunk was full of this week's groceries, meals planned like each week before. I was supposed to be gone by now, unreachable, untouchable. But instead I was going through the motions as if nothing had changed, as if the plan had simply been a dream. It was no one's fault but my own. I had my chance and blew it.

My cul-de-sac was one right turn up ahead, but I slowed down to a crawl. I hadn't felt like facing Owen since Sunday night; he knew my tells by heart, and I wasn't ready to, well, tell.

I'd spent the last hour balancing out the pros and cons of explaining to Owen what I saw Ryan doing to our little girl. As much as I wanted to protect this secret from getting out and spreading like wildfire, it wasn't my secret to protect. It wasn't even Aria's secret, because she had no idea it happened. The truth was locked and sealed. Hidden in fog, all she seemed to remember was watching some stupid science-fiction movie with Ryan, both of them drinking on the sly and getting silly and "a little" flirtatious, and waking up hungover. She couldn't recall how she got home, then woke up vowing never to drink again. Well, that was one good thing at least. It only made her angry whenever I mentioned Sunday night. I was lucky I had gotten the information out of her that I did.

But was she being honest with me? Kids were notorious

liars when they thought they'd get in trouble. Part of me wished I knew the truth, but the other part preferred the ignorance. I banished this pointless line of reasoning before it unspooled. To tell or not tell Owen—this should be my focus.

One thing about that fateful night nagged at me. Some pain . . . and bleeding. It had to have been her first time. Ryan had taken her virginity. How could she ever trust a boy again after what her friend of fifteen years did to her? How could she ever overcome this? It wasn't my cross to bear, but it sure felt heavy on my shoulders.

Telling Owen was a last resort. With Owen came vengeance. With vengeance came publicity. And right now, Aria seemed blissfully unaware of how close her life was to being shattered. If she never found out what really happened, I hoped she could move on to be healthy, happy, whole. But if I told her . . . what would be left of her? No mother should ever be faced with this heartbreaking choice. And yet it was all I could think about.

Up ahead, my two-story brick house came into view, the windows glowing against the evening's gray descent. I rolled up to the driveway, first noticing the unfamiliar mud-brown Honda heap parked at the edge of my lawn. Eaten away by rust along one side, the door on the driver's side was painted a garish green in contrast with the rest of the hooptie's hen-turd brown, like my mamma used to say. Next I saw who it belonged to—the woman dashing across my lawn toward it. I jumped out of my car.

"Excuse me, do you need something?" I called out.

She only ran faster as I jogged over to her. I couldn't get

a good look at her face, but she was a scrawny little thing with mousy brown hair.

A moment later her tires screeched across the pavement as she nearly ran me over.

"You've got a helluva nerve, almost hitting me!" I screamed at her car as it was rounding the corner and then out of sight.

I hauled the groceries inside, finding Owen in the kitchen. After grabbing bags out of my arms, he began putting things away while I stood with my hand propped on my outthrust hip, the don't-bullshit-me stance I always used to demand his attention.

"Who was that?"

"Who was who?" He continued casually opening and closing cupboards and refrigerator drawers as the bags of food disappeared into their usual organized compartments.

Oh, he wanted to play games, did he?

"The woman I just spotted running from our house. She seemed awfully scared to meet me. You better damn well have an explanation, Owen."

It didn't escape me, the accusatory tone with which I reprimanded him, when what I was doing in secret was so much worse.

"Wrong house. She was looking for someone else. Sorry to disappoint you that it's not something more scandalous." He said it so matter-of-factly I almost believed him.

"Who was she looking for?"

"I don't remember. I just know it wasn't a name I recognized. Might have been the previous homeowners. Oh, wait. I almost forgot." He reached behind the drying rack and pulled out a shiny metallic cone of wrapped flowers. "Got you these."

His eyes sparkled as he waited for my reaction. When his smile faded, I realized I hadn't reacted at all.

"Oh, honey, thank you. What are these for?" I sniffed the flowers as any grateful wife would do, then began unwrapping them from the crinkly paper.

"Just because I love you. Do you like them?" Did he even care if I liked them? Or did he care more that he liked feeling like a doting husband? I guess control freaks needed affirmation too.

"I love them. You're so thoughtful. Thank you." I tenderly placed them in a vase, admiring the bright splash of color they gave the room. I always was a sucker for flowers. The vibrancy, the sweet scent, the warmth they promised. Even weeds, with their twisted, choking nature, could be beautiful. You just had to look for their beauty. I knew the feeling.

"Anyway, babe, I'm going to watch some TV until dinner. I'm beat." His kiss stung my forehead as he passed me on his way to the living room.

Flowers could make up for a squabble. Their bright heads peeking out from the edge of a vase could even hide the darkness that lived in our home. But they couldn't make up for the emotional sinkhole that grew bigger every day and would eventually swallow us whole. If I let it.

Owen, Aria, and I ate a silent dinner that night. A brooding presence hung in the air, and we all felt it. Later, in the living room, Owen fell asleep on the sofa watching a Pittsburgh Pirates baseball game. Aria retreated to her room, where she'd been spending an inordinate amount of time lately. I sat on my bed, neatly made with burnt orange decorative pillows that added a splash of color against my boring white walls that Owen insisted was a tinted shade of Chantilly lace. White was white was white, in my opinion, but it didn't matter. Tinted or not, he vetoed my request for turquoise. Said it was too "beachy for a house in Western Pennsylvania." As a little girl I adored a beautiful turquoise bracelet Mamma had given me, a family heirloom supposedly crafted by an honest-to-goodness Navajo Indian. I lost the bracelet and caught hell from Mamma for my carelessness. I wish I still had that bracelet. Well, like Mamma always said: "If wishes was horses, honey, we'd all take a ride."

My cool palms sucked the heat out of a mug of coffee that was now lukewarm. It was probably too late to be drinking caffeine at almost nine o'clock at night, but I wouldn't be sleeping tonight anyway. The pros and cons of having the conversation with Owen looped endlessly in my head.

Pros:
Ryan learns lesson
Justice
Prevent another girl from getting hurt
No more secrets
Aria should know the truth

Cons:
Truth destroys Aria
Aria feels unfixable shame
Owen kills Ryan
Owen goes to jail . . . or should this be in the Pros list?

The list of reasons to tell him was long. There was only one significant downside, but it created the biggest aftershock. Should Aria know? What if she had mentally blocked it for a reason? What if telling her utterly destroyed her? Telling her could strip her of all confidence, all innocence, all joy . . . and there was no way to return her to her former well-adjusted self.

I had seen what depression did to Robin. It was an ugly, unrelenting beast that would feed and feed and feed until there was nothing left to devour.

I sipped the cold coffee as Owen shuffled in, shutting the bedroom door behind him. He settled on the bed next to me.

"Have a good nap?" I asked as pleasantly as I could manage.

"Yeah. The Pirates lost. Again. What are you doing in here?"

"I've just been . . . thinking." I stopped, wanting to say more, afraid to say more.

Owen's eyes narrowed with concern. "Thinking about what?"

Now was the time. I had to do it—the list couldn't be wrong.

"I need to tell you something, but I don't know how."

Worry all over his face, worry in the awkward way he scooted away from me, worry in the way his hand adhered to my knee. I imagined what he was thinking—that I was about to confess to an affair, or financial troubles, or cancer. I wondered if he'd be relieved to discover the truth, or if it would be as devastating to him as it felt to me.

"Mackenzie, whatever happened, we'll get through it together."

"You don't even know what it is. So how can you promise that?"

"Are . . . are you leaving me for someone else?"

It had been a constant question of his, even after eighteen years of marriage. As if I had the time or the means to find another man. I was literally home all day every day, with Owen always watching me. When he was at work, our security cameras captured my every move, any comings and goings. A waste of money when you live in a gated community, but "you can't put a price tag on safety," he'd say. When I headed out, he clocked my mileage like he was my auditor. He checked my phone records, browsing history, everything . . . everything that he knew about.

It was the things he didn't know about that I could hide. Something so much worse than an affair.

It was ludicrous that his thoughts always turned to infidelity, because I would need to already have a life in order to chase a new one.

"Seriously, Owen, that's what you think I need to talk about—that I'm cheating on you?"

"I don't know. You sound anxious about whatever it is. I'm grasping at straws."

"No, it's not an affair."

"Then spit it out already." He was losing patience, and so was I.

"First promise me that you won't fly off the handle." The promise was laughable, but it was worth a shot. Owen was anything but calculating. Overreaction was his middle name. Never thinking anything through.

"Okay, okay, I promise, but this is getting exhausting. Just tell me what's going on."

"On Sunday night at Robin's dinner party, I walked in on

104

Aria and Ryan in the basement. Ryan was . . . I can't say it, Owen." I choked on the word, like it was sharp glass stuck in my throat. *Rape.* I couldn't say it. It was too revolting a word to speak aloud.

"Can't say what? Did Ryan do something to Aria?"

I nodded. That was the best I could do. I needed him to follow the trail on his own.

"Did they have sex, Mackenzie?"

I nodded again, then shook my head. I set the coffee cup down on my nightstand, unable to steady it in my trembling hands. "I don't think it was consensual."

And cue the grief all over again. My face fell into my palms as I sobbed, waiting for Owen to wrap his arms around me in comfort. But all I felt was the cool empty air around me. I looked up, the room wavy through my tears.

Owen stormed toward his dresser where he kept his gun, and suddenly I was more afraid for Ryan than angry with him.

"Owen, stop! You can't do this!"

"Just watch me."

He tossed his folded boxers aside as he unearthed his gun safe. His fingers frantically tapped the password in, then he opened it, brandishing the weapon, a Glock 19. I only knew that because Owen had drilled gun safety into my head, even dragged me to the shooting range a handful of times. I knew nothing about guns otherwise, nor did I care to learn.

"Please, stop. Somebody's gonna get killed."

"That's the point, Mackenzie! That little punk deserves to die. I'm going to make sure that happens."

"Do you seriously want to go to jail for murder? You'll never see the light of day again."

"They'll never find his body once I'm done with him. No body, no crime, no jail." It struck me that Owen knew exactly what he was talking about. That thought sent an icy chill through me.

"Owen, be logical. For once in your life think about your family. Aria doesn't even know what happened. She's already lost so much. Losing her father too . . . please stop!"

I was becoming hysterical now. Begging, pleading, trying to reason with him. "You will go to jail for life, Owen! They'll find out. Ryan's a kid. You're angry, yes, but we need to figure out what to do first. Not just freak out. Okay? This isn't like last time." Owen shot me a knowing glance. "Please, honey, give me the gun . . ."

I reached for the weapon, scared it might go off in the exchange. I knew what this gun was capable of; I'd seen Owen use it in anger before, seen what a man gripped by jealousy and rage could do. It was the one secret I'd hoped would eventually slink back into the depths of my memory, forever forgotten. And yet it still lived.

I had hoped to bury the past, but every once in a while, like in this exact moment, the memory would climb out of its coffin for a visit. The metallic odor of gunpowder on his hands, the distant crack of the bullet zipping out. Unfortunately, I knew Owen's volatility firsthand, and as much as I hated Ryan for what he'd done, I couldn't condemn him to death. If Ryan didn't survive this, none of the rest of us would either.

"The gun," I pleaded.

"So that you can defend him, Mac? I don't think so." Owen lifted the barrel, then aimed it at me.

Chapter 15

Robin

Winter in Western Pennsylvania hurt. It bit your cheeks, chapped your lips, stung your throat. Worst of all was when you didn't wear weather-appropriate shoes. Then it froze your toes numb until they felt like blocks of ice weighing fifty pounds each.

Trudging uphill with feet so encumbered was another torture winter sadistically enjoyed. I had just finished my last class of the semester, of the year actually, and I couldn't wait to reach my dorm where I hoped Lily and Mackenzie had mugs of steaming hot cocoa waiting. Boxed mac 'n' cheese, popcorn, and hot cocoa were about the only things we used our kitchenette for, and even the mac 'n' cheese usually tasted inedible when we didn't have milk and butter on hand. If you've never tried watery mac 'n' cheese, don't start now. The box tastes better.

"Hey, wait up!" someone yelled behind me, but I didn't recognize the masculine voice. A crowd of freshmen rushed along the sidewalk around me, but no one else stopped. I certainly wasn't about to.

"Chick with the long brown hair and impractical shoes!" So it was me he was calling to. I turned around. By the glow of a solitary streetlight I could just make out the figure approaching me in the dusk through the cascade of falling snow.

"Do I know you?" I asked.

His eyes widened with excitement or recognition, I wasn't sure which. "Yeah, I'd know a face that pretty anywhere. We've definitely met."

He stepped into a patch of light along the curb, giving me a better look at him. His cheeks were rosy from the cold and his hair was flocked with snowflakes. He looked faintly familiar, but not anyone I knew. Not from my classes, at least.

"Are you a student here?"

By *here* I was referring to the only college in Beaver Falls; it was the only thing that put the small town on the map.

"No, but I know I've seen you before. You ever eat at Pizza Joe's?" he asked.

Bingo. That's where I knew him from. I'd probably seen him countless times, since the pizza shop was a local college favorite, especially for those of us who only knew how to cook watery mac 'n' cheese and popcorn.

"Oh yeah. I think I remember you now." It was Cute Waiter Guy. His name began with a *juh* sound, but it flittered at the edge of my tongue. *John? James?*

He was still cute—cute enough to introduce myself to, but not quite cute enough to be memorable. College life was full of new crushes, and even I could admit I was a tad boy crazy. He looked about my age, maybe a couple years older. I suddenly felt naked without makeup, so I pulled out my metallic lip gloss and puckered up, swiping my lips before pocketing the gloss.

"I'm Robin."

I stretched out my arm, offering my gloved hand. With cheap faux charm, he kissed my knuckle and I chuckled at his old-fashioned display of chivalry. It actually worked, though. He was instantly cuter.

"I'm Geoffrey. Friends call me G."

"How original, *G*." I rolled my eyes, lacing the letter with sarcasm.

"Aw, don't judge. I can't help what generic nicknames other people come up with."

"Know what my friends and I used to call you? Cute Waiter Guy."

Cocky as ever, he smirked as if he thought that was apt. "Oh, yeah? That's funny. Where you headin'?"

"To my dorm. Then I'm going to grab dinner in the cafe-teria. I'd invite you, but it's students only." I shrugged, resuming my stride. My dorm was still a long half-mile uphill from the main campus and I was wearing high-heeled tennis shoes, the worst possible choice for walking in slippery snow but all the rage in 2000.

Technically G could have purchased a meal ticket, but there was no way I was bringing this stranger into my judgmental world just yet. He'd get eaten alive. If my friends saw me show up with some new guy at dinner, the interrogation would never end. Plus I wasn't sure I was interested enough to force myself through a whole meal with this guy just yet.

I'll admit, he was intimidating. And alluring at the same time. Definitely a bad boy with streetwise swagger. I wondered how much preparation went into getting his hair to look so carelessly disheveled. He wore a Kurt Cobain-ish flannel lumberjack shirt and frayed jeans, but no coat. That just wouldn't be cool, even when temps were in the twenties. Then it occurred to me: maybe he had fallen on hard times. Maybe his grunginess wasn't an affectation. Maybe he was homeless. It was a wickedly provocative notion—showing pity on a cute homeless guy, maybe showing him a good time. But I wasn't that kind of a girl, though people sometimes made that assumption because I was a notorious flirt.

As Geoffrey matched my pace, he turned and walked backward, keeping step with me as he talked. "How about instead of shitty cafeteria food you join me for dinner?"

Don't do it, apprehension told me.

Then Geoffrey smiled, his blue eyes icy and penetrating. *Get bent, apprehension.*

"If you say Pizza Joe's the answer is no. You're not allowed to take me where you work."

He shot me a strange, almost guilty look. "Why not?"

"Because it's lame and unoriginal. If you can suggest someplace more original, I might say yes. But no promises."

"You drive a hard bargain, but I think I can win you

over. I know a really good place right outside of town. Like Italian?"

"Who doesn't like Italian?"

"All right then. It's settled. My treat. My car's parked right over there." He pointed across the street at a narrow alley that ran behind the soccer field.

"Now?" I glanced down at my bedazzled jeans and stretchy gauze shirt, the latest trend I'd borrowed from Britney Spears, bundled under a thick fur-lined coat. "Hell no. I don't know you well enough to go to dinner with you."

"Isn't that kind of the point of a date? To get to know one another?"

"No, you're supposed to call me first. Woo me with your words. Then a date might be on the table."

"Wow, old-fashioned, huh?"

"Yep, I'm a lady."

He laughed. "Why do I doubt that?"

"What's that supposed to mean?"

"Girls who wear jeweled pants and high heels like that"—he pointed at my shoes—"generally aren't ladylike. But I could be wrong."

"And you're such a gentleman, huh?"

"I never said that. But I'd be willing to prove I am."

"How so?"

The wind was picking up, along with the snowfall. It stirred my hair into a halo and bit my skin. Geoffrey must have noticed me shivering.

"At least let me give you a ride home, and then I'll follow all the proper protocol for winning your heart, milady." He swept the air with his arm in a gallant gesture.

"Does that actually work on girls?"

"I don't know. I've never had to try this hard before. You tell me. Is it working?"

His cheeks, ruddy from the cold, lifted with a grin I couldn't resist. A warm car sounded really good to my frozen toes. Maybe dinner wouldn't be so bad either. I hadn't had authentic Italian food since Lily last cooked for me and had got me hooked. The overcooked noodles and canned marinara our cafeteria served were barf-worthy. How could I say no?

"All right, I'll tell you what. I'll let you buy me dinner, but this better be damn good for me to blow off my friends."

"I promise it's to die for."

As we walked to his car we chatted about how eggplant parmigiana got an undeserved bad rep for being slimy, and agreed that alfredo was the tastiest among the sauces. In the alley several cars were lined up against a crumbling brick wall. As an extension of campus parking, usually faculty and athletes parked here, and it didn't occur to me that Geoffrey wasn't either of those.

"I'm the green sedan," he said, pointing to the crookedly parked car—a nondescript Japanese import, in rough condition—at the end of the row.

"Nice parking job. I'm guessing you didn't pass your driver's test on the first try?" I teased.

"Hey, be nice! You try parking against a brick wall with zero forgiveness if you're too close. I didn't want to scratch up my nice paint job."

I laughed, because the car looked older than me . . . and not in the cool classic car kind of way. My mind flashed back to my earlier impression of G, and I wondered if perhaps he was living out of the ratty car. When we reached it, my suspicion was all but confirmed when I glanced in the back window and saw a tattered pillow and blanket draped across the back seat. Suddenly this didn't feel right.

He pulled out a set of keys from his pocket and led me to the passenger-side door. "Allow me." He poured the words into my ear as if this was a typical date. "See? I told you I was a gentleman."

"I don't know, Geoffrey," I said lamely. "Maybe this isn't such a great idea after all. I should be studying—"

His gaze tripped down my body with greedy hunger. I shuffled back a step, but not quickly enough. He threw me up against the wall and pinned me, awakening a legion of goose bumps that crawled over my skin. "Don't hand me that shit, you cockteaser."

His breath was thick in my ear. His tongue shot out and flicked the lobe leaving wet residue.

"What the hell are you doing?" I tried to push him away but he was too strong. "Please don't," I begged, but my words were a mere puff of smoke in the cold air.

One hand covered my mouth as the other jabbed his car key against my throat. I scraped at him with my fingernails, but the pressure of his heavy chest against mine limited my reach. I screamed into his hand uselessly, then tried to bite it as my breaths grew shallow. He jabbed the key harder.

"Try that again and I'll puncture your goddamn throat!" he warned. Hot spittle sprayed my face. "You wanna breathe? I'll let ya. Don't want you to pass out. I want you to be awake when I'm fucking you."

He adjusted his hand on my mouth, giving me a tiny gasp of air, the other ripping the button of my jeans loose. He tugged my pants roughly to the ground and his hand groped between my legs while snowflakes carelessly danced around us. I struggled, but the key returned to my throat.

"If you just let me finish, it will go a lot better for you." He drizzled the words across me. "But if you fight, well, I can't promise I won't fucking kill you. Got it? Nod if you understand."

I didn't want to nod, didn't want to give him the satisfaction.

"I said nod or die, bitch!" he hissed.

I nodded frantically, tears filling my eyes. As he boosted me up against the wall, my skull smacked against the jagged brick. I winced at the stabbing pain of him entering me. But the emptiness filling me felt worse. Falling into a black abyss, I prayed for death.

Chapter 16

Robin

TUESDAY NIGHT

Sticky with sweat, I bolted upright at the sound of my bedroom door squeaking open. When was Grant going to get around to oiling that? I'd only mentioned it a thousand times already.

The nightmare was still vivid in my head, though ripped around the edges. Early evening moonlight streamed through the blinds, casting jail bars on the wall. The glow hung on a silhouette by the door.

The bed was a disheveled mess, Collette snuggled in a nest of rumpled sheets hanging off the mattress and pillows strewn everywhere. I had only gotten halfway through straightening it this morning and never got back to it before falling asleep with the baby at my breast. How ironic that it seemed so important to make the bed every morning when the rest of my life was in shambles.

"Mom, are you okay?"

It was Ryan. Even in the darkness I sensed his apprehension. I caught it in the way his voice tilted. I knew my son so well. And yet maybe I didn't know him at all.

"Yeah, sweetie, I'm okay," I whispered, code for *baby sleeping so don't wake her.*

"I heard you crying."

"Oh. I fell asleep while nursing and had a bad dream." I hadn't realized anyone heard me crying. I wondered how many times my family had heard me suffer through that same nightmare over the years.

I admit, I was surprised. I hadn't expected Ryan to come to me. We rarely interacted these days. By the time he turned fourteen he became a stranger in our house, always off at a friend's, or at baseball practice, or out celebrating a game-winning play, or holing up in the game room with his latest video game.

I smiled grimly at the recollection of Ryan at age four, a little boy who would cling to my leg as if it was his life support. He was my little shadow. And when Willow came along, oh boy, watch out! The fits of covetous rage as he temper-tantrumed on the floor, legs flailing, fists pumping because I couldn't hold him while I nursed his sister. Back then I had thought it was so sweet, his jealousy over me, but now I wondered . . . I wondered if it was a sign of something darker. A demon that lived in him, growing stronger over the years until it finally took full form in our basement two days ago.

I tossed a pillow aside and patted the empty space next to me on the bed. "Come sit, honey."

"What's going on?" Ryan sat, stiff and awkward and uncertain, like he hadn't been knitted inside my body. He was part of me, and I part of him. Didn't he realize that?

Tonight he wasn't the careless teenager whose shoulders slumped casually and whose eyes held a dull gaze, as if he were perpetually just waking up.

"I need to ask you something, and I need you to be honest with me." I searched for affirmation in his pale blue eyes. They weren't Grant's eyes, or my eyes either. I could only assume they belonged to his sperm donor.

"Okaaaay." The elongated word meant he was scared. I could only imagine the thoughts racing through his head. I needed to get this over with.

"I want to know what happened Sunday night—with Aria in the basement. Tell me everything, and be honest. Because I already have an idea of what happened, but I need to hear it from you first."

There. It was out. My shoulders stiffened. I prepared myself for whatever came next.

"So you know." He shifted away from me, head hanging. Shame? Fear? I couldn't read him.

"No, Ryan, I don't know. That's why I'm asking you to tell me what happened from your perspective." I grabbed his chin, forcing him to look me in the eyes. "I want to know exactly what you did, what Aria did—every detail. Even if you did something wrong, I need to know so I can protect you."

He nudged my hand away and it fell on his knee. I needed that physical connection, because he needed it too.

"I . . . I . . . I don't want to talk about it."

"Please, honey, whatever happened, we can deal with it together. But if you try to keep it a secret from me, it's only going to get worse."

He sighed. "Me, Willow, and Aria were all hanging out, until Aria wanted to try some wine. So we told Willow to leave, you know, so she wouldn't see us drinking and tell on us. Anyway, I drank more than I should have. Aria did too. We were both feeling pretty buzzed and we ended up kissing."

"So you were drinking *alcohol*?"

He nodded.

I shook my head. "I don't expect you to be perfect, but you should know better than that, Ry."

"I didn't even want wine. Aria just wanted to try it. We were only having some fun."

"Yeah, and look where that got you. Anyway, continue. What happened after you kissed?"

Ryan picked at a loose thread on the bedspread, concentrating on it. "She kissed me back, and I thought she wanted to, you know, have sex. I mean, she seemed into it. So we started to, like for a minute, when her mom showed up. I swear, it happened so fast, but I didn't think Aria was upset or anything about it. Did she say she was upset?"

The weight of guilt clearly hung on him like a noose, but I had no consolation to offer. He couldn't see what bubbled beneath the surface of his life. Possible rape charges. Imminent jail time. A sexual offender record following him for life. These worries curled around me, squeezed every maternal bone in my body.

I didn't want to tell him, but I had to. He needed to know the truth.

"Ryan, honey, Aria doesn't even remember what happened. I think she was too drunk to know what she was doing."

"No, Mom, she was into it, I swear. She kissed me first."

"But did she verbally say she wanted to take it further—to have sex?"

Ryan examined his bitten fingernails, a nervous habit we shared, then looked up at me. His eyes were confused and unfocused. "Oh, God, I don't know, Mom. I don't remember. We were drinking and talking and having fun. It started with a kiss . . . and I don't know. Did I do something bad?"

I couldn't speak, and he read my silence.

His breathing escalated into shallow panting, and his gaze darted around the room. "What did I do? Mom, am I in trouble?"

I placed a hand on his shoulder, and another one grabbed his palm. "Calm down, Ry. Breathe." My voice was calm, soothing, but he lingered on the verge of panic. "Nothing is happening. I just want to get your side of things so that we can sort it out. Are you okay, Ry?"

His eyes lowered, then met mine as I talked him off the ledge.

"I know this isn't easy, but we just need to get to the bottom of this." I thought back to my confrontation with Mac. She didn't know if Ryan had used protection. I dreaded asking him, but I had to. "Ry, I assume you still have condoms in your underwear drawer."

His hand rose to rub his forehead, shading his embarrassment. "No secrets around this madhouse."

"Yeah. I have to ask you: did you . . . have one on?"

He hesitated only a moment. "No, Mom."

I felt my heart drop to my shoes. "And did you . . . ejaculate?"

"Geez, Mom! I don't . . . I mean, I'm not sure. Maybe . . . a little. Mrs. Fischer came in and—"

"That's okay, Ry. Can you answer one more question for me?"

He nodded.

"Did you specifically ask her if she wanted to have sex?"

"Um, no, I don't think so."

"Okay, well, that's important. But you know she's only fifteen. And you're eighteen. You . . . took advantage of her, honey." As if *honey* sugarcoated the four-letter reality. The reality that could put my son in jail. He was an adult. Aria was a minor. But I couldn't utter it. This was my son, not a rapist.

"Mom, I swear I didn't mean to. She didn't push me away or say no or anything."

"Not saying no isn't the same as saying yes, Ryan. You know that, right? Just because a girl doesn't fight back doesn't mean she wants it. Please tell me you understand that!" I was yelling now as my own trauma needled every nerve in my body. Hands pressing against my mouth. Fingers squeezing my neck closed. Pressure, then a snap of pain as he forced himself inside me.

My face fell into my palms as I pushed the images away. *Please, not now. I can't fall apart in front of my son!*

"Mom, I love Aria. I've always loved her. I would never do anything to intentionally hurt her. I didn't know—I didn't think. Are you saying I . . . I raped her?"

Ryan was crying now, and I cried with him. I pulled him into a hug, because I couldn't say anything more. I couldn't pacify his fear. I couldn't free his conscience.

"I don't know, honey, I don't know." I shook my head sadly. "Mackenzie is going to tell Owen, and God knows what he'll do. He could take matters into his own hands, or press charges . . ." My fears piled one on top of the other.

"And then what?"

"And then it's up to the court to determine what happens. I'm so sorry, Ry."

We sat huddled together, Ryan sobbing into my shoulder for his sins, me weeping into the darkness for my son. Finally Ryan sat up, looking more intense than I'd ever seen him.

"I've got to talk to Aria. I need to tell her I'm sorry. I need to make things right with her. And if Owen kicks my ass, so be it. I'll get what I deserve."

"Honey, Owen could turn you in to the police! What you did is a crime. And you're not allowed to see or speak to Aria—not until things cool down. Or until we speak to a lawyer. We need to figure things out first."

"Mom, Aria needs to know. It's not fair to her to keep her in the dark. And she needs to hear it from *me*."

"No, Ryan. Some things are better left unsaid. When it's something that could really hurt someone you care about, it's not always best to tell them. Sometimes secrets protect others." Like the secret I couldn't tell Grant, the secret I couldn't tell Ryan.

Ryan looked at me, confusion stamped on his young face. It broke my heart to see him so broken like this.

"I don't know, Mom, I think you're wrong. I don't think lying protects other people. I think lying protects only yourself. So if you want me to lie, I'm sorry, but I can't. I've got to tell the truth. Aria deserves to know."

I had to stop him from doing something he'd regret, something that could destroy his chance at a future. Any admission to Aria could convict him. I could plead with him, but he wasn't listening.

The words tumbled past my lips before I could pull them back.

"Ryan, your dad isn't your biological father."

Chapter 17

Mackenzie

It wasn't the first time Owen had pointed a gun at me.

The first time was shortly after we'd gotten married during a vicious reaction after I told him I wanted to go on a girls' getaway with Lily and Robin. That night I learned two important things: placate, then extricate.

"Owen, I'm not the one you want to hurt." Although my voice remained calm, fear exploded inside me. "Together we can deal with Ryan, but not like this. Think about the risk. Think about Aria. There's another way to handle it, but not with a gun."

Owen's gaze shifted to his trembling hands, then flicked

123

back up at me. I'd managed to soothe him from his rage, but prying the handgun from his tense fingers was another matter.

"I'm here for you, honey," I assured him. "You and me, a team."

When his arms slackened, I stepped forward, then lured the weapon from his grip, dewy with sweat.

I carefully placed it on the dresser, then pivoted the barrel toward the wall. I was too distracted to secure the safety switch, which was probably best. Considering how violently my hands shook, I'd probably end up firing off a round instead.

Ever since *that day*, the day Owen's real nature clawed its way out of his charming costume, I had developed a fear of guns—well, guns in the wrong hands. After all, I was a dyed-in-the-wool Southerner who grew up with rifles and shotguns, went target shooting with my daddy, always maintaining a healthy respect for a firearm's power. But then Owen showed me what a gun could do beyond a hole in a wildly flapping target hanging from a branch, or an empty beer can perched on a tree stump. That tiny conical projectile could shred flesh, tear sinew, splatter gray matter. I didn't want it anywhere near this rampaging Hulk version of Owen.

"I want to kill him, Mac. God help me, I want to hurt him like he hurt my baby girl." Owen was pacing a hole in the carpet, but at least he was calming down a little.

"Hold your horses, honey. I know you're angry, but we have to figure out a better way of dealing with this that doesn't involve killing a kid."

"A kid? That's what you think he is? He's a man now, Mackenzie, and men are supposed to protect women, not hurt them. He deserves what he gets."

"And what do you think he should get? A bullet in his brain?"

"If it were up to me, yes. That's what he deserves. Put predators like him six feet under where they belong. God only knows what he's done to Willow."

"Owen! She's his little sister!"

"And Aria was like a sister. Don't you see? He's grown up with Aria all his life, and yet the second he got a chance to . . . God, when I think of him on top of her—"

He screamed like some wounded beast. His eyes were crazy and a huge blue vein stood out on his temple. I instinctively moved away from him.

"Whoa, babe, it's all right. Had to get that out of my system." He reached out and squeezed my shoulder—a rare display of tenderness.

"You're not helping matters, Owen. We need to figure out what to do now. Do we tell Aria? Do we just let it go away? Do we go to the police? I don't know what to do, or what's best for Aria."

"I'll tell you what's best. We've got to press charges. That boy shouldn't be allowed to get away with this scot-free."

"*That boy* is my best friend's son. We've known Ryan since he was born. This isn't some stranger we're talking about. If we press charges, he could end up in jail. His life will be ruined. There goes college and a decent job and a normal life. You don't bounce back from something like that. Plus everything that happened will be made public, which would be devastating for Aria."

"Then what are you saying—we do nothing? Because doing nothing is the same as saying it was okay. And one day Aria *will* remember—one day it'll all come back to haunt her, and do you know who she'll be most mad at? Us. Us for knowing and not telling her. Us for turning a blind eye instead of protecting her. Will knowing the truth hurt her? Yes, for now. But she'll heal, she'll move on. But us lying to her about it—she'll never forgive us. You think about that before you go trying to sweep secrets under the rug."

There were so many secrets hidden there already; was there room to hide even one more?

"What about your secret, Owen? The one you made me swear never to tell. The one that could have put you in jail. The one I've kept for you for eighteen years. You want me to tell everyone what you're hiding? Get down off your high horse, Mr. High and Mighty!"

I seldom stood up to him. He glared at me, his jaw clenched like pliers chewing on a nail. I had hit a nerve. He grumbled angrily, then headed for the door.

"Where are you going?" I asked.

"I'm going out. Clearly you'd rather protect a rapist than your own husband."

He was as mad as a hornet, and it'd only get uglier if I didn't stop it. I tugged on his arm, hoping my touch would somehow connect with his emotions. Unfortunately, Owen had only two emotions: protective and angry. He pulled away.

"I don't want to fight, honey," I said gently. "I want to figure it out—together. But we can't make a hasty decision. Whatever we do will impact Aria. All I'm asking is that we work through the options."

"I know what I'm going to do. I'm going to the police, and I'm going to make sure Aria knows the truth about what she did."

"What *she* did? What do you mean by that?"

"Something just occurred to me, Mac. Yeah, Ryan is a degenerate, but he didn't do this alone. She was drinking—she needs to learn from this. It's your fault she's in this mess, because you've given her no boundaries. *You.*" His pointing finger was a blur between my eyeballs.

I couldn't let him do this, not him, not now. It needed to come from me, but he was determined. It was only a matter of time before his misogyny reared its ugly head and he blamed me for everything.

"I'm sorry! Let me fix this." I stepped in front of him, hugging his chest. I didn't want this closeness with him, because I knew where it led. But it always worked on him. "Please let me talk to her first. Please," I begged.

There was only one apology he would accept—my body. I didn't want to give it to him, but I needed to for my daughter, for my friend, for everyone but me. He needed power, and I needed time. It was the only way.

I cupped his groin. His body stiffened, then relaxed as I kissed his neck.

"Let me take your mind off of everything. You need this." I massaged him. His iron will melted. Grabbing my biceps, he flung me around and threw me to the bed. I bounced against the edge, waiting for the inevitable—my pants ripped downward in a puddle at my feet. The tear of lace panty seams. My shirt whipped upward, discarded on the floor. My bra snapping against my back as he clumsily fiddled with the clasp. Then the unzipping of his jeans.

He'd always been careful not to leave bruising on my neck or arms, but tonight felt different. Angrier. Rushed. Careless.

I closed my eyes, barely holding on to the string that connected me to earth as my mind lifted me into the inky sky. Tonight he didn't care what marks he left behind, what physical bruises matched the ones on my soul as he pumped me raw until I silently wept.

When he finished, I winced as I slid back into my torn panties. There was no forehead kiss of gratitude this time, my payment for being an obedient little wife.

"Are we okay now?" I squeaked.

"I don't know. I need time to think."

Brood was more like it. And brooding only led to more anger.

"Let's just sleep on it and consider the options tomorrow." *Please work, logic.*

"Options?" He laughed flatly. "The options were stripped from us when Aria decided to get drunk. You know, the more I think about it, it's clear both of you women are to blame for this. No common sense! She shouldn't have put herself in that position, practically begging to get taken advantage of. What decent girl gets blind drunk unless she's trying to be reckless? Trying to be a whore?"

I gasped in horror at the man's chauvinism.

"As a husband and a father, you actually think that about women—that we're *asking* for it when we drink too much or dress a certain way? That's seriously your view of women?"

Why I was shocked to hear this from the man who ravaged me night after night—that was the real shocker. Yes, I was a proud Southern gal, but I'd always known chivalric honor à la *Gone With the Wind* was a load of crap. Southern or otherwise, some men wanted women to be maids in the living room, cooks in the kitchen, and whores in the bedroom. Owen's devotion to this backward thinking made me want to throw up.

"I'm just saying that if you ever dressed like a slut or acted like one," Owen said, "I would have never married you. Or I'd have put you in your place."

"So by that logic, as long as a girl dresses conservatively, even if she sleeps around, she's not a slut, right?"

"No, she'd be a slut too." More blatant misogyny.

"But men can dress how they want and sleep with however many women they want and that's just the accepted norm?"

"Men are the dominant gender, honey. Look at how ducks and chickens mate—the males practically gangbang the females. And that's part of animal nature. The males do the conquering; the females are the submissives. Haven't you ever wondered why women only have a narrow window of fertility, while men can procreate almost twice as long? Men are meant to spread their seed; women are meant to be our incubators. It's just how it is; I don't write the laws of human nature, I just observe them."

"You're not observing them, Owen, you're twisting them to justify your caveman logic. You're basically saying that Aria asked to be raped because she made herself vulnerable. But if women are the weaker sex, that pretty much means we're always vulnerable."

"Exactly. Now you're getting it." He patted my head like I was a good little doggie. "That's why I always protect you— from the predators out there and from yourself."

Of course he didn't mean the predator in my own home.

He shook his head at me. We were both growing weary of this pointless *Me Tarzan, You Jane* conversation.

"I don't want to get into this debate with you, because

you won't win, Mac. It's futile. All I'm going to say is that as the mother, you're the one who raised Aria. I don't know where you went wrong with her, but she should have known better than to get drunk with a boy alone in a basement. If those are the kind of loose morals you've instilled in her, then that's on you."

My palm flew out and slapped him on the face. I only realized it after the fact when I pulled it back and felt the sting. I instantly regretted my mistake. His eyes widened in alarm—no, it was fury—but for once he knew better than to speak because my words were flying like darts at him now.

"I'm sick of it! I'm sick of how you're blaming us! How dare you blame me or Aria for what Ryan did! That's your daughter, you asshole. And I'm your wife. If you ever speak about her like that again, it will be the last thing you say."

I couldn't believe what I'd done. Standing there, naked except for a tattered pair of underwear, screaming at the man I dared never defy.

He lifted his hands in surrender. Had I won?

"Fine. I'm done. I'm going to spend the night at a hotel. You decide what you want to do about this mess. And before you think about spreading my secret around, just know you were there too behind the wheel, babe. I'm not the only one who knows where the bodies are buried, Mackenzie. You'll go down with me, and Aria will lose any chance at a decent life."

He left before I could get another word in, although I was tapped out anyway. He was right. I could never tell anyone about what we had done all those years ago. Because while Owen may have pulled the trigger, I was the one who gave the order.

Chapter 18

Robin

The skeletons in my closet didn't just rattle, they danced, bones clanging like a symphony so everyone could hear. And now they were loose, twirling in sinister pirouettes around my bedroom.

"Dad isn't . . . he isn't my dad?" Ryan grimaced like the words tasted sour on his tongue. He pushed away from me on the bed and his body shook as he wept. I cradled him in my arms. He was still my little boy, would always be my little boy, no matter how much taller than me he grew.

His world had just been rocked sideways, and I had no idea how to stabilize it.

"I wanted to tell you for so long, but it's a difficult part of my past, honey. I didn't know how to tell you. Your father doesn't even really know the details."

"I don't understand. Did you cheat on him?"

"No! No, of course not. I met your dad when you were two years old. He was so amazing with you and fell in love with you instantly, so when we started to get serious, I asked if he'd be willing to be your father. In every sense of the word. I wanted him to embrace you as his own. Of course he was thrilled with that—he'd always wanted a son, and that was that. He adopted you the first chance he got. But technically, he isn't your biological father. Your biological father was a piece of shit who I never wanted to tell you about. The only good thing about that man was that he gave me you."

I stopped, unwilling to let the memory torment me again. I was done wrestling with demons today. There was a long pause, and Ryan finally looked up at me. The sharp iron in his eyes had been pounded smooth, replaced with forgiveness.

"Why do you say he was a bad person? What did he do?"

I would never tell him. It wasn't something he should ever know—that his mother was raped, that he was the product of violence. What possible benefit could anyone get from that?

"He was a sleazy guy who preyed on women. I should never have slept with him, but like I said, I got you out of it, so I have no regrets."

"What if he changed? What if he's a good guy now?"

"Honey, some people don't change. Men like him don't change. They take what they want from the world and then spit the rest out. If I could erase him from this earth, I would. But I can't."

"Can I at least meet him? I think I have a right to know who my biological father is."

He was eighteen. He could do whatever he wanted. But meeting Geoffrey meant excavating the truth. It wasn't his truth to explore. It was mine, and I wanted to keep it that way.

"Ry, I wish I could agree to that, but I simply can't. That man hurt me. He doesn't deserve to know you. Please, for me, let it go."

"Mom, I don't know that I can do that."

As I weighed his headstrong words, Willow stepped into the bedroom carrying her lacrosse uniform. She had heard too much, based on the confused look she wore.

"What's going on?" she asked.

Ryan wiped his tears, and I stood up to guide Willow back out the door, bribing her with a snack.

"Nothing, sweetie. We're just having a private conversation about something. How about I make you some popcorn then it's bedtime, okay? It's a school night."

"Okaaay." But it was too late. Her curiosity was piqued. "Doesn't sound like nothing."

"Just some school stuff we're dealing with. Go on, scoot. You too, Ryan. Before Collette wakes up."

I shooed the kids out the door, heading for the kitchen. On the way down the hall Willow handed me her lacrosse uniform.

"Can you clean this by tomorrow? I need it for a scrim-mage."

"By tomorrow? It's getting late. I was about to head to bed."

"Sorry, I forgot to give it to you earlier," she whined.

"Honey, next time don't wait until the last minute. I've

got to sleep tonight too, you know." I kissed her forehead and ushered her to the living room to watch some television while I nudged Ryan into the pantry. I couldn't risk him poking around in our past, *my* past.

"Look," I whispered, "I don't want you to meet him right now. Let me think about it, okay?"

"At least tell me his name. Please, Mom?"

"I don't know . . ." I wavered.

"You drop this bomb on me that my dad isn't my dad. You owe me a name."

"Ry, I'm only looking out for you. You don't want to know him. He's nothing to you and I'd like to keep it that way."

"Fine, I'll ask your friends. I'm sure they know, don't they?"

He could be impossible sometimes. The last thing I wanted him doing was asking *them* questions.

"There's a lot you don't know, Ryan, a lot I don't want you to know for good reason. It's not just about you—it's about me too. Why can't you let it rest?"

"Could you, if you were in my position? If you just found out your father was someone you've never met, wouldn't you want to know who he was? Please, just a name. I promise I won't do anything without talking to you first. I just want to know his name."

I couldn't deny him this request. Ryan was persistent, if anything. I first discovered that about him when he was five years old and he attempted to hitchhike to the North Pole to find out for himself if Santa Claus was real. It was a terrible, horrible decision, but I spoke the name I hadn't uttered for years: "Geoffrey Faust."

A flash of Geoffrey's face collided with the name on my tongue, but I willed it away.

"But don't forget your promise, Ryan. Don't go contacting him without talking to me first. Anything we do, we'll do together. And I want your father's input too. He'd be really hurt if he knew you were looking up that sperm donor asshole without talking to him about it."

"I promise, Mom."

But if there was one thing our family was good at, it was breaking promises.

Chapter 19

Willow

Willow might have been young, but she wasn't as naïve and innocent as her family seemed to think she was. At twelve years old, she knew how to read the room. The averted gazes. The whispers. The unexplained tears. The many secrets. Everything was falling apart around her, and she didn't know what to do.

She hadn't forgotten what she had seen Sunday night, or what she heard tonight. Should she tell Mom that she caught Dad kissing Aunt Lily in the pantry? Or ask Dad why they kept Ryan's biological father a secret all these years? It wasn't fair that her family had to be so messed up when everyone else's was normal. It simply wasn't fair.

137

Korn's "Falling Away from Me" thrummed against Ryan's closed bedroom door where Willow stood tapping with her knuckle. He wouldn't hear her over the cacophony of guitars, so she tested the doorknob—it wasn't locked—then peeked inside.

"Ry?" Her voice was a hum lost in the apocalyptic power chords and suicidal lyrics.

Ryan lay on his bed tossing a ball in the air. He glanced over at the movement by the door, then aimed the ball at an empty garbage can near his desk, missed the shot, and sat up.

"Hey, Will. Turn that down, would ya?"

Willow searched for the volume button on his stereo and adjusted it to the low drone of background noise. She stood there motionless, unable to put words to thoughts.

"What's on your mind, sis?"

Ryan had always doted on Willow. For the last six years, as far back as her memory went, he'd been her protector, her hero. If a kid at school made her cry, he'd take care of it. If she got in a fight with Mom or Dad, Ryan came to her defense. They had a special bond that nothing could break . . . until now. Now it felt like her whole world was breaking, and her brother was soon to be swallowed up with it.

She sat on the bed next to him, ignoring the funk peculiar to teenage boys' rooms—a heady mixture of dirty laundry and raging hormones—pushing herself back with her heels until she met the wall. Ryan joined her so that they were both leaning against the wall, socked feet splayed in front of them against rumpled gray-striped sheets.

"What did you mean when you asked Mom about your biological father?"

He didn't answer at first. In fact, he didn't say anything. Finally: "So you heard that, huh?"

"Yep. Does that mean you have a different dad than me? Or is Dad not my dad either?"

"Hey," Ryan said, enfolding her small hand in his, "no matter what, we have the same parents. And yes, Dad is your dad. It's just that before Mom met Dad, she dated someone and that's where I came from. But apparently he's not a good guy, so that's why Mom never told me about him. Nothing changes, though. We're still a family."

"But if Mom kept that a secret for so long, how do we know there's not other secrets they're hiding? What else hasn't Mom told us?"

Ryan's hand, with Willow's tucked in it, dropped to his lap.

"I don't know, Will. I wish they wouldn't have lied, but we all have secrets. I guess we're entitled to have a few, don't you think? Especially if keeping the secrets means not hurting others." Ryan grew somber as he said this, as if haunted by something.

"What do you mean?"

"Well, what if telling a friend that she sucked at singing was the truth, but telling her would make her feel bad about herself? Is it better to be honest and hurt her feelings, or lie and let her feel good about herself?"

"I don't know. I guess let her feel good about herself."

"Right, because what's the point of hurting her feelings if it's not going to serve any good?"

"But it's not a stupid little thing like being able to sing.

139

It's a pretty big deal to have another dad. What if he has other kids, and you have other brothers and sisters? You could have a whole other family and not know it. And worst of all is they kept it from you—from us. Aren't you pissed about it?"

He shrugged, so cool and collected, as if he hadn't been sobbing his eyes out only an hour ago.

"I haven't really thought about that. And besides, I know it seems big, but it doesn't change anything, because you're my family, not some stranger."

Willow's chin hung on her chest. Bumping shoulders with her, he drew her gaze upward. "Hey, you know that, right?"

She looked away, wordless.

"We don't always have to tell each other everything. I'm sure you don't tell me everything about you—like what boy you like at school."

"Sure I do. I like Jamison Burke because he's funny. So yeah, I do tell you everything."

Ryan chuckled. "Really, everything?"

There was that one secret, the pantry secret. The secret she hadn't told her bestie, or written about in her diary, or mentioned in her bedtime prayers. It seemed too heavy and delicate, like voicing it would make it explode, taking her whole family down with it. It was like the dominoes Grandpa used to play with her. Each domino stood perfectly aligned in a pretty pattern, but when you knocked that first one down, the whole creation fell. Putting it back together was long, hard work. That was the pantry secret—a dangerous game of dominoes.

She couldn't let their family be destroyed or let her parents' mistakes ruin them. The pantry secret would be hers to keep, even if it meant lying to her brother right now.

"Fine, I guess there are things you probably don't want to know about, like how I'm getting boobs now and stuff like that."

Ryan playfully covered her mouth with his hand.

"Exactly—I don't want to know my little sister has boobs."

They both laughed away the gravity of the conversation.

"What do you think he's like—your biological father?"

"Mom said he's an asshole. But I don't know. You can't sum up a person's entire character in one word. It's a matter of perspective, you know? He might not have treated her well, but maybe now he has a whole new family that loves him and he treats them great."

"If you have other brothers and sisters out there, don't you want to meet them?"

His eyebrow rose, as if the idea of meeting them wasn't so bad.

"I suppose so. But you're all I need, Will." He hugged her, but it offered her no comfort.

"If he turns out to be a nice guy, are you going to leave our family to be with him—your other dad?"

"Will, he's not my *other dad*. He's no one to me. Geoffrey Faust is just a name, a person who knows nothing about me. Don't worry about it, okay? I'll probably never meet him anyway."

Maybe that was true, but maybe it wasn't. Willow knew the allure of opening boxes to discover what's inside. He'd want to know eventually. And when he did finally open that box, *kaboom*! Everything would fall apart.

Willow might have been young, but she wasn't helpless. Ryan had protected her for all those years. Now it was time for her to protect him. Geoffrey Faust would stay far, far away. She'd make sure of it.

Chapter 20

Lily

Never pick one of your favorite hangouts to tell your friend you've been cheating with her husband. Because when it's all over, you'll never be able to go back there. It's like splitting up friends after a divorce—there's always casualties.

As the sun emerged, wakening my riotous thoughts, I called Robin for a gossip session at our usual coffeehouse, and I had made my *first* mistake.

Something about the South Side brought me to life as I wove through the bustling sidewalks, my flip-flops slapping against the cracked concrete. The rows of two-story brick buildings with their cluttered shop windows always held an earthy, hipster charm. I would never be as cool as the millennials who shopped and partied and tattooed themselves on this long stretch of storefronts, but I could still appreciate their culture. It revitalized me, gave me my youth back if only for as long as it took me to finish this cup of coffee.

Italians and coffee were a package deal, like Pittsburghers were with their Steelers football. You couldn't have one without the other. Espresso was my weakness, and on some mornings, it was my reason for living.

Big Dog Coffee was a favorite of mine, not just for the savory brew but also for the oatmeal bar. An ingenious invention, if you ask me. A healthy, delicious, and perfectly customized breakfast. Though, as a fitness instructor, maybe I was biased.

Midmorning was always one of the busiest times of day, but today only a handful of patrons were scattered at square wooden tables around the trendy coffee shop. I preferred the hubbub of conversation to hushed emptiness where my conversation echoed off the walls. It felt cozier, more private in a room full of chatting people. Don't ask me why, because I couldn't explain it if I tried.

Robin sat across from me beneath a gorgeously chaotic painting of oranges and blues and yellows that resembled a bridge leading into downtown Pittsburgh. She sipped her latte while I admired the froth shaped like a flower floating on my espresso.

Her ponytail bounced, just like her personality. Peppy bangs shiny and conditioned, wearing formfitting yoga pants and a cute matching athletic top. She wore it for style; I wore mine for purpose.

As my gaze wandered, I regretted picking this spot to do this. This memory would spoil any good feelings I'd had, because I'd never be able to walk back in here without the rush of guilt following me. But it was too late for regret and a small price to pay losing my favorite coffee shop after what I'd done behind Robin's back.

I was readying myself, armed with only my dark roast. I was too nauseous to eat. We'd delivered our morning greetings, complimented the perfect May weather, and nestled into idle conversation. Getting around to the confession was all that was left to do, but it was the hardest part.

"I'm glad we could get this girl time together. It's never just you and me anymore," Robin observed. After dropping Lucas off at school, she'd left Collette home with Grant, who had cleared his schedule for a much-needed day off. I knew because he had texted me about it, hinting at seeing me. Luckily I had already planned to tell all, or I might have actually considered his offer.

A weak-willed Jezebel. That's who I am.

I'd rehearsed my lines in my head, then pictured the aftermath. Robin would storm home to Grant, who'd be there to win her back with apologies and fine jewelry. My timing would be perfect, unless he didn't come through for Robin as I hoped.

"Sorry about that. I've been a bad friend lately. My business has been crazy—lots of new clients, plus I'm working on creating a few new dietary programs. But I'm glad we could sit down and catch up today."

I didn't know how to segue into the part about sleeping

with her husband. There was no natural transition from *my work schedule's insane* to *but I made time to sleep with your husband and please don't kill me.*

"That's great, Lil. So business is booming, huh?"

"Well, it pays the bills. But that's not what I wanted to talk to you about. There's something I need to tell you."

Just as the courage erupted to get it over with, my cell phone rang. I glanced at the number—not one I recognized. Perhaps a new client referral I shouldn't pass up.

"One sec. I should probably get this." I answered the call, pressing the phone to my ear. "Hello, this is Lily Santoro for Workout Wonder."

A long pause.

"*Ciao*?" I asked again.

I almost thought the caller had hung up until I heard a breathless, "Fuck. You."

"Hello? Who is this?"

Then dead air.

"*I malano miau*, they friggin' hung up!" I muttered.

The voice was wispy, like a ghost from the past. I couldn't quite make out whether it was male or female, but who would call to cuss me out? An angry client? I had none that I knew of, not *that* angry . . . except for Irving, the lawsuit-happy bastard.

"You okay?" Robin asked.

"Yeah." My hands trembled as I turned off my cell phone and pocketed it. I didn't want whoever it was calling me back. "Sorry about that. Must have been a wrong number. So, how about you? Are you staying busy?"

Robin dropped her chin on her hands, giving me a forlorn

vibe. Oh *merda*. She needed a favor. "Not really, no. I need a job. Desperately."

I fell back against my chair. Robin—a job? She hadn't worked since meeting Grant, which was fifteen years ago. Since then she lived for making home-cooked meals, dusting, mopping, baking, nursing . . . all that selfless wifedom and mommyhood crap I couldn't stand.

"What about retail again? You did that for a bit after college. Flexible hours, mindless work—no offense— employee discount . . . you were good at that, weren't you?"

"Lil, I was awful with customers! Remember? I was per-petually late, I hated running registers, and I got in trouble for talking too much with coworkers. It wasn't the right fit for me."

"What about waitressing?"

"No way. Remember last time I had to run around carrying trays of food? I'd get fired on the first day. You know how clumsy I am."

She flung out her hands in a self-deprecating gesture, sending her full coffee mug crashing to the floor. An idle barista came over to fetch Robin a fresh cup and to clean up the mess. Robin mouthed a mortified *sorry* at her.

When we'd both finished laughing at this demonstration, she added: "Besides, I need to make more than a buck fifty an hour."

"Plus tips," I added with mock enthusiasm.

"Which I never got. I think I lost money with waitressing because my boss would dock my pay when I'd break stuff."

We both laughed as I recounted the time she'd spilled hot coffee on Tony's crotch the first time she met him.

From that moment on, whenever she offered him coffee he covered his groin.

"So anyway, Lil, I was glad you called me this morning. I've been wanting to ask you something."

"Okay." I gulped my espresso, anything to avoid eye contact. Did she know about me and Grant? I inhaled a cleansing breath and prepared myself for the worst.

"I seem to have gotten myself into a bit of debt. Actually, a lot of debt."

Thank God, thank God, thank God. This was about her, not me. I was all ears.

"How much debt?"

"Over $42,000 . . . on my credit card . . . at a huge interest rate."

"What?" I exclaimed. I knew Robin could be an impulse shopper . . . there wasn't a sale she could resist. But debt of this magnitude? "Are you serious? Robin, that's major. What credit card even has a limit that high?"

She groaned and dramatically flew back against the chair, face creased with worry. "I don't know how my line of credit got extended so much. I think maybe it was part of a home equity line, but all I know is my interest rate is crazy high. Like twenty-one percent high."

"Robin, you'll never pay that off. What the hell were you thinking? And does Grant know?"

"No, that's why I wanted to talk to you. I can't tell him. He'll flip out. He works so hard and we're barely scraping by. We live paycheck-to-paycheck because we're still paying off his student loan debt and all the medical equipment costs.

He's a doctor and we're broke! How did I get into this so deep? I need help, Lil."

"No kidding. You're spending hundreds if not thousands of dollars each month on . . . what? What shit are you buying anyway?"

"You know how I started selling stuff?"

Oh yes, I remembered those days quite well, especially since she'd always come begging me to purchase something, anything. The numerous online business ventures she'd tried on like swimsuits in a fitting room, none of which "fit." Each one required upfront costs, and each one ended in a flop. From selling makeup to jewelry to leggings to essential oils to cleaning products to God knows what else, I'd lost track.

Rule number one in friendship: Don't try to sell stuff to your friends. They'll resent you for it later.

"Well, I was buying all these starter kits and then the product costs started adding up. Then I was selling that clothing line through Facebook parties, but that was almost a thousand dollars in start-up costs. Those online businesses cost money, but you've got to spend money to make money, you know?"

I shook my head, and her lips drooped in a disappointed frown. "Robin, you change jobs like you're changing underwear. If you're telling me you've spent forty-two grand on makeup and clothes, then there is something bigger that's wrong here." I tapped my temple. "Up here. You need help."

"Oh come on. It's not like it was just makeup and clothes,

Lil. Some of it was toward vacations, new furniture, random stuff around the house."

"So Grant probably has some idea of the debt if he knew you were buying furniture and making home improvements, right?"

"I don't think so. He's oblivious about the financials. He never looks at our bank accounts—and I mean *never*. I'm in charge of all of that. He's already uptight about the two car payments, both our student loans, and a mortgage we can't afford . . ."

"Wait, you're still paying off your student loan debt too? You're forty years old, Robin! What the hell?"

"I deferred it. And deferred it again. I can't defer it anymore, though."

"You've got to tell Grant. He needs to know. Together you can come up with a budget to pay it off."

"That's just it, Lil. I need to get a job before I tell him to show him I'm serious about helping to pay it off. Something tolerable. Would you be willing to hire me to do something? Maybe admin work? Answering phones? Setting up appointments? Anything?"

Robin would be the absolute worst thing for my business. She was scatterbrained and unreliable. But how could I say no? Truth was, I owed this to her. I owed her anything she wanted, considering my betrayal. But she didn't know about that yet, and I was having second thoughts about telling her. She needed a friend more than she needed my honesty. After all, she was climbing out of a pit of debt. Maybe telling her now wasn't the best timing.

And then an idea knocked. I could help her out with her

financial crisis, win her favor, then maybe the blow wouldn't be so hard when I told her. It could all end up okay. It had to.

"Of course, Robin. Whatever you need, you know I'm here for you. I could use a personal assistant right now, at least until you find something more suited to you."

"This is why you're my best friend, Lil. Thank you. I promise I won't let you down."

"That's what friends are for."

I knew I was playing with dynamite. Never mix friends and business—everyone knew this rule (even those who didn't know the rule about not selling stuff to friends). Smart people followed this rule. But I didn't have the luxury of playing it smart, because guilt was taking the wheel. I'd be placing my carefully nurtured fitness company into the hands of the terribly undependable Robin, whose flighty attitude when it came to business could ruin me. But I ruined her first, didn't I? The only difference was that I deserved it.

I could anticipate the end before it began. It'd be a miracle if our friendship survived.

Chapter 21

Robin

THURSDAY

A phone call from the school in the middle of the day was usually not a good thing. A phone call from the principal was even worse.

I picked up the phone on the first ring, expecting it to be the office telling me Willow was sick and to come pick her up. But when I heard the nasally voice of Principal McConnell, my heart sunk.

"I'm calling to let you know that Willow seems to have left after first period. She was present in homeroom, then . . . well, vanished."

"Vanished? What do you mean?"

"Exactly what I said, Mrs. Thompson. No one has seen her since then, and she wasn't checked out through the office." Principal McConnell sounded more irritated than concerned as her words snapped at me. "Did you come to pick her up and forget to sign her out?"

My heart thumped frantically. It wasn't like Willow, who prided herself on perfect attendance each quarter, to play hooky.

"No, we didn't pick her up. Did you check the bathrooms, locker rooms, places like that?"

"Of course, Mrs. Thompson. No one has seen her. And no one saw her leave."

"Did you ask her friends? Maybe they know where she might have gone."

"We spoke with all of her friends, but no one knows anything. And no other kids have gone missing, which means she went on her own. Her bag and books are still in her locker, though, which is odd. I imagine she would have taken them with her if she went home."

"And you searched the entire school premises for her?"

Her umbrage was totally undisguised now. "Yes, Mrs. Thompson, when we realized she was missing that was the first thing we did—before calling you."

"Thanks for letting me know, Principal McConnell. I'll figure it out. And if you hear anything more, please let me know right away."

"Absolutely, Mrs. Thompson. We hope to see Willow back in school tomorrow."

As I hung up, I teetered between immobilizing fear and resolute action. I didn't have time to worry; I needed to find her. Figure out where she went. It was a matter of deduction. She'd never leave school unless it was for something important. The only things that mattered were her friends, who were all accounted for, lacrosse, and Ryan.

Then it clicked, like a lock cracking open.

I wondered if this had anything to do with my conversation with Ryan two nights ago. It's possible Willow heard more than she let on, or maybe Ryan had told her about it. That was the more likely scenario, since they were as thick as thieves; it didn't surprise me that Ryan would confide in her. I decided to call him on his cell phone to see if he knew anything about Willow's disappearing act.

I dialed his number, listening to it ring once, twice, three times, then again before the call dropped me into his voicemail.

"Ry, honey, it's Mom. Call me the moment you get this. It's about Willow and it's urgent."

His phone was an appendage, so I decided to text him in case he was in the middle of class and couldn't take calls.

Willow is missing. Call me ASAP.

I waited a minute, then another for a reply, then realized I hadn't called Grant yet. I had a feeling he'd tell me I was overreacting, that when he was Willow's age he often skipped school. But that wasn't Willow. Willow was a straight-A, goody-goody, perfect-attendance kind of girl. She never missed school unless she was on the verge of being deathly sick, and even then I had to force her to stay home. *Hooky* wasn't in her vocabulary.

Grant picked up on the first ring, God bless him. "Everything okay, honey?" He spoke with the anxious concern that my rare calls to his office always engendered.

"No, Willow's missing. She showed up at school, but the principal just called to say she disappeared—even left her book bag at school. I'm thinking about calling the police."

"Don't do anything until I get home, okay? I'm on my way."

He hung up before I could say anything else.

By the time Grant got home fifteen minutes later I had no call from Ryan, no update from the school, and no idea where my twelve-year-old daughter was. I had slipped from a Sarah Connor badass take-no-prisoners heroine into a panic-mode mom. So I called the only other person who could help me through my terror: Mackenzie. Despite our fight, despite what had happened between Ryan and Aria, I needed my best friend now more than ever. She was the only one who understood, one mother to another, that when it came to our kids, we put them above all else. Above any drama that came between us.

My butterfingers fumbled around my cell phone screen as I misdialed once, twice. Third time's the charm.

I could barely hold the threads of my sanity together as I spoke. "Mac, it's me, Robin. Please don't hang up. I need your help."

Nothing but silence for a long moment, then a sigh. Thank God she hadn't hung up on me. "What do you want?"

"I'm freaking out here. Willow's missing."

"Oh, Robin. What happened?"

In an instant my friend had returned. No matter what happened between us, I knew she'd be there when I needed her most. "She was at school this morning then suddenly disappeared. No one knows where she is. If you can think of anywhere she might have gone—"

The front door swung open and Grant rushed in, his eyes wild with worry. He saw me on the phone and immediately started pacing the room, swiping his hand through his hair and muttering underneath his breath. He was so agitated it was a miracle he made it home in one piece. He waved me to hurry up.

"I can check Eat'n Park, the mall . . . local hangout spots," Mac offered.

"Sure, that'd be great."

"Hey—" Mac's momentary silence sounded louder than her words. "We'll find her."

"Thanks. I gotta go. I'm heading to the police station now with Grant, but if you hear anything, please call me. I'm so scared, Mac."

"Don't worry—I'm sure she's fine. I'll call around and get the word out. Hang in there."

"Thanks." I was about to hang up, then said, "I love you, Mac. I'm sorry for everything."

"This doesn't mean we're okay, but that's not what matters right now. Let's just bring Willow home."

The call ended and I slipped my phone in my back pocket. I wiped the stinging tears away, staining my finger black with runny mascara.

"What exactly happened?" Grant asked. I'd never heard his voice so tense, so emotional. He was just as scared as I was.

"Nothing—that's exactly the issue. I can't get a hold of Ryan, and Willow's not here or at school. We need to report a missing child."

"All right, let's go. You grab Collette. I've got pictures of Willow on my phone I can give the police."

Sharing missing child photos. Filing a police report. None of it felt real, and yet I sped through each moment on auto-pilot. With Collette firmly pressed to one hip and a diaper bag bumping against my thigh, I ran to meet Grant at the minivan.

My fingers fumbled over the car seat clips as I hurriedly adjusted Collette in place. The clip was stuck shut with some-thing sticky, and the more I fidgeted with it, the more stubborn it became.

"Please fucking click shut!" I screamed at the lock, sending Collette into fearful tears.

"Shhh, I'm sorry, sweetie," I tried to soothe Collette, but she was already pink-faced crying now. Her wails grew louder and louder, and everything crashed in on me all at once. The insurmountable debt. Grant's aloofness. My out-of-control family. Lies piling on top of lies. And the sleepless nights trying to calm the cries of a colicky baby. Love held no sway over exhaustion, frustration, and pent-up anger.

"Shut up! Shut up! *Shut up!*"

"Get a hold of yourself!" Grant jumped out of the car and ran to me, pulling me against him. "It's going to be fine. I promise we'll find her."

He led me to the passenger-side door, guiding me into the seat.

"Try to relax, Robin. We'll deal with Collette when we get there." He swiped a dangling toy from the rearview mirror, handed it to Collette, and fastened the buckle with an easy click. "You're all worked up. Close your eyes and breathe."

I did as he said, my chest aching with each painful gasp.

By the time we pulled up to the Monroeville Municipal

Center, my breathing had returned to normal. A wall of glass three stories high loomed beyond the placard directing visitors to the various departments.

"I think we need to pull around back," I said, pointing to where the gray brick wrapped around toward a lower parking lot. A line of parked cop cars led the way. We found several parking spots in front of a large sign that read Monroeville Police Department. Grant pulled into the spot closest to the glass doors leading inside the lobby.

A honeysuckle-fragranced breeze followed us inside. I ran up to the front desk receptionist and said breathlessly, "I need to report a missing child. This morn—"

"One second. I'll let you speak with an officer." She picked up the phone and turned away from us slightly as she spoke quietly into the mouthpiece. When she hung up, she waved us to follow her, weaving around cubicles until we reached a desk in the corner where a cop in uniform stood waiting. "Officer Montgomery will help you. I hope you find your child," she said with a grim smile.

The policewoman extended her hand, giving us each a firm shake as Grant set down Collette's car seat next to a metal chair. The woman's hair was pulled in a tight blond bun, secured at the nape of her neck. I randomly wondered how many pins were required to keep it so neat all day.

"I'm Officer Courtney Montgomery. Please have a seat."

Other than a picture of Officer Montgomery and two other women in front of a sprawling vineyard overlooking a lake, her desk was sparse compared to the cluttered ones surrounding us. I wondered if this meant she was extremely efficient or extremely new at this job.

Collette cooed as Grant handed her a plush bunny toy, its ear half chewed and wet from Collette's teething.

Officer Montgomery grinned sympathetically, then picked up a pen and paper. "You're reporting a missing child, correct, Mr. and Mrs. . . . ?"

"Thompson," said Grant. "Yes, our daughter Willow."

"What is your child's full name and age?"

"Willow Eve Thompson. She's twelve years old."

"I'm sorry you're going through this. What time did she go missing? And where was she last seen?" Officer Montgomery looked up, her eyes sincere and compassionate. I liked this woman, perhaps a mother like me, and I instantly felt like she'd bring my little girl home. Anyone who cared this much had to be good at her job.

"Willow went to school this morning—Gateway Middle—like usual," I explained. "But it was right after first period"—I mentally calculated the time—"maybe around ten o'clock or so, when she disappeared. The teachers and staff looked all over the campus for her but couldn't find her. That's when I got a call from her principal, about thirty minutes ago, telling me what happened. No one has seen her since."

Officer Montgomery scribbled something down, then glanced back up. "Have you checked with her friends to see if any of them have heard anything or know anything?"

"The principal told me they did, and none of her friends are missing from school. As soon as I found out I called Grant and we came straight here."

"Is it unusual for her to skip school?"

"Willow loves school—she's a straight-A student, as

160

dedicated as they come," Grant interjected. "She's never done anything like this before. She's perfect."

Officer Montgomery smirked as if she heard that a lot. "Does she have a cell phone?"

"No, we don't believe kids that age should have a personal phone," Grant said. "She uses our home phone for calls."

"That helps. It eliminates the possibility that she might be connecting with someone you don't know about—a secret boyfriend, for example." Officer Montgomery's glance strayed from Grant's face to mine, where it stayed. "Anything traumatic happen in your home lately? A fight? Sibling issues?"

I didn't want to tell the cop about what Willow might have overheard, but what if it mattered? What if it led me to her? But it also might not.

"Um, nothing that would make her run away," I answered, a second too late. Officer Montgomery searched my face. I had taken too long.

"Well, since she's only been missing a couple hours, I suggest you call her friends, see if any of them know anything, and have the principal and homeroom teacher contact me so I can take their statements. In most cases with girls this age, they're skipping school, hitting the mall, doing what rebellious teenage girls do. Let's give it a couple more hours and see if we can figure out where she might have gone."

She handed me her card, and a wave of disappointment swept over me.

"That's it? That's all you can do? What if she was kidnapped?"

"It's highly unlikely she was abducted from the school property, Mrs. Thompson. With the security they have, someone would have seen something. Most likely she left on her own to go somewhere to meet someone. She had a specific purpose for leaving the school grounds. We just have to figure out those two details."

My mind immediately jumped to the only logical answer: she had left school with Ryan; that's why he wasn't answering his phone. But what was the specific purpose? Of course: they were looking for Ryan's biological father.

I decided not to mention it to Officer Montgomery, not yet. Not until I located Ryan first. The truth would disrupt all our lives. It'd put a spotlight on Ryan, which was the last thing he needed right now. And God forbid Grant find out like this. No, I couldn't bring Ryan's past into this. There had to be another way to find Willow without sacrificing my son.

"Thank you for your time and help," I said flatly.

"Try not to worry. We have a lot of missing child cases and almost all of them get resolved within a couple hours. Kids tend to wander off, get into mischief." She grinned at Grant, adding, "It happens quite a bit, even with perfect kids." She turned back to me. "If you don't see or hear from her by dinnertime, call me on my cell. We'll find her. Okay, Mrs. Thompson?" Her hand rested on mine in a silent promise to bring Willow home. I wanted to believe that promise, but I couldn't.

Down at Grant's feet Collette began to squirm and squawk, her face wrinkling with irritation. Grant sensed I was a powder keg about to explode.

"All right. We appreciate it, Officer Montgomery," he said, rising to his feet. "You'll hear from us one way or another this evening."

I picked up the car seat while dangling a toy in front of Collette. She only cried louder as she strained against her confinement. I hurried down the corridor past open cubicles, faces turning at the sound of my baby's earsplitting shrieks. Grant silently speed-walked behind me. He knew better than to speak. Never mess with a mom on a mission—or one dealing with a fussy baby.

As we slid into the car, my phone rang. An unknown local number. I picked it up before the second ring.

"Hello?" I said, my voice trembling.

"I have your daughter," a man said. And in that cold, eternal moment, every mother's worst fear stabbed me in the heart.

Chapter 22

Lily

I couldn't tell if it was real or a dream, the pounding in my head. The *thrum thrum thrum* quickening, throbbing against my skull as it intensified.

"Lily, please open up!" a tinny voice commanded.

It sounded distant, like someone screaming from the depths of outer space. I felt myself being sucked into a black hole . . .

And then my eyelids fluttered open.

"Lily, it's me, Mackenzie. Please, it's urgent!"

It took a moment for my world to reassemble itself. I was

in my apartment, passed out on the couch. I had no idea what day or time it was, and for a moment I felt scared. What had I missed?

The banging on the door continued.

"Please open up!" She sounded frantic, spooked.

"Coming!" I yelled. I hefted myself up, feeling my legs wobble as the apartment shifted underfoot. Suddenly the world fell on its side. I clutched the arm of the sofa to regain my balance, waiting for the room to stop spinning. Closing my eyes, I inhaled deeply. A few seconds passed, along with the vertigo.

I shuffled to the front door, unlocking the dead bolt. Before I could even crack the door open, Mackenzie pushed her way past me into the entryway.

"Willow's missing." Her face was pink and flustered, like she'd jogged the whole way here. But I recognized it as hysteria. Mackenzie often got this way when Owen pushed her to the breaking point. My job as best friend was to level her out, talk sense back into her. I knew how to navigate the spousal *merda*, but runaway kids were not in my wheelhouse. It was information overload for my fried brain to process.

"Wait—start over. What's going on?"

I led her into the living room, then settled on the edge of the sofa while Mackenzie paced the floor.

"Willow was at school this morning but went missing. Robin's at the police station right now. We need to help in any way we can."

"What can we do?" I had never had kids. I had never dealt with the police. This couldn't have anything to do with me and Grant in the pantry, could it? Was I to blame?

I didn't want to ask, didn't want to know. I felt useless. Worthless. Depressed. Miserable.

Guilty.

And it had nothing to do with Willow but everything to do with what I'd done.

"I don't know what to do," Mac fretted. "I just feel horrible for Robin, especially since the last time we spoke we got into a major fight." She paused. Knowing her for so long, I could tell she was hiding something.

"What'd you fight about?"

She shrugged halfheartedly. "Nothing."

I wasn't buying that.

"Come on. You know I'll always listen to you."

"Fine." She hesitated, and for a moment I wondered if she had decided not to spill. Finally, pay dirt. "I caught Aria and Ryan having sex."

"What?" The word escaped while I was still processing the news. Little Aria, not so little anymore.

"But Aria has no recollection of it. And Robin's acting like it's no big deal."

"They're teens, Mac. It's a rite of passage to make dumb decisions."

"I don't think you understand, Lil." Her voice had an edge, her blue eyes darkened. "Ryan took advantage of Aria. She had no idea what was happening, and she still doesn't know what happened."

"Are you sure she doesn't remember? Maybe she's not being honest with you because she's embarrassed."

"No, not Aria. She wouldn't lie to me. She was pretty drunk and oblivious."

"But Ryan adores her. I'm sure it's a misunderstanding." I walked a tightrope playing devil's advocate, but there was no way this happened the way Mackenzie painted it. These kids had been friends forever. "Maybe—"

"Stop defending him!" she blurted. "For once will you listen to me? I'm telling you that Robin's son victimized my daughter, and you're more concerned with keeping the peace! Well, there is no peace anymore. Robin refuses to accept the truth, and apparently you do too. So I guess I have no real friends."

"Wait, stop that!" I jumped up from the sofa and grabbed Mackenzie in both arms, pulling her into a hug. This was spiraling away from me faster than I could reel it in. I leaned back so that I could meet her eyes. "Mac, I'm listening. You got my attention, okay? What can I do? Should I talk to Robin?"

Mackenzie had always been the peacekeeper, but I'd wear the negotiator mantle if it meant fixing this schism.

She dismissed my question with a wave, then stepped away from me. I had an unsettling feeling like I was losing both her and Robin. "Until Robin sets things straight with Ryan, I'm not speaking to her. So if you want to say something to her, be my guest. But I'm done with that whole family."

"What about Willow? They need you right now."

"I'll be there to help find Willow, but then I'm done. What if Willow found out about Ryan and Aria and took off? She idolizes her brother."

"You think that might have caused her to run away?" I had pulled my fair share of disappearing acts as a teenager, but I wasn't a mother, so what did I know?

"That's my guess. Kids her age don't usually get abducted in the middle of class. It's more likely she left on her own free will."

"Do you have any ideas on how we can help? Put up flyers? Post her picture all over Facebook? You tell me, I'll do it."

"We could start with that and . . ."

Mac's shrill voice dulled into the background as guilt slammed into me hard. It was all too much. I could barely listen to her without my skull splitting wide open. My head reminded me that I was due for another pain pill, but I couldn't take it in front of Mackenzie. The moment it knocked me out, she'd be all judgy about it. I'd learned my lesson the last time she chastised me for hours about how painkillers were addictive, a gateway drug to something worse. But what was worse than this?

I leaned back, blindly feeling for the wall, then propped my head against it while my forearm covered my eyes from the sun streaking through the room.

"You okay?" Mackenzie asked. "You look like hell warmed over."

"I've seen better days."

"Lily." Her voice turned all maternal, the way she spoke when she was prepping for a lecture. "I know you. Something's not right."

She thought this was about painkillers. She could offer to help me get through the withdrawal, keep me accountable on my path toward sobriety. If only it was that simple. Sorry to burst your bubble, but this was about being a home-wrecker. There was no quick fix for a family torn apart by infidelity.

"You can tell me if something's going on." Oh sweet, naïve Mackenzie.

Could I? Could I really tell her? Because more than anything I wanted release from the shame that constantly suffocated me in my own misery.

I rehearsed it in my head: *I'm sleeping with Grant.* No, if it didn't sound right in my head, it wouldn't sound right coming from my mouth.

"You'll feel better once you talk about it. I promise." She led me to sit down beside her, propping my feet on her lap. She patted my legs like I was her child, and it felt nice to be coddled for once. I was tired of having to play fiercely independent all the time. Sometimes a girl just wanted to be doted on.

Willow was missing, possibly because of me. I was in love with a married man. My drug addiction was eating me alive. And the self-hatred was gnawing on my remains. What else did I have to lose by confessing?

"Swear to keep this between us? No telling Robin. Or Owen."

"I swear. What's going on? It can't be as bad as all the other crap going on."

I chuckled mirthlessly. "Oh, it's that bad. You'll never forgive me."

"Try me." Mackenzie fixed her gaze on me, the same one Mamma used to give me. I closed my eyes. I couldn't look her in the face while I said it.

"I fucked Grant."

And there it was. Out in the open. Her shock deflated the air out of the room. As the unnerving silence lingered, I wondered if she was even still there. I opened my eyes, glanced over at her. Mackenzie sat stunned, unblinking, her breath held.

"Please say something," I begged.

"Wow, what can I say? You screwed your best friend's husband. I don't even know how to reply to that. What do you want me to tell you? That you really messed up? That you destroyed the marriage of someone who loves you like a sister? Lily, it's unforgivable what you did. You realize that, don't you?"

"Yes, I know I'm a horrible person. I know it's unforgivable."

"How did it happen?"

The question of the day—and I didn't have an answer. "I don't know. It just happened. Are you going to tell Robin?"

She didn't answer at first. She wanted to make me sweat. And it was working too.

"No, I'll keep your secret, Lil, because it's not mine to tell. But you're going to have to come clean at some point, because you owe her the truth. She's your friend, and friends tell the truth even when it hurts."

Was my friend, she should have said, because once I told Robin everything, I would lose her.

Mackenzie threw my feet off her lap, stood up, and headed for the door.

"Where are you going?" I asked. She was angry. Beyond angry. Uncharted-territory angry.

"I can't stomach being in the same room as you right now, Lil. Look, I'm glad you were honest with me, but Robin is the one you really need to confess to. Not right now, obviously. Let things with Willow get resolved. God knows Robin doesn't need more to worry about. She's already hurting enough."

Mackenzie flung the front door open and tossed one last pitying look my way.

"I'm sorry, you know. I wish I could take it back," I said. And it was true, but impossible. There was nothing I could do to repair the damage I'd done.

Mackenzie's gaze turned flat and cold. "One of these days you're going to regret pushing away the people who loved you most—first Tony, now Robin. They actually cared about you, but all you care about is the momentary high. Whether it's the pills I know you're still popping or the sex, it's all fleeting. People aren't, though. If you sabotage every good thing, you'll have nothing left but a wasteland. I love you, Lil, but not enough to watch you self-destruct."

She slammed the door behind her, and all I could think about was the orange bottle of pills containing my sweet release from this prison I confined myself in.

2015, Pittsburgh, Pennsylvania

I hated driving downtown: endless bumper-to-bumper traffic; aggressive assholes behind the wheel; idiot pedestrians racing out into busy intersections, their overcoats flapping behind them. But sometimes it was a necessary evil to venture into the belly of the beast. Especially when you were about to meet with a potential business investor.

Everything was ready to fall into place . . . before everything was about to fall apart. I had drafted the bank-requested proposal for my health and wellness company—

Workout Wonder, *Don't wonder if you can get healthy when we'll help you do it!*—networked and found someone with loaded pockets who was equally excited about the prospect, even located an affordable start-up site. Tony had given his stamp of approval, willing to work whatever extra hours were needed to supplement our income until I got things up and running. My dream was becoming a reality, with only one step remaining.

The contract sat on the passenger seat, ready to be signed by my new partner—who I was ten minutes late to meet. I had circled the same block three times with no luck finding a parking spot until, lo and behold, Lady Luck smiled on me. A spot right in front of his office, and I'd be damned if I let anybody else get it before I did.

I inched my car forward at the red light, cussing the knot of businesspeople rushing through the crosswalk. My front fender skimmed the intersection when the truck slammed into the side of my Honda Accord, smashing through the passenger side and hurling my car into oncoming traffic. My neck snapped to one side. My airbag crushed my cheek. The competing forces twisted my body into a Z. The pedestrians and skyscrapers spun crazily like a carnival ride.

As the car slowed to a stop, everything else stopped with it. My dreams. My future. My health. My marriage. That day was the beginning of the end.

Chapter 23

Robin

I hadn't recognized Geoffrey Faust's voice when he called to tell me he had Willow. Why would I? It had been nineteen years ago, after all. Nineteen years of burying his face somewhere in the tar-black depths of my mutilated soul. Nineteen years of erasing him—his voice, his body, his smell, his ghost. And now here he was, back from the dead to haunt me. As if he hadn't destroyed me enough, now he was with my daughter.

The drive to the address I had scribbled down on a scrap of paper was a blur of passing trees and houses. I couldn't tell you if I ran any red lights or sped through any stop signs.

I drove with red fury guiding me, set on getting Willow back from the last person I had ever expected to see or hear from.

I felt bad for lying to Grant, telling him Willow's "friend" had called and that sure enough, they had skipped school together. Collette was overdue for a nap, I insisted, and Lucas would be home from kindergarten any minute. I threw in that I needed to stop by the store for sanitary pads. That instantly convinced Grant to stay home.

I had my reasons for the lies. I couldn't tell him the truth. Never. He wouldn't understand. He'd fill up on rage, and God knows I'd had enough rage to last a lifetime. It was better left unspoken, a secret locked away that only I held the key to . . . well, me and Geoffrey Faust.

The apartment building was as average as they came. A line of redbrick buildings with tiny concrete patios creating adjoining corridors separated only by a rusted railing. Decorative bistro sets and colorful pillows adorned the front porches of several dwellings in a vain attempt to personalize the cookie-cutter homes. Potted flowers welcomed spring, and a lone black cat stood sentry in one of the doorways. A forbidding omen?

Geoffrey had directed me to number 206. Second story. Six doors in. I found it easily, although my steps were wary as I approached. Was it stupid of me to have come alone? There was no other choice, was there? I couldn't possibly bring Grant to meet the father of his son, or Mackenzie when things were still awkward between us. I'd considered calling Officer Montgomery, but involving the police didn't seem like a good idea either. Besides, part of me wanted to do this on my own. To show Geoffrey he hadn't defeated me. To prove to myself I was stronger than my pain. I could run from my past, playing a game of hide-and-seek with my demons. Or I could stomp the smug little devil into dust. Dust it was.

Willow was safe, he'd assured me over the phone. Willow had confirmed it with an annoyed, "Just come and get me, Mom!" shouted in the background. She had turned up on his porch; I didn't ask for an explanation as to how she got there. After my initial fear subsided, I had put two and two together: somehow Willow had learned about Geoffrey Faust—from eavesdropping, or Ryan directly—and came here looking for him on behalf of the big brother she idolized. But that didn't explain Ryan being incommunicado. Surely he wouldn't have just dropped his little sister off at the home of a man he'd never met.

Of course, it could be a trap. That distressing thought occurred to me as I glanced through a dirty window, cupping my eyes to peer inside. Closed blinds blocked my view, but my ears picked up on a television blaring inside. Laughter. Clapping. Some kind of game show, it sounded like.

I knocked on the door and it rattled partway open. I pushed it wider and peeked in. The apartment was clean and well furnished, the television entertaining an empty sofa and two cushioned chairs. Not what I had expected from the likes of a scumbag like Geoffrey.

"Willow?" I called.

The man who came around the corner was not the man I remembered from my past—so much had changed about him. A shaggy beard hid the cut of his jawline, and his head was bald and shiny. A few extra pounds rounded his face.

The march of time could change a person's looks, but instinct couldn't be outsmarted. In my gut, I knew it was him.

"You're Willow's mom? Nice to meet you," he said, hand outstretched. "She's in the bathroom."

I ignored his offer of a handshake. "You don't remember me?" Not that I wanted him to, but how dare he forget.

"Should I?"

I pulled out my phone and flipped to a picture of Ryan. I lowered my voice to a fierce whisper so Willow wouldn't overhear. "See this boy? He's your son, you asshole. How can you stand there and look me in the eyes and have no clue who I am or what you did to me, to your son? You came, you conquered, you destroyed, leaving me to rot like a sack of garbage. I wonder if you've had one moment of remorse for all the misery you've caused, you son of a bitch!"

His expression remained impassive. His dark eyes flicked from the picture back to me. "Ma'am, I'd know if I'd had sex with a fine-looking woman like you or had a kid running around. You have me confused with somebody else. That's not my son."

Just then Willow came around the corner, her face downcast with remorse.

"What the hell, Willow?" I ran to her, scooped her into my arms. "Where's Ryan? Did he have anything to do with this?"

"I don't know where Ry is, Mom. I came here by myself."

"Why, Willow?" I thought I knew why, but I wanted to hear her explanation.

"Ryan told me everything. You lied to us all. Ryan said you said he was a jerk." She smiled apologetically at her host.

"I wanted to see for myself, so I could tell Ryan what he was really like. So I looked on the internet, got the address, hired an Uber, and came here. That's it, Mom."

She made it sound so matter-of-fact. I had to admire her resourcefulness even while I cursed her foolhardiness. I looked at Faust and then back at Willow. "He hasn't hurt you, has he?"

"Hurt her?" Geoffrey interjected. "Ma'am, I've let your daughter take over my apartment and extended her every hospitality."

"He's been super nice to me, Mom. Please don't be mad."

"I have a right to be mad at you. What you did was dangerous. You have no idea who this man is. He could have killed you!"

"Whoa-whoa-whoa. I'm no killer, lady." Geoffrey waved his meaty hands in my face. "Like I said, I've never seen either of you in my life. And I think it's about time both of you got the hell out of here." He walked over to the apartment door and opened it. We'd worn out our welcome big-time.

I studied him, holding the door open impatiently. Maybe he was being honest. Maybe he was lying. I might even be married to a cheating liar, which I never saw coming. Clearly I wasn't the best judge of character.

"I'm sorry we bothered you," I muttered halfheartedly as we exited. He didn't answer, and shut the door decisively.

In the hallway, I didn't hold back. "That was stupid, Will. Never ever do something like that again. Come to me if you have a question rather than running off to a stranger's house searching for answers. You scared us to death—we reported you missing to the police!"

Reality must have hit her then, a sudden realization of the risk she had put herself in. Her eyes glazed over and she cried into my chest, her tears soaking through my shirt.

"I'm so sorry, Mom. I didn't think . . ."

"Shh. It's okay." I ran my hands over her sweet blond head, my fingertips catching in her mass of curls. "Everything's okay now."

If only I could believe that myself.

Chapter 24

Robin

It was after ten o'clock before Willow finally fell asleep in my arms. It'd been so long since I held her like this, her not-so-small body cuddled into my side as I stroked her soft hair, inhaling the scent of her coconut shampoo. When had my baby girl grown up? Somehow I had blinked and missed it.

It had been so much easier when she was younger. No skipping school. No comprehension of the drama that surrounded our family. Blissfully naïve and eager to please. A daddy's girl, mommy's little helper. But now . . . now she was scheming behind our backs, sneaking out of school, asking questions I had hoped to never have to answer.

181

Back then it was lollipops and playgrounds. Now it was secrets and disappearing acts. And lies. So many lies.

If the kids had ever gotten around to doing the math, they would have figured out the truth eventually. Grant and I had met when Ryan was two, married when he was three, and Willow didn't come along until he was six. But what twelve-year-old notices those tiny discrepancies? Hell, apparently eighteen-year-olds don't even do the calculations. I guess Grant and I had been vague enough about when we had first met that they never questioned if Grant was Ryan's biological father. But did it matter, really?

Grant was his dad. Willow, Lucas, and Collette were his siblings. One big happy family. Period. Except to Willow, apparently it did matter. Enough to send her digging in the remains of my past.

The creak of floorboards drew my attention to the hallway. Grant stood there, his body lithe and toned from after-work gym workouts. At least that's where he told me he spent his time. Or were those chiseled pecs and that flat stomach the result of extraordinarily athletic sex with his equally agile paramour in seedy hotels?

I hated Grant for his perfect body and youthful face while I wore my exhaustion like a burial shroud.

"Hey, honey. I have a surprise for you." Grant wiggled his finger at me to follow him.

"A surprise, huh?" I knew what that meant. A surprise for me meant sex for him. And I was so not in the mood.

Two kids ago we were sex-crazed lovers who couldn't get enough of each other. Four kids, two car payments, and a mortgage later we were dull strangers who shared a bed.

Grant blamed me; I blamed the kids. When you're barely surviving on a couple of hours' sleep, and spending all day grocery shopping, folding laundry, prepping meals, nursing, and helping with homework, well, it gets old. It drains you of that passion for life you once had.

It didn't help that I felt self-conscious when naked around Grant. He looked like a Greek god while I still carried the mushrooming tummy of a pregnancy eight months ago. And my boobs, while huge with milk, crawled with stretch marks and blue veins popping through creamy skin. I thought nursing would help shed the pounds, but by the time you hit forty, skin's elasticity doesn't bounce back like it does in your twenties. My flat ass was evidence of that as the skin sagged where my thighs met my butt cheeks. If you had this worn-out body, would you want to flaunt it in front of your hot husband? I think not.

My body became my journey, each wrinkle and flaw a dubious milestone in my life. That scar under my lip was from that weekend we went camping in an RV. When Lucas woke up screaming from a nightmare, I bolted upright into an overhead cabinet, bumping my head, then reflexively ducked down, smashing my tooth right through my lip on Lucas's bunk bed frame. Every time I saw that scar I thought of three-year-old Lucas and that trip we took. I consoled him through the bloody lip and bruised forehead that night because his comfort was more important than my pain.

It always was that way when you're a mother.

Every cell in me had contributed to their life. Sometimes I felt like a cow or a chicken, my body and my time exploited by my children. My blood was theirs, my sleep was theirs, my milk was theirs, and now my life was theirs. I loved my little leeches, but damn if they didn't suck every last part of me dry.

And then there was Grant, wanting the leftovers.

I kissed Willow's forehead and tucked her blankets in, a habit I had relished when she was little. I tiptoed out of her room, following Grant to our bedroom. I wasn't exactly wrong, but I wasn't exactly right either. Scattered along the hallway were rose petals, the path lined with votive candles leading into the bedroom, straight into the bathroom. I grew excited as I entered, the bath drawn and bubbles glistening in the glow of scented candles arranged around the garden tub's rim.

"What is this?" I asked coyly. I knew exactly what this was. Romance wasn't dead after all.

"How about you settle in, relax, enjoy some wine." He lifted a crystal glass poured to the brim, the wise man. "Maybe read or whatever, and I'll join you in a bit with dessert."

He winked—because dessert always meant sex. But now I was actually in the mood, God bless his effort.

"Ah, I think I know what we're having." I giggled like a horny teenager.

"If you're thinking chocolate-covered strawberries, you'd be correct."

"Oh, you sly dog! I hope they come with a side of you." I gave him an exaggerated wink.

He laughed and I remembered how much I missed the sound of it. "We'll see, you dirty girl. Now get in there."

He slapped my ass on his way to the kitchen, and I couldn't wait for the night to begin.

Five minutes later I couldn't wait for the night to end.

This time it wasn't Collette crying or Willow and Lucas fighting. As I stepped out of my pants, I heard the front door shut and the slap of Ryan's sneakers against the hardwood stairs. They grew louder as he rushed past Willow's room, and a few moments later a door slammed shut. The sound of water running, the telltale complaint of air in the pipes. He was in his bathroom.

Something was wrong. And he had never called me back after my message about Willow, which was a huge red flag. That was his little sister, the one he would go to the ends of the earth to protect. I hesitated in the doorway, dueling between ignoring it and enjoying my bath, or finding out what was going on with my eldest son. Parental duty won once again, damn it.

Stepping into a crumpled pair of sweatpants, I tiptoed upstairs to his bathroom door and tapped on it with one knuckle.

"You okay, sweetie?" I spoke to the white compressed wood.

"I'm fine, Mom." Ryan sounded short and annoyed, which irritated me to no end. Why did the kids instantly go on the defense with me at a simple question? I was sure they saved these voices just for me, because I never heard it toward their father or their friends.

The sink water was still running a couple minutes later, and I wondered what he could possibly be doing in there.

"When you're finished, I need to speak with you. It's important."

"Can't it wait until tomorrow?"

"No, it can't wait. I left you a message about your sister, to which you never replied. Then you were out all night, with no phone call, no text, then you breeze in here and say you don't have two minutes to give your mother? Until you start paying rent, I own you, kid. So open the door."

"Please, Mom. I don't want you to see me right now."

What the hell did that mean? "Get decent because I'm coming in."

I rattled the doorknob as Ryan yelped, "Okay, Mom! Stop—I'm opening the door!"

As the door swung open, Ryan shuffled back a few steps, his hand shielding his face. I tugged his arm down and examined him. A growing purple and yellow bruise blossomed under his eye socket.

"What happened? Who did this to you?"

My fingertips gently probed his face as he winced and jerked away from my touch.

"Nobody. I got hit with the ball during baseball practice."

Liar, liar, lips on fire. I could smell a lie a mile away. I'd been a teenager before, a deviant one at that, and I knew how to spot 'em.

"Don't bullshit me, Ry. Who hit you?"

"I don't want to talk about it. You'll flip out."

"Does this have something to do with Geoffrey Faust—and Willow going to see him today?"

"What? Willow went to see him?" His face paled, jaw dropped. "Is she okay?"

"You didn't know about that? Didn't you listen to any of my voicemails I left you or check your texts?"

"No, I forgot my phone today. It was at home. What happened?"

I didn't want to get into it. But Ryan wouldn't quit until he had answers. Just like his sister.

"Willow must have overheard us talking about Geoffrey Faust and decided to look him up." I paused and added leadingly: "Or else you told her about him."

Ryan smiled wanly. "Guilty as charged. You know how close we are."

It was my turn to smile. "Not important right now. Anyway, the rascal hired an Uber and showed up at his apartment. Wanted to see what he was like."

"Kid's got more nerve than we give her credit for," Ryan said admiringly.

"You're right about that. But the man swore he's not the same Geoffrey Faust I knew." I shrugged. "And it was so long ago, maybe it's not him. Anyway, she's afraid he's going to take you away from us, so she went there to beg him to stay away in case you went looking for him."

"Oh, Mom, I'm so sorry. I had no idea she would do that. Is she okay?"

"Yeah, I think so. She's still wrapping her head around everything, but then we all are. How about you? That news was pretty big. You doing okay with it?"

"Honestly, it doesn't change anything for me. I'm Dad's and your son; I don't know Geoffrey, and I can't say that I'll ever want to know him. He walked out on us. Why should I give him a second thought?"

I hugged him like I'd never get to hug him again. When

I released him, I held his face in my hands, the first face on this earth that I truly loved with a sacrificial love that only a mother knows, the first face that gave me purpose in life. He had taken the worst of myself, chiseled away the misery, and unearthed a pure love I didn't know existed. A love that saturated me. The moment I met my baby, I knew all the heartache wasn't in vain, because he made my heart whole. Something beautiful had come from something so ugly.

"I'm proud of you, Ry. But I'm not buying the whole baseball accident thing. What really happened?"

"Promise you won't tell Dad? And that you won't over-react?"

"I can't promise that, Ry. I'm your mother. I'll do what needs to be done to protect you. Always."

"Mom, just swear you won't do anything without talking to me first. Please."

"Fine, fine. I promise." So what if he and a buddy got into it? Testosterone and competition don't always bring out the best in boys. I didn't understand why he was being so secretive about this.

"Mr. Fischer stopped me after baseball practice tonight . . . and had a few things to say to me—"

My hand flew up to my mouth, stopping Ryan's explanation mid-sentence.

"Owen hit you?"

"He was angry about what happened with Aria, Mom. It's understandable. I got what I deserved. Please just let it go. If you confront him, it'll only make things worse."

A grown man hitting a teenage boy . . . no, I couldn't let

Owen get away with this. But I couldn't let Ryan know what I was about to do. He'd never tell me anything ever again. So I played it cool, as cool as I could as I lied through my teeth.

"Ry, you don't deserve that, and technically we could press assault charges for what he did to you, but I'll let it slide—for you. Because you asked me to. But if that man ever goes near you again, I'll . . . ooooh, I love you, you know that?"

He sighed like he had just released the weight of a heavy secret. "Thank you for being cool about this and not killing anyone."

I hadn't made any promises on that.

"Moooommy!" Lucas's tattletale voice called from my bedroom. "Someone threw leaves all over the floor and made a huge mess! They're gonna get a big spanking!"

The flower petals. I'd forgotten about tonight's romance fail. It looked like I wasn't going to be the one getting a spanking tonight after all.

Ryan looked at me quizzically.

"I better go deal with the munchkin," I said.

I kissed Ryan goodnight on the cheek, then headed back downstairs. Grant was wiping off the counter from the chocolate-covered strawberries I'd probably forget to eat, so I tucked Lucas into our bed—Grant would grumble about it later, but neither of us wanted to deal with the exhaustive effort of relocating him—and popped on a movie, *Wreck-It Ralph*. The kid could never fall asleep for long before he'd climb his way into our bed. We'd given up on ever having the bed to ourselves until Lucas reached puberty.

I grabbed my keys and told Grant the timeworn cliché

that I had a quick errand to run, then off I went to pay Owen Fischer a little visit.

Ten minutes later I rang the doorbell, pacing the patio that Mackenzie had spent hours decorating. She always went a little overboard with her outdoor motifs, but her current hummingbird theme full of purples and teals was quite eye-catching. A hummingbird feeder dangled from the awning, along with hanging baskets of fuchsia petunias and violet geraniums. A rustic bistro set inlaid with colorful tile had given us many spring mornings enjoying coffee and chitchat over the years. I wondered where she had purchased the décor, and if I could pull off a similar look on my own back porch.

When Owen answered the door, I couldn't remember all the curse words and threats I had practiced on the drive over. I couldn't speak. I glared up at him in fist-clenched, sizzling wrath, our eyes dueling.

"Come to thank me for setting your son straight?" His face was so eerily expressionless that I struggled to hold myself back. Then his lips curled in a nasty smirk. "Don't worry. Becoming some thug's girlfriend in jail will make him think twice about raping another innocent girl."

I slapped him across the cheek with every ounce of strength in me. His head swung back, and when he turned to face me again, his hazel eyes smoldered.

"Tell your son he's going to need a damn good lawyer, you bitch."

That was a choice word coming from Owen, the man who never swore.

"Never come near my family again or you'll be fertilizing

the new lilac I just planted." I stormed down the walkway to my car, a mixture of satisfaction and adrenaline pulsing through me. I'd had the last word, and I meant it. Owen could swing his big gun around, hiding behind empty threats and violent words. I didn't need the fanfare, though, because I was the sniper who would pull the trigger.

When I got home I found Grant in bed reading and Lucas gone. The rose petals had been cleaned up, the candles blown out, bathtub drained.

"I put Fizz to bed," Grant mumbled.

"I'm sorry about tonight," I said. "But something happened that I had to take care of."

He barely looked up at me, then returned to his book. "It's fine."

But it wasn't.

"Owen punched Ryan in the face. I had to confront him, Grant. I couldn't let it go."

That got a reaction. Grant closed the book and looked at me hard. "He did *what*?"

"He attacked Ryan."

"Why would he ever hit Ryan? I don't understand."

I didn't know how to explain it. Ryan had enough to worry about; he didn't need a lecture from Grant on top of everything else. "Ryan and Aria had sex, and they had been drinking. Owen thinks Ryan forced himself on Aria, but I talked to Ryan and it doesn't sound like that's what happened."

Grant's fury flattened and he shook his head. "Oh geez. As a father of girls, I can understand why Owen would be angry. No father wants to think of his daughter having sex."

"But hitting a kid? Grant, you have to agree that's taking it too far. He's becoming unhinged."

"Maybe I could talk to him, man to man. I'm sure it's not as bad as you think."

"It's too late for words. He plans to press charges against Ryan. He's got a vendetta and wants to ruin his whole life; I can feel it. He's going to put our son in jail, Grant!" I felt hysterics bubbling up.

"Are you sure you're not misreading things? Mac and Owen are our friends—they would never do that." Oh Grant, ever the optimist.

"Owen told me to get a lawyer for Ryan. This isn't going to blow over. Mac's not even speaking to me."

Grant tossed off the bed covers and came to me, folding me into a hug. "It's okay, honey. We'll figure it out. We just need to know the facts. Is Aria saying that he—he raped her?"

"I don't know what she's saying. Aria won't answer Ryan's calls—even though I told him not to contact her—and Mac's like the Great Wall of China. I have no idea what's going on behind closed doors over there. I don't know how to stop this from exploding."

I stood in the middle of the room wrapped in my husband's arms, and yet I felt so cold. I couldn't stand the silence, but I had nothing left to say.

"I know how to stop it, Robin."

"You do?" I was willing to entertain any idea at this point.

"It'd put a stop to Owen forever, though."

Grant returned to the bed, and I shuffled behind him,

sitting in the crook next to him. I'd never seen such broody darkness in Grant's eyes before, but there it was, the hazel deepening into a pool of black.

"I don't care, if it saves Ryan."

"You know, of course, about my handy-dandy prescription pad." I nodded, and Grant's features tensed. He blinked, slowly. "Well, I can think of a dozen prescriptions that if consumed in high enough quantities could put a man his size down. I'm not saying we should . . . but we could."

"No, we couldn't . . . could we?"

"It wouldn't be difficult. I could easily justify writing Ryan a prescription for an anti-anxiety medication. Something that's known to trigger an adverse reaction when overdosed. Somehow it ends up in Owen's food. Just sayin'."

"We could go to jail if they traced it back to us."

"And Ryan could go to jail if we don't."

It sounded so logical sitting here discussing it like we were chatting about dinner plans.

"What do you think the chances are of us getting caught?"

"You, none. You wouldn't know anything about it. Me, well, I'd take the fall in a heartbeat if it meant protecting you and the kids." He placed a hand on my knee, squeezed, and kissed my cheek. "Worst-case scenario, if the cops do tie it back to us, I'll say it was all me." He cupped my chin, tilting my face toward his. "I'd do anything for you. Anything."

Grant was willing to put his life on the line for Ryan, for our family, for me.

A chill ran up my arms—a chill caught between adoration for the man who would go to jail for me, and fear of the man who would kill for me. Who was he? Lover. Adulterer. Liar. Provider. Killer. Protector. The answer didn't seem so black and white anymore.

After all of his secretive calls, then catching him lying about "poker with the guys," I'd been shocked to find out he might be a cheater . . . but a killer too? And yet I admired his nobility, his willingness to take the fall. He could solve Ryan's problem with the scribble of a pen, a pickup at the pharmacy, a visit with Mackenzie, where I'd discreetly poison Owen's food. Without sanctimonious Owen leading the charge for Ryan's crucifixion, Aria and Mackenzie would drop it. I was sure of it. It'd be over; Ryan would be safe.

As my own scheme unfolded, maybe I wasn't as innocent as I thought. The things a mother would do for her child were unspeakable. As I contemplated the murder of my friend's husband, I didn't know if I should feel proud or scared of myself.

Chapter 25

Lily

Mistakes come in threes.

I had been trying to avoid Grant like he was a germ-infested kid, I really had, but when Robin called to invite me to Ryan's Gateway Gators baseball game, I couldn't say no. She *needed company*, she whined, saying that she wasn't really into baseball, never understood the game, and seven innings were just so damn long while dealing with Collette and Lucas that she'd blow her brains out if I wasn't there to keep her company. So I said yes, I'd meet her at the ball field.

That was mistake number one.

Mistake number two happened two innings, three

sneak-in-your-own-beers, and one nachos-and-cheese later as poor ignorant Robin sat between me and Grant chatting like everything was fine and dandy. Because as far as she knew, it was. Her marriage wasn't crumbling around her, her friendship wasn't stained with betrayal; her biggest concern was the cheese droppings on her jeans that she hoped wouldn't stain.

When Grant left to greet the dad of one of the other players, Robin turned her full attention to me.

"Seeing anyone lately?" she asked while Collette squirmed in her arms and Lucas whined for more candy. The kid had a one-track mind when it came to sweets.

Your husband, I could have said but didn't. "No, not really. No one is as good as Tony was for me. I still miss him, you know?"

"Tony? Really? He was an average-looking chub. What was the appeal there anyway?"

Robin meant no cruelty by her remark. Sure, Tony was fat. We could call it what it was. But I loved that about him. Fat guys knew how to please a woman because they had more to prove. Tony worshipped me, treated me like a goddess. Tony loved to satisfy me, in and out of the bedroom. And I reciprocated. Because when someone goes out of their way to make you happy, you can't help but return the favor.

We were perfect together, him with his insecurities that made him attentive, and me with my egotism that demanded he always be mine. It worked for a long time . . . until it didn't. But that was my fault, not Tony's. And I still hadn't gotten over it. Or over him, for that matter. Maybe if he hadn't told me to wait for him I wouldn't still be waiting. That was a year ago.

"I liked feeling small in his arms. He was like a big teddy bear."

"More like being smothered in his arms, but hey, to each her own."

I knew what Robin was doing. It was a thing girls did. Insult the ex to lessen the loss.

"It doesn't matter anyway. Tony's gone and now I'm alone." It was a fact I still hadn't accepted, if I was being honest.

"Have you tried any dating websites? You might meet someone nice that way."

I rolled my eyes. "Is there ever anyone *nice* on a dating service?"

"I'm sure there is. Don't knock it until you try it, Lil."

"All right, full disclosure here. I've tried this dating app a few times and the guys are hit-or-miss, but mostly miss." I opened up the app on my phone and scrolled through the pictures. "Let's see, this guy had a creepy foot fetish." I swiped to another picture. "And this one was still obsessed with his ex." Then a third. "And this one's coke nails didn't inspire much confidence."

I was sick of meeting deadbeats looking for a sugar mamma. I wasn't that girl.

"Here, let me pick one for you." Robin took my phone and began swiping through pictures, speculating over this guy's weird fixation, that guy's personality disorder.

When Robin's laughter stopped suddenly, I looked over her shoulder and nearly choked on my mouthful of water. There, on my screen, wearing a charming grin and striking a macho shirtless pose, was Grant. Not only was he cheating on his wife, but he was cheating on his mistress too. Not that I had any room to judge, but still . . . the *stronzo*! I glanced up at Robin, whose face was drained of color.

She scrolled down to his profile description, and I covered the screen with my hand. "Are you sure you want to read that?"

"No, but I have to, don't I? My husband's back in the dating game, apparently. As his wife I should know what he's marketing himself as, right?"

Okay, she was handling this a little too well. Screaming, sure. Yelling, of course. Crying, obviously. But the icy demeanor she wore didn't fit. I removed my hand and watched her eyes fly over his profile, again and again:

Fun-loving pediatrician looking for casual no-strings with similar interests.

"What does that even mean, *similar interests*?" Robin muttered under her breath.

I knew exactly what it meant. Someone who wanted discreet, uncomplicated sex. Nothing more, nothing less. But I was pretty sure Robin didn't need to hear that; she'd fill in the blanks on her own.

"And as if mentioning he's a doctor will score him brownie points?" she added with bite.

It probably would, actually. More likely to get hits if you had money. There were plenty of promiscuous single girls looking for a sugar daddy to take care of them.

When she looked at me, I wasn't sure if it was for

affirmation or denial. Did she want a *that cheating bastard* or *that's probably not him*?

"So he wants to play games, huh? I'll play a game." Her voice was saturated with a darkness I couldn't read. What was she planning?

"Robin, honey, what are you doing?" I almost didn't want to know, but I needed to protect her from herself. Vengeance led to the grave.

"I'm creating a profile. Then I'm gonna trap him and use that to take him down. And when I'm done with him he'll be ruined professionally and won't have a penny to his name."

Spoken with the calm of a breezeless day. So matter-of-fact it sent a chill up my spine. I'd never seen this side of Robin—the sinister, ruthless side. God help me if she ever found out what I did. Grant was her husband, the father of her children; I was just a friend.

Within minutes she had created a profile, uploaded some random beautiful woman's picture she found online, and created a profile description:

Single nanny looking for a casual encounter. Must be a gentleman who knows how to treat a lady.

She clicked to activate her profile and *whoosh*! Off it went into cyberspace. A few minutes later she found Grant's profile again and sent a private message requesting to meet in person. A hot nanny and a kid doctor both looking to bang— the perfect match. Damn, Robin was good. Scary good. It was only a matter of time before my neck was next on the chopping block.

"Mommy, I have to go pee." Lucas tugged on her shirt, bouncing on the balls of his tiny tennis-shoed feet. His arms and legs never stopped moving, like a windup monkey.

"Okay, sweetie. I'll take you." Robin sniffed Collette's rear and frowned. "Looks like sissy could use a fresh diaper too."

Lucas looked up at me and smiled widely, showing off a gaping hole where he'd recently lost a tooth. "Guess what, Auntie Lil! Guess what! Guess what!"

"What?" I barked, but when his face contorted with hurt, I sweetly covered it up with a syrupy, "What's up, little guy?" I hated when he repeated himself again and again and again. How Robin managed not to duct-tape his motormouth shut was beyond me. I guess that was why I didn't have kids and she did.

"I can pee standing up!" Lucas proudly chirped.

"Oh, you're a big boy now?"

"Yup. I peed on the wall, and in the garbage can, and on the floor, and on the toilet seat all by myself."

I gasped, horrified. "Really? That's . . . uh . . . great."

"And you also managed to pee on Mommy's jeans," Robin added, "and that's why Mommy said you need to sit down when you pee, since Mommy had to clean all that up." Robin looked at me with a stiff grin that said *Motherhood isn't for the weak*. "C'mon, Lucas, let's head to the bathroom where you'll *sit* when you pee."

Robin stood up, managing her way down the bleacher aisle. One arm was full of baby, the other burdened with an overstuffed diaper bag, while dragging an easily distracted Lucas who kept zipping away from her and getting tangled up in the legs of the crowd. Superwoman, that was Robin.

It made me feel even worse about betraying her. But not bad enough to avoid mistake number two when I showed Robin the damn dating app.

Minutes after Robin left Grant filled the empty seat.

"Hey, gorgeous," he said, brushing his finger against my leg.

I scooted away. "Behave. Robin will be back any second."

"What if I told you I didn't care if she saw us?"

I rolled my eyes. "I'd tell you you're an *idiota*."

I wanted to warn him about Robin's ruse to catch him with that dating app, but it wasn't my place to do it. I was done playing piggy-in-the-middle. Plus I didn't want to dive into the conversation about him seeing women other than me. Jealous mistress wasn't my thing.

So instead I avoided looking at his strong hands that knew how to touch me, or his sweet mouth that had tasted the terrain of my body. It was excruciating making platonic small talk with him, us both knowing what we knew, feeling what we had felt. Not to mention my pang of jealousy that he was also seeing other women. The rush of his heat still tingled my lips even now. I was addicted and I didn't know how to get sober.

When Grant watched me stand up, I said, "I'm heading to the concession stand. Need anything?" Yes, I was legitimately hungry, but finding a moment alone with Grant always lingered in the back of my mind.

"I'll join you." Then he smiled. *Merda!* It was that glint of mischief in his eyes that got me in trouble in the first place. But I didn't stop, couldn't stop. Have I mentioned that I'm an addict?

We headed to the food booth, but when we reached it, he grabbed my hand and pulled me behind it. In the back, the booth was supported by stacks of concrete blocks, creating a secret and shadowy nook, just barely tall enough to stand up in. It was common knowledge teen girls and boys used this spot for make-out sessions. Luckily for us, it was currently unoccupied.

We wasted no time with words. His lips immediately engulfed mine, his hands cupping my ass and lifting me up until I straddled him. I knew Robin would come looking for us soon, but I couldn't stop. His lips trailed down my neck as his hands roved over my breasts. Dry humping like two horny teenagers, I saw a shadowy shape approaching.

"Shh," I whispered, hopping away from him. "Someone's coming. Hide!" We scrunched back deeper into the nook. As I crouched in the shade, it took me back to ninth grade when I had made out with Brian Bahn under the bleachers, my first real boyfriend. First love lingered a lifetime.

I straightened my shirt and rebuttoned my pants—I hadn't even realized he had made that smooth move. Breathless with mingled excitement and trepidation, I casually waited for Robin to pop into view. But she never did. No one did. The shadow simply idled, within eyeshot but too indistinct to identify. Was whoever it was listening to us? Waiting to catch us in the act? I crept forward and peeked out just as the shadow retreated. I could see people milling around the baseball park. A moment later I spotted Robin's back among the crowd, her hair falling in loose waves around her shoulders. I didn't know if our little eavesdropper was her or not, but I'd be damned if I came crawling out of the shadows while she stood right there.

"Is it her?" Grant whispered in my ear.

"I'm not sure if she saw us, but she's standing right there." I nodded in her direction. "Just wait until she moves."

And what if she saw us? What would happen then? Question after question plagued me, worry heaped on top of guilt and regret. I didn't want to feel this way. I wanted to be happy. I wanted to be free of this burden. But I couldn't stop, and I didn't know how to stop. For the first time since Tony I felt alive. But Tony was gone, wasn't he? I had pushed the best thing in my life away and there was no returning to that life. I'd lost everything that mattered all because of the accident, the pills, the depression—a hungry cycle that swallowed me whole.

People judge addicts as weak, but they have no idea what it's really like. Speculate all you want, but until your life depends on something, you'll never know. For years I tried to figure out how people just "quit" their drug of choice, but it wasn't so easy. My thoughts were always on my next high, whether it be pills . . . or, now, Grant.

Maybe Robin catching us was what I needed to straighten my life out. Maybe if I got my life together Tony would take me back. But in that scenario I'd lose Robin. I'd lose my friend in order to gain myself. I wasn't so sure it was an even exchange.

"We gotta go back out there," Grant finally said, ripping me from my self-loathing. "I don't want her finding us here."

"Is it better if she sees us both coming out of here together? That's going to look pretty damn suspicious."

Then I had an idea. It was a stupid one, one that would probably turn Robin against me, but it was better than getting caught. As Grant headed out into the open, I lingered behind.

Welcome, mistake number three: kissing my best friend's husband while she stood mere feet away.

I pulled my phone out of my back pocket and swiped to unlock it. It rang twice before Mackenzie answered.

"Hey, Mac. Are you free right now?" Holding my phone up to my ear, I waved Robin over as if I was excited to finally find her. "Sorry," I mouthed to Robin, "I was behind the concession stand trying to hear my phone. I'm on with Mackenzie. She might be joining us."

Her chin lifted slightly, and she didn't exactly look happy about the news. I read what she was thinking—*don't you dare make me share space with Mackenzie*—but at this point I didn't care about their feud. I needed Mackenzie here, and fast, before I finished what Grant and I had started. I didn't trust myself anymore. Only Mac knew about the demons I was battling, and I needed her to fight them with me.

I paced out of earshot before Robin had a chance to object.

"Why?" Mackenzie asked slowly. Curiously, as if she knew I was up to something. "What's going on?"

"We're all at Ryan's baseball game and we wanted you here."

"Seriously, Lily? I told you I'm pissed at Robin. I'm not going anywhere near her family."

"Come on," I begged. "We've been friends for decades. Stop acting like children and let's deal with it like grown-ups. I think Robin wants to make amends."

"Robin said that—she wants me there?"

"Of course, we all do." A tiny white lie for the sake of friendship. "You both need to stop letting this rift come between you and discuss it, figure it out together for the sake of the kids. Put on your big-girl pants and talk it through."

"I wish I could, but Owen would kill me. He and Robin had sort of a . . . falling out last night."

"What are you talking about, a *falling out*?" How much drama were these two involved in? I felt like I'd missed an entire season of *Real Housewives of Monroeville* starring Robin and Mackenzie.

"Honestly, I don't want to get into it right now, but it's pretty bad. I don't think I'll be seeing you girls for a while until Owen cools down. Sorry."

Merda! There went my protection from myself. And Robin's scowl while Collette squirmed in her arms wasn't helping. Screw sobriety, I needed a pill to get through this night, because I could guarantee Robin would be giving me an earful about Mackenzie the moment I hung up.

The pills were in my car, so I mouthed an *I've gotta run to my car real quick* to Robin, listening to Mac vent while I crunched my way along the gravel parking lot.

"Are you going to be okay at home with Owen being all riled up? You know the plan still stands—*la mia casa è la tua casa*. I know how he gets when he's angry."

"I'm fine, Lily, really. I just need a bubble bath, a glass of wine, and a book. By the end of the weekend things should hopefully calm down."

By this point I found my car, digging my keys out of my pocket.

I hadn't noticed it until a sliver of light glinted on my tire, catching my attention.

"Oh my God," I said, forgetting I was on the phone.

"Lily? Is everything all right?"

"No. Someone slashed all my tires."

I could have shrugged it off as mischief-making teenagers, except for the handle of a blade jutting out of the front driver's side tire. A message—and a creepy one at that. Was this saying I was next? The worst part was that it could have been any number of enemies I had recently made. Irving? Willow? The mysterious phone breather?

The mistake underpinning all of my others: making enemies out of friends.

Chapter 26

Mackenzie

They say love and hate go hand in hand. They're right, you know. In this world there is nothing as inspiring as love. The poetry it has created, the artwork it has motivated. But if a husband stole it away and replaced it with apathy, there is nothing as vindictive as a wife's hate.

I heard the front door slam shut. Not the gentle, calm click of the latch returning home, but a brash, irritated *bang*. The master was home, and surprise surprise, he was in a bad mood. When Owen had a rough day at work, the whole neighborhood knew it. He made sure of that with his speed-driving and slamming the front door off its hinges. What they didn't know was what he did behind closed bedroom doors, safe from Aria's view but not safe for me.

"*With your disfigurement you should be happy I like screwing you,*" he'd tell me when I made excuses for why I wasn't in the mood. Not like my mood mattered. He always got what he wanted, when he wanted it. My *disfigurement*, as he put it, always kept me in the passenger's seat. I would never be the driver of my life, because I wasn't pretty enough.

Owen stormed past me into the kitchen, where he threw open the fridge door and grabbed a beer.

"You okay, honey?" I called from the living room where I was folding laundry.

Six neat stacks—one for me, one for Owen, and four for Aria. How that girl managed to go through four times as many clothes as a normal human was a mystery. I decided to have her start washing her own laundry just to make a point. She'd agree, do one load to humor me, then I'd be back to doing it. Not that I minded. I loved the purpose it gave me. Sometimes Aria playfully accused me of being like those mindless commercial moms on TV, finding fulfillment in cleaning up little messes with the latest miracle product. I wondered when Procter & Gamble would come out with something to clean up really big messes. Like my life.

"Just work stuff. Nothing worth talking about. You?" Owen leaned against the island counter and cracked open the bottle, guzzling half the beer in one gulp.

As a manager at a publicity firm, it was usually smooth sailing at a job he loved, unless he lost a client. Today seemed like one such day.

"Lily called me earlier today. Invited me to Ryan's baseball game. Apparently Robin wants to make up. I'm thinking we should—for the sake of the kids."

He exploded. "Are you kidding me? Have you lost your mind? If you even see or speak to that family again, I promise you, you'll regret it." Owen's threat echoed against the kitchen cabinets.

I regretted mentioning it as I watched his face redden and eyes go dark like windows in an abandoned house. To me, Owen was a haunted house, with layers of decay and demons playing hide-and-seek inside its bowels. He often scared the shit out of me.

"They're my best friends. I can't just stop being friends with them because of what happened with Aria and Ryan. Besides, once emotions cool off Robin and I will deal with it—together." His gaze narrowed on me in a nonverbal warning, but I kept going like a runaway train. "And it doesn't help that you had to escalate things. Why do you have to be such an asshole?"

His eyes widened. "First of all, there's no need for profanity, Mackenzie."

I noticed the use of my proper name, which was usually reserved for when I *acted like a child*.

He continued: "I am the man of the house and you don't speak to me that way. You know better, don't you? And secondly, they are no longer your friends. You're forbidden from seeing them again."

I hated it when he scolded me. I'd swear if I wanted to, damn it. I'd pick my own friends, thank-you-very-much. I was a grown woman. I could make decisions for myself.

But I didn't say any of that. I didn't say anything but a

mumbled "sorry," because that's what I always did. Apologize. Obey. Rinse. Repeat.

The irony wasn't lost on me, that despite Owen's anger issues—which he referred to as being the "man of the house"—he never swore. Not a single cuss word, ever. In fact, it violated his moral code. And yet belittling his wife of eighteen years, turning me into his personal servant, there was nothing in the code against that. If you looked up *hypocrite* in the dictionary, you'd find Owen's picture. While my brain recognized this, my heart couldn't compute. I was frozen in place, because I had no choice but to take the bad with the good. He was a great provider, reliable, loyal, even loving, in his own way. But there were those few occasions— well, maybe more than a few—when the love turned sour. In those moments I was scared to death of the demons lurking inside the man I'd given my life to.

I was sleeping with the devil, and I had no idea how to break free . . . or even if I could. When half of your face looked like mangled meat, your confidence took a hit. If you don't believe me, try lighting your head on fire and see how you feel once the scar tissue heals. I guarantee you'll love yourself a little less.

"That's right, you're sorry," Owen added. He always had the last word. He made sure of this. "And before you start vilifying me, you do realize their son raped our daughter, don't you? For you to stay friends is like approving of what he did."

"And what about us—what you do to me?" The words tumbled out before I could stop them.

"What do I do to you other than provide a beautiful home

for you, give all of my time and energy and love to you? Exactly what do I do to you, Mackenzie, that you find so disagreeable and offensive?"

I felt my courage dwindle. There was no point trying to force my point; Owen would always win.

"Never mind," I murmured.

"No, I'd like to hear it. I don't give you everything you want or need?"

"I didn't say that."

"Tell me what it is I do that's so horrible. Do I cheat on you? Do I run off with my friends every chance I get to leave you all by yourself?"

Touché.

"No, you don't."

"Then please enlighten me as to how I'm such an awful husband."

You hurt me. You force me to do things I'm uncomfortable with. You make me fear you.

"I love you with every part of my soul, Mackenzie," he continued, "and I think I've done a pretty thorough job of showing you that. I dedicate my whole life to you and Aria, my family, the only ones that matter. I wish you had the decency to love me the same way, as completely as I love you."

"I do, Owen. I love you more than anything. But sometimes you . . ." I couldn't say what I wanted to say. I couldn't tell him that I felt like a prisoner, that I felt like a victim, that I felt like his toy to play with whenever and however he felt like it. I couldn't say those things because they sounded silly even as I considered them. I was his wife, who vowed to love him the way he needed to be loved. So he was rough in the sack. Why did I make such a big deal about it? Maybe because—and it was so hard to even think about it—his preference for vicious, impersonal doggy-style sex, with no face-to-face contact . . . felt an awful lot like *rape*.

Despite his flaws, he loved me when no one else had. He was the pill I swallowed to feel happy. It tasted bitter going down, but once that panacea took hold, I felt whole again.

I needed to stop before I drove him away and ruined my family.

"Sometimes I *what*, Mackenzie? You need me just as much as I need you. I do everything for you. How would you survive without me? Would you even want to? You have the life most women dream of. You get to stay home and raise our daughter, you have no stress, no worries. How could you dare accuse me of not doing my best for you, for us?"

"I never said that. I know you do. I just wish you considered my feelings when it came to certain things, Owen."

"What things?" he asked. He genuinely had no clue.

"Things like . . . sex. You hurt me."

"I *hurt* you? Because I want to make love to my wife?"

"Is that what that is—making love? Because it doesn't feel like it to me."

"Wow, I ask for one thing from you, one thing. Sex. A little passionate lovemaking between husband and wife. And you can't even give me that? You want to begrudge me intimacy? How about I do what other husbands do and find it somewhere else, with someone else? Would you prefer that, Mac?"

"No, of course not."

"Then what? Tell me what it is you want me to do." He stomped toward me now, grabbing both my arms, lifting me off the sofa, squeezing until my muscles ached. After this his thick fingers would leave long blue bruises, which I would hide with sleeves until they faded enough that no one would notice . . . and then a week or two later there would be new ones.

"I . . . I want . . ." I knew the script by now. I was supposed to tell him I'm all his, take whatever he wants, do whatever he wishes. But yes doesn't always mean yes, and silence doesn't always mean yes. "I want you."

"Come with me. I know what my girl wants." Spittle flicked along my cheek and ear. He dragged me into the laundry room, closing the door behind us so Aria wouldn't hear. He liked doing it in different places, as if marking new territory. "Now tell Daddy how much you want me. How much you need me inside you."

I coughed to hide a sob. I knew better than to cry; tears only made things worse, fueled him.

"I need you, baby," I whispered instead.

He bent me over the washing machine, his hands gripping my neck, and the rest I blocked out as best I could as the edge of the cold metal machine dug into my stomach. My active participation wasn't required; it never was. All that he needed was a body to inject himself into, to overpower and control. My body was as good as any to him. Except with me it was "pure" and "good" because I was his wife; it was noble with me.

By the time he finished, a folded stack of laundry placed on the dryer had fallen to the floor. As he zipped up his pants, he said, "Make sure you clean that up, Mac. Thanks for the release."

He kissed me on the forehead, because that's what you did with a *release*. You didn't snuggle or ask if it was good for them too, although even if he had asked, I would have lied and said that it was. The lies would be over soon, because I saw the end game up ahead.

After the laundry was refolded and Owen was planted in front of the television watching the news, I decided to check in on Aria. I had been worrying about her the last couple of days, keeping a close eye on her in case she showed signs of depression. But if she was anything like me, she knew how to hide it well.

The shower was running, so I decided to put away the clothes. I carried Aria's basket into her room, opening and closing drawers as I tucked her garments into neat little stacks. Pants. Shirts. Socks. Underwear. As I set the pile of panties and socks in her drawer, I heard a curious rustle.

There, tucked between a pair of cheeky striped undies and a floral pair, I discovered a plastic baggie and lifted it up to the lamplight. Shredded dried leaves, similar to tea leaves but more likely something illegal. No teen hid tea leaves in her underwear drawer.

I'd never smoked pot, had no clue what it looked like in real life, except for the cartoonish marijuana paraphernalia I'd seen on hats and shirts during my 1990s adolescence, when pot was still considered rebellious. Now every stay-at-home mom and even the grandparents had jars of cannabis oil in their cupboards.

I opened the Ziploc bag and sniffed it. Again, no clue what I was smelling or if it was felonious or not. But a baggie hidden in an underwear drawer didn't scream *harmless* to me.

As I resealed the bag, Aria walked in, wrapped in a towel, eyes wide with horror.

"Mom, what are you doing with that?" she yelped, snatching it out of my hand.

"The bigger question is what are *you* doing with . . . whatever this is."

"It's not what you think." She shoved the baggie back in her drawer.

"Honey, I wasn't born yesterday. Is this pot?"

She hesitated, avoiding my glance. "It's not a big deal. You know kids my age are doing it all the time."

"I don't care what the other kids are doing. I care about what *you're* doing."

"Have you ever done it?"

"Me? God, no. It wasn't legal back in my day, and none of my friends did it. I didn't even know anyone who had access to marijuana." At my high school the rebellious kids were into drinking and general hell-raising, not drugs. Not among my small circle of friends, anyway.

"Not even in college?"

"Ha! Can you imagine your father?" I'd met Owen early on as a freshman and we spent our college years trying to impress each other. "He would have had a fit if I even went near the stuff or anyone associated with it. He probably would have dumped me on the spot."

"Good old judgy, controlling Dad."

"Oh, come on. So your father prefers to abide by the law. What's wrong with that?"

"It's not that. It's how he treats you, Mom, controls you—controls all of us—that's what bothers me."

"Seriously? You're giving me grief because I've never smoked illegal substances? Do you hear how you sound? I'd prefer you never did them either. They're a gateway drug to worse, Aria."

She rolled her eyes and slipped into her pajamas. "See, this is what is so frustrating about you. It's not about the pot. It's about you and how you let Dad dictate everything for you. You're going to judge something you haven't even tried all because of Dad's feelings about it."

"I'm not judging it because of Dad. I'm judging it because I know what drug addiction can lead to."

Aria's laugh was hollow. "I'm not a drug addict, Mom. I've never even tried pot before. But would it be so bad if I did? Just to take the edge off of life?"

"Take the edge off? What edge?" She was fifteen. No fifteen-year-old should have an edge to her life. Of course, I couldn't discount the fact she was undergoing a huge personal crisis—yet one she didn't seem to be aware of. I prayed this *edge* had nothing to do with her knowing what happened with Ryan.

"Never mind. I'm just saying stress, that's all. Sometimes it sounds nice to just . . . drift away for a bit."

Okay, that worried me. Drifting away sounded an awful lot like drowning, which sounded an awful lot like a death wish.

"Is all this morbid talk because of Ryan?" I couldn't avoid

this conversation any longer. It was due. "I know you're avoiding him. I see all the missed calls on your phone."

Aria shrugged, then sat cross-legged on her bed. "Maybe a little. I don't remember every detail, but I know we made out. And I feel really weird about it now."

"Why would you feel weird?"

"I'm embarrassed about it! First of all, I was drunk so I don't know if I was throwing myself at him, and I'm petrified he's going to think less of me now. And then I was worried Dad would find out. It's just a big mess, and I don't know where Ryan and I stand. It's all so confusing, Mom."

"I know, it always is with matters of the heart." I sat next to her, wrapping my arm around her side as she rested her head on my shoulder. I hadn't lost my little girl after all.

"Does it ever get better?"

I wanted to tell her yes, of course it did, but it wasn't my reality. "I don't know, honey. Maybe you should talk to someone—a therapist who can help you sort through all of these feelings."

She heaved an exasperated sigh. "No, I just want to talk to *you*. Connect with *you*. Sometimes I feel like I don't really know you. I only know the version Dad has molded over the years."

"Oh, sweetie. This is the real me. And you can always talk to me." I touched her cheek, and her fingers rested on mine, holding my hand against her damp skin.

"Everything feels so . . . chaotic right now. I just wish I could go away for a little while."

"Don't we all. Hey, what do you say to us both doing it together?" I pointed to the baggie sticking out of her drawer, then headed toward it. "I'm not saying I want to make this a new bonding thing, but right now I could use a hit. Mommy-daughter bonding over a joint." I was being facetious, of course, but in this moment it didn't sound like such a horrible idea.

Aria chuckled and followed me, swatting my reaching hand away. "No thanks. I think I'm just going to flush it. I don't want to be responsible for turning my mother into a *drug addict*, after all. Can you imagine Dad walking in on both of us high?" We both laughed until our cheeks hurt.

I watched her move across the room, her blond hair dark and dripping, her cheeks pink and drizzled with water. The scent of fresh vanilla wafted behind her.

"Are you using my body wash again?" I sniffed her head, and she ducked away from me with a grin.

"I like yours better."

"Then I'll get you some, but stop using mine, because you never return it and I'm stuck using your dad's man-smelling stuff. I end up smelling like Old Spice all day."

Aria's nose wrinkled and I loved her for it. She made me feel so normal, so human.

"Mom, can I ask you something?"

"Sure, honey. What?"

"Do you love Dad?"

"Of course I do."

"Even after how he treats you?"

I wondered what she had seen over the years. I thought I had hidden the dark side pretty well.

"What do you mean? He's good to me, to us, Aria. We

have a beautiful home, never go hungry, never want for anything."

"It's just that . . . he treats you like a servant. Like he owns you or something. Do you not even notice . . . or care?"

"Honey, your father has more . . . *traditional* . . . views of husband and wife. The husband is the provider; the wife is the homemaker. I agreed to this when I married him. He's the head of the house, but I'm the neck, holding the head up. He only calls the shots because I let him. It works for us."

"But does it really? You're actually happy living like this? Because if I wasn't allowed to see my closest friends because my husband told me no, I'd be kicking him to the curb. But that's just me, I guess."

So she had heard the fight. I really hadn't wanted her exposed to that, but she was growing up and becoming more observant every day. Maybe this was good. I wouldn't have to lie to her about the plan to leave Owen. Heck, maybe she'd even support it.

"Aria, marriage is complicated. Feelings are complex. Sometimes a person can love someone who isn't good for them. The heart can't always be tamed or controlled. I wish love would be simple, but it isn't always that way."

"I guess. But I think you could do better, Mom. I don't know why you stay with him. Why you even love him. He's mean, he's constantly telling you what to do or not do . . . I know he's my dad and all, but I have no relationship with him. He doesn't give a shit about me."

"Aria!" I warned. Owen had never abided swearing, and I found myself seeing that his rules were followed. "Language please. And your father does love you, even if he doesn't show it."

"I just wonder sometimes if we'd be better off without him—just you and me."

"Honey, don't say that! That's a horrible thing to say."

And yet I'd been plotting it for weeks. Slowly taking money out of the bank account every time I went grocery shopping. Scheming with Lily on how to execute it perfectly. The plan was simple and doable. Set up my own private checking account. Trickle money in over several weeks, enough to afford a couple months of rent on a place for Aria and me while I searched for a job. Then one day just disappear, leaving nothing but a note telling Owen that it was over. Lily had offered us her spare bedroom until we got on our feet. It was foolproof and I'd followed it through . . . up until that last step. The biggest one. The one that took courage I lacked.

"We both know Dad can be pretty horrible to live with. And the day you can truly admit that is the day you'll be free. It's what you deserve, Mom."

My daughter had faith in me, so why didn't I? Maybe it was time to tell her about the plan. Maybe it was time to be free after all.

Chapter 27

Mackenzie

After my conversation with Aria last night, I couldn't sleep. With Owen beside me snoring, all I could think about was what my marriage to this man was doing to my daughter. But would leaving him do worse?

A girl needed her daddy. She needed him to build her confidence, instill courage in her, show her how a potential boyfriend should treat her, protect her, one day walk her down the aisle, and give her away to the right man, because he had spent his life showing her what the "right man" should look like. A good, supportive father led the way for a girl to find her own happily ever after, whether with a good man or on her own.

Taking Aria away from her daddy didn't seem right, even if he wasn't doing any of those things.

Owen had always been hands-off when it came to the infant period. Changing poopy diapers? He'd run to the bathroom and dry-heave simply at the smell. Handling the feedings? To him, that's what God gave women boobs for. The toddler years were an endless page of the same conditioning: women handle the kids; men handle the moneymaking. I had been fine with the arrangement, since motherhood suited me. In fact, it suited me so well that I wanted another, and maybe even another after that. But kids cost money, and one kid was plenty, according to Owen. One vasectomy later, the option for more kids was out of my control.

It was almost eight o'clock when I couldn't keep the morning sunlight from blinding me even through closed eyelids. I decided to get out of bed and make pancakes, a home-cooked breakfast that we didn't have time for on weekdays. Within fifteen minutes I had dark roast coffee brewing and most of the ingredients mixed, until I realized I was one egg short.

"Shoot," I mumbled under my breath as I searched the fridge again, just in case I hadn't seen an extra egg hiding somewhere behind the milk.

"What's wrong?" Owen asked, sneaking up behind me and wrapping his arms around me, kissing my neck—the good side. I always loved when he did that while I cooked. I felt so safe in his arms in those moments, in ironic contrast to how unsafe I felt in his arms at other times.

I loved how he inhaled me, holding me against him

protectively as his heart drummed against my back. In these moments I soared.

I turned to face him. "I'm an egg short. I'll run next door to see if Miss Barbara has any."

He smirked. In the north adults didn't precede a first name with *Miss*. That was a Southern thing—or *thang*—and he couldn't let it slide.

"No, don't ask *Miss* Barbara. It makes us look like beggars. Just run to the store and buy a dozen."

"She won't mind at all, Owen. It's what friendly neighbors do. It's not a big deal."

"Yes, it is a big deal because it makes us look irresponsible. You represent the family; you represent *me*, when you leave this house. I'll not have you making a fool of our family by begging for eggs from our neighbors."

I was still in my pajamas. I hadn't even enjoyed my first cup of coffee. There was no way I was going to get dressed to run out to the store for one damn egg.

"Fine, I'll go to the store wearing my pajamas. Would that suit you better?"

"Mackenzie, I don't find that funny, and you know it. Get dressed, get yourself presentable, and go shopping like a decent human being."

What he didn't understand was that without my morning coffee, I didn't feel like a decent human being. I didn't want to pretend to be one either. I wanted to bolt over to Barbara's, grab a single egg, run home, and lounge in my pajamas while I sipped my vanilla-flavored coffee and ate pancakes slathered in butter and syrup. But when it came to Owen, it wasn't worth the battle because he always won the war.

I headed to the bedroom to change, my anger festering. The echo of my parents' warning twenty years ago still bounced around in my head year after year like a never-ending death knell.

2000, GODWIN, NORTH CAROLINA

My daddy was your typical small-town Southern daddy: overprotective and ever hopeful that I'd become a nun. Picture a man on his front porch chewing tobacco with a shotgun sitting on his lap—that was Daddy. No matter what breed of boy I paraded in front of him, they were never good enough for his little princess. Even when his princess was twenty years old.

"Daddy, I swear on Grandpappy's grave that Owen's a good guy. You'll see." I was anything but persuasive when it came to winning Daddy's favor with a potential boyfriend.

We had just finished eating Mamma's baked ham and au gratin potatoes while Owen praised her cooking with every bite and Daddy smirked. Mamma sent me outside to talk to Daddy while she finished putting leftovers in Tupperware.

The scent of lilac enfolded Daddy and I, sitting on the porch swing, sipping tea. They had flown me home for Easter break, inviting Owen to join me. I was surprised when he accepted the offer. As the swing squeaked back and forth, I felt nostalgic for the days when Daddy and I had done this daily. I'd tell him about school while he just listened.

Daddy glanced at me and lifted a skeptical eyebrow. "He's a damn Yankee. You know how I feel about them."

I shook my head. "You never change, do you?"

"You'll always be my little girl, Mackenzie. I can't just turn off being protective of you. Especially from boys like Owen."

The trend started back in first grade when I invited Louis Douglas to come over one Saturday to find frogs to add to my terrarium. It was the least I could do after Louis had asked for my hand in marriage via crayoned note: *Will you marry me? Circle yes or no.* I emphatically circled yes in bright pink, my favorite color back then. Watching from my bedroom window, I remember how cute Louis looked galumphing down the dirt road to our house, wearing wading boots that swallowed him whole, and carrying a big plastic bucket and a fishing net on a telescoping pole. Daddy waylaid the poor boy, and in the course of his interrogation reduced him to tears.

The next Monday I found Louis's marriage proposal on my desk, ripped in half. He studiously avoided me from that day on while I pined away for his attention. Sure, it was just puppy love, but I never got over it. Or the fact that Daddy, even when I was at that tender age, was already steering my destiny.

I stayed away from boys all the way through middle school until Jeb Miller, a fellow ninth-grader at Cape Fear High School, showed up on my front porch to pick me up for a date. When Daddy answered the door with a shotgun in hand, Jeb dropped the Whitman's Sampler he'd bought for me at Walmart and ran for his life. Daddy ended up eating the assorted chocolates while I listened to his tirade about how I was too young to be dating.

Word soon got around school that Mackenzie Kirkland had a crazy father who shot first and asked questions later.

It would have done no good to explain to anyone that the shotgun wasn't loaded, or that Daddy got some kind of perverse pleasure out of perpetuating the stereotype of the shotgun-totin' Southern patriarch hell-bent on protecting his daughter's chastity. Daddy was a proudly unreconstructed Southerner, a monument to bigotry and isolationism who always voted Republican, hated anybody who hailed from above the Mason-Dixon Line, and championed the myth of the Lost Cause. Like a lot of white Southern men, he had a chip on his shoulder because the South had lost the War of Northern Aggression—Daddy refused to call it the Civil War. He was secretly ashamed of that incontrovertible fact; it made him a little mean.

But the shotgun was just a prop; he wouldn't hurt a fly. He didn't even go deer hunting with his buddies because he thought the creatures were so beautiful, and should decorate woods, not walls. (This was an opinion he had once shared with me in a tender, unguarded moment, and he'd sworn me to secrecy.)

At school I became the object of ridicule, and not just because of the shotgun incident. Daddy wasn't shy about broadcasting his often-outrageous opinions on religion and politics that his friends echoed, but other, more liberal-minded folks found ignorant and uncouth. Chief among his beliefs was the benighted notion that all boys, even ones from devoutly Christian families, were spawns of the devil. Preachers' sons, he maintained, were the horniest boys of all. My family earned the reputation of being backward hill-billies, and all because my father was a throwback to a bygone era. I accepted my fate as The Undateable Mackenzie Kirkland and thought it was just a matter of time before Daddy fitted me with a chastity belt.

By tenth grade my mamma intervened on my behalf. "Don't forget that we were high school sweethearts," she reminded Daddy. "Let her have some fun for once."

It worked . . . until it didn't.

One brave soul, Darren Williams, accepted the challenge to ask me out and managed to pick me up for dinner at the local Waffle House unscathed. Promptly returning me home on time that evening, he scored enough points with Mamma and Daddy to keep me on the hook from tenth grade all the way through to senior year. Darren, figuring Daddy was always skulking in the shadows (which he was, pretty much), never got up the nerve to do anything more than kiss me a few times, and even then he kept his lips pursed tight and his eyes open, lest he find a shotgun in his face.

The "romance" fizzled when I decided to head north for college, my chastity intact, while Darren found work at a big poultry farm. Daddy complained vehemently about the decision, suggesting that I thought Southern colleges weren't good enough for me. That wasn't entirely true. Based on the brochures, I thought I could get a quality education at a college in the quaint Pennsylvania town of Beaver Falls. But I could not deny that I was anxious to get as far away from North Carolina—and Daddy—as possible. Daddy put his foot down, but luckily Mamma talked some sense into him.

"Mac's pretty, she's smart, and she should be allowed to make her mark in the world," Mamma had told him in no uncertain terms. "Tying her down to this one-horse town is a death sentence. Don't you want your daughter to have a better life than you and me've had?" The truth stung, but Daddy listened. After all, his baby girl was going to be a doctor or lawyer or some other "highfalutin career woman." He meant that in a complimentary way, even though it never quite sounded like it.

The next semester off I went to good ol' Beaver Falls, a stone's throw from the big city of Pittsburgh, with its rolling mountains and three rivers and bustling nightlife of dance clubs and bar crawls. With Daddy no longer micromanaging my social life, I came out of my shell and thrived. I found out there was a big, wide world outside of Godwin where people liked me for who I was, Southern accent and quaint ways and all. I discovered that real friends—like Robin and Lily—regarded differences as virtues to be celebrated, not faults to be vilified.

I rested my hand on Daddy's. "Owen's not like most guys at college. He wants to marry me."

"Marry you?" Daddy grumbled. "Hell no, don't you be talking about marriage already. You hardly know him."

Daddy wasn't exactly wrong. I had only met Owen my freshman year. But he was athletic and good-looking and sure of himself, maybe a little cocky. All right, a lot cocky. It wasn't every day a girl met someone intelligent, articulate, fun to talk to, and who could make me laugh. He projected the aura of a guy who knew what he wanted and how to get it. But I think the main attraction was the plain and simple fact he was the first young man who'd showed any interest in me since high school, and who wasn't in danger of being chased off by Daddy. I was my own woman now, free to date anyone I chose.

"Just give him a chance. He's courteous, and he doesn't curse. And he treats me good, Daddy."

I didn't add that I suspected these traits were only pretensions to gentility. I started noticing the shift in the little things. Like how he delighted in mocking the way I talked, the way I dressed—privately, usually, but occasionally in front of our friends. He took great sport in dismissing all Southerners as inbred, barefoot infidels. When I described my upbringing in rural North Carolina, and mentioned Daddy's well-meaning overprotectiveness, he said it only proved his point. It was easier to laugh along with him than to deny these hurtful charges. I thought back to all the suitors Daddy had "discouraged." I guess I was afraid Owen was the only one I'd ever get on the hook, and I wasn't about to let him get away.

"What kind of man don't curse? It ain't natural. Sounds like he's hiding something."

Maybe Daddy was right, but I didn't want to find out. Ignorance was bliss.

Despite my enthusiasm, Mamma had seemed curiously lukewarm about Owen. When Owen started talking marriage, I was both excited and scared. Deep down I knew that if Daddy didn't approve of my mate, the union might as well be cursed.

The porch door swung open, and Mamma peeked out. "Owen's waiting for you in the living room. And no more talk about politics."

Daddy, who could smell bullshit a mile off, was not

impressed with how Owen agreed with everything he said. "Your boyfriend does have one talent, Mac. He can talk out of his ass and kiss somebody else's at the same time."

Mamma hung by the door waiting for me. I could tell she wasn't fond of being left alone with Owen. I stood up, kissing Daddy's cheek before heading inside. "You'll see, Daddy. Eventually he'll grow on you."

"A boy shouldn't have to *grow* on me, Mac," Daddy grumbled. "I can tell in my gut if a boy's good enough for my daughter, and Owen ain't. He's already runnin' your life. Uppity Yankee bastard thinks his shit don't stink."

"Oh, Daddy," I said, "Owen is not running my life. No man can do that—my daddy taught me that."

"You don't see it now, but you will," Daddy warned. "He's made you give up your friends, quit your extraparticulars." I smiled but didn't bother correcting him.

"He's right," Mamma chimed in. "He made you change your major . . . where's it all end, Mac? You wanted to be a nurse, and now you're studying communications."

"I decided I'm not cut out for medicine. I hate needles and get queasy at the sight of blood. That had nothing to do with Owen."

"Since you were a bitty little thang you talked about traveling and working with Doctors Without Borders," Mamma clucked. "You were so passionate about doing that, now suddenly you don't want to? When did that dream die?"

"It didn't die; it just . . . changed. I'm not sure I'm cut out for travel, constantly living out of a suitcase. I'm thinking something more administrative might be a better fit . . .

until we have kids. Then I'll stay at home like you did with me, Mamma."

"Well, there's nothing wrong with staying home with the kids if that's what you want," Daddy said. "I just don't know if I can ever give that boy my blessing. I can't trust him. Even your friends don't seem keen on him, so your mamma tells me."

I glared at Mamma. "You just had to go and stir the pot, didn't you?" I accused her.

"Don't go gettin' smart with me, young lady, or I'll snatch you baldheaded," she said, using her favorite Southern threat to pull out all my hair. "I talk to Lily and Robin on the phone when I call and you ain't home. It's your fault for never pickin' up. But I'll tell you, Mac, they don't have anything good to say about him."

"They're just jealous because we don't spend as much time together anymore. But it's not my fault. I don't have enough time to go around. The little free time I have left after studying I like to spend with Owen. He makes me happy."

"He'll ruin you, that's what he'll do," Mamma warned. "Mark my words, Mackenzie Marie Kirkland. Owen Fischer will crush your dreams and control you until you're a miserable shell. I've seen it with my own two eyes when it happened to your aunt Carol. Don't think it can't happen to you too."

"Listen to your mamma, Mackenzie, she's talkin' sense," said Daddy. "You don't want to let nobody run your life."

I should have listened to the warning back then. I should have followed my heart, not my fear. But I didn't see the difference between the two back then, because young love is blind. And when we're blind, we follow the voice we trust, even when that voice isn't trustworthy.

It would be years before it dawned on me that in marrying Owen, I had in effect married a version of my father. A psychiatrist could have gotten rich off of dissecting that disturbing realization—if I'd had the money.

Chapter 28

Robin

Saturday afternoons are my favorite time of the week, especially during that sliver of time when the house is unearthly still, hovering between two modes of chaos. It's during this brief hour when Grant busies himself with mowing the yard or some other outdoor project, Ryan and Willow get caught in video game warfare, and Lucas and Collette are finally down for some synchronized napping. After squeezing in a couple hours of work for Lily, I was ready for *me* time—the only time of the week I get to myself. A glass of wine, my favorite Netflix binge, feet propped up on the sofa, and it's all about me.

I placed my wineglass next to a fresh bouquet of flowers Grant had bought me. Presumably guilt flowers for his online dating excursions that I hadn't yet confronted him about but planned to soon. Tomorrow, in fact. He had accepted my alter ego's invitation to meet for drinks at Boot Scooters, a bar he knew I'd never go to without him. I'd told Ryan it was a surprise date night I had planned and I needed him to babysit. Grant had already lied through his teeth about meeting up with *a friend* for a beer. I'd even picked out my sexiest silk black dress to make sure it still fit—and I looked damn good in it too.

I played it like a movie in my head, rewinding it over and over. He'd be sitting at the bar watching for his temptress, then lo and behold, here I'd come, placing a hand on his shoulder, looking like a million bucks. His eyes would widen, searching for a hiding place, and he'd stammer through a series of lies and excuses about why he was there. I'd play along for as long as it took to finish a martini, then I'd cut to the chase.

I'd want half of everything, plus the house. Alimony payments until I felt like supporting myself, plus full custody of the kids along with a healthy child support check. And if he denied me? Well, I knew how to spread gossip like spreading dirt on a wall. Especially since most of his patients' moms were friends of mine in the PTA. Grant's reputation would be ruined, taking down him and his thriving medical practice. So really, what choice would he have?

I didn't want to be *that* kind of woman—the woman scorned. But he'd forced me here, hadn't he? It was merely a matter of payback's bitchiness at work.

No, I wouldn't dwell on such things anymore. Today I would enjoy the calm before the storm, then tomorrow let the thunder come. Sixty minutes all for me. The temptation to online browse Wayfair's "must-have clearance décor!" pulled on me, but I resisted. I could refuse my urges, just like I would refuse Grant's begging for forgiveness tomorrow night. Instead, I set down my phone and prepared to vegetate. It was the most precious time of week, but when the phone rings, may God smite the person who interrupts *me time*.

I had just queued up *Stranger Things* when the doorbell rang. If I weren't worried it'd wake up Collette and Lucas I might have ignored it. Muttering my way to the door, I answered it, prepared to politely tell the Jehovah's Witness I expected to go peddle their *Watchtower* someplace else. What I didn't expect was to see a police car parked in my driveway and a plainclothes detective standing on my front porch.

An impulsive breeze blew in behind him.

"I'm Detective Rossi looking for Ryan Thompson. Does he live here?" The detective flashed a badge, then returned it to his jeans pocket. He was wearing an orange button-down shirt that darkened his olive complexion. He wasn't much taller than me with gelled curls that I imagined crunching between my fingers.

"I'm his mother. What's this about?" I knew what this was about. I just never thought it would actually happen. I steeled myself for the worst.

"Please show me to your son, ma'am. I'm going to need to bring him to the station for questioning."

A force cut through the air like a guillotine. Somehow

I managed not to faint—or to hit Rossi in the mouth. I couldn't believe this. Owen Fischer was most certainly behind this. After what he had done to Ryan, smashing his face, he had the gall to press charges now? The shock shook my anger loose.

"Is this about Aria Fischer? Because he didn't rape that girl. She's a family friend and it was consensual."

He didn't flinch, didn't blink. "Ma'am, we'll be speaking with everyone involved to get the facts. If you want to bring your son to the station, we'll get all the details and figure it out together. I understand this is difficult for you, but I need to speak with your son."

As his words draped one over another, it felt like a red-hot brand to my brain.

"Did Aria press the charges, or was it her parents?" I demanded fiercely.

"I'm not at liberty to say at this moment, ma'am. Like I said, I need to speak with Ryan in person, down at the station, now. Once we get his statement we can get to the bottom of it. Right now no one is in trouble."

"So he's not under arrest, right? He'll be coming home after your interrogation?"

"No, ma'am, he's not under arrest. We only need his state-ment. If the DA feels the charges are legitimate, there will be a formal arrest. But for now, all we need is to ask him some questions, get his side of the story. Is he home?"

"Yes, he's in the basement. I'll go get him." I opened the door wider, letting the detective step inside the foyer while I headed toward the stairs. I paused as something occurred to me. "Do we need an attorney?"

"If he hasn't done anything wrong, there's no need for one. Like I said, we just want to know what happened from his point of view."

As I turned the corner to head down to the basement, a turret of dark brown hair slid into view. Lucas, awake from his nap, eyes wide with confusion and worry. No child should have to watch his big brother, his idol, being hauled off in a cop car.

"Hey, Fizz," I said, lifting him up and smoothing down his bedhead. I grunted as I hugged him against me. My little boy felt so big in my arms. "Why are you awake, buddy? Naptime isn't over yet."

"I saw the policeman through my window. Is Ryan going to jail?" he asked.

"No, sweetie, of course not. They just want to ask a couple questions, Fizz. No biggie."

I could tell my words held no comfort as his eyes dampened. I pressed my lips to his sweet naïve head, channeling his warmth to my heart. I loved him more than life itself, and I would do anything to protect my children. Anything.

"Hey, I promise everything will be fine."

I shouldn't have made that promise because nothing was fine. My husband was cheating on me. My son was being accused of rape. Everything spun out of control and I couldn't right it. I had no idea what Ryan would say in that interrogation room, and I was petrified to find out the truth. Because I knew better than anyone that sometimes the truth didn't always set you free.

Chapter 29

Lily

SATURDAY

Hiding my head under my pillow, I had ignored six phone calls and four text messages from Robin in the past hour. Only two days into her administrative job for Workout Wonder and already she had double-booked two clients, overcharged another one, and scheduled a prospective client on my only day off. If it was anyone but Robin, I would have fired her ass on the spot and shredded her with words.

"With everything going on, why not wait until things calm down?" I suggested this morning upon discovering the mix-ups. "You're dealing with too much all at once."

But she was adamant about needing a distraction.

Anything to curb the anxiety of watching her life crumble around her. So I agreed. Guilt held me captive.

Guilt and withdrawal, that is.

My temples throbbed, my eyes hurt too much to read the texts, and whatever emergency Robin had created would have to wait. After last night's tire-slashing drama, I couldn't sleep. I couldn't stop wondering and worrying who did it, and why. Normally I would have muted the anxiety with a pill or two—slept it off. My newfound sobriety couldn't have had worse timing, but I was useless when I was high and I needed to stay clean if I was going to figure out who was behind the threat.

When the tow truck arrived, the driver chalked the incident up to a teenage prank. Either that or someone really hated my guts. I didn't laugh, because I had an ill feeling that it was the latter.

Rolling onto my back, I wrestled my pillow underneath me and stared at the orange prescription bottle of painkillers taunting me from the bedside table. I picked it up, popping off the lid. Inside the plastic they rattled a Siren call.

"No!" Pills scattered across the floor as I tossed the bottle toward the garbage can and missed.

The glisten of a knife's blade caught a stray sunbeam. I had pulled it out of my tire and considered taking it to the police for fingerprinting, but I was sure they'd laugh me right out of the station. A minor vandalism dispute was nothing compared to the murderers they were probably chasing.

My first thought was Robin. If she had seen me with Grant, making out with her husband, maybe tires wouldn't be the only thing she'd slash. Maybe the admin mistakes were intentional—an underhanded tactic to bring down my business. But throughout the rest of the baseball game she had acted nothing but normal around me—chatty with gossip, annoyingly occupied with Lucas and Collette, bursting with excitement over working together. Robin couldn't fake happy if she tried, wearing her emotions like a scarf that either adorned her or swallowed her, which led me to eliminate her from the list.

Slashing tires seemed pretty juvenile, which put Willow under the spotlight. Plus she knew what kind of car I drove. But sweet little Willow wreaking havoc on my car didn't sound like her at all. Plus, after Willow tracked down Ryan's biological father, Robin had kept the poor girl on a very short leash.

Who else was there? And what had I done to deserve it? There was only one client I could think of who would have motive to get back at me. Irving was a typical grade-A asshole with unrealistic demands and a penchant for threats. After two months of working with him on his diet and exercise regimen, when he didn't get the results he wanted and demanded a full refund, I told him where he could shove it. He didn't like that too much and threatened legal action. Fortunately for me and unfortunately for him, my contract was pretty clear-cut . . . along with his threats of getting back at me.

I ignored his calls and texts until he huffed off, tail between his legs, never to be heard from until his most recent legal threat last week, to which I told him to have his lawyer talk to my lawyer. Rather absurd, since neither of us actually had lawyers. It would be just like Irving to resort to this kind of childish vindictiveness, just to boast he had gotten the last word.

My brain hurt from going in circles, but I had vowed not to take my drug of choice to ease the symptoms, no matter how good half a bottle of painkillers washed down with Jack Daniel's and Coke sounded. I'd be a trouper and suck it up like a good little addict in recovery.

Cold sweat soaked my T-shirt, but I was shaking too much to strip it off. Grabbing the damp edge of the bedspread, I pulled it up over my head and curled my knees to my chest.

Another chime from my phone. Then a knock at the door.

I threw a pillow at the bedroom door in anger. "Dammit, Robin, go the fuck away!" I screamed at nothing, at everything. I couldn't move even if I wanted to, but I wasn't about to invite Robin's drama into my home.

"Liliana, it's me, Tony. Please let me in."

Tony? What the hell was he doing here? I hadn't seen him in months, though my memories of him never strayed far. Some days I missed him like crazy, but I couldn't tell you why. We were toxic together. Maybe I was a *little* conceited— okay, a lot—but our volatile relationship always reminded me of Cleopatra and Mark Antony. *Fool! Don't you see now that I could have poisoned you a hundred times had I been able to live without you?* Cleopatra reportedly said to her lover. I know just how you felt, Cleo baby. Tony and I fought battles time had forgotten, but our makeup sex was epic, sheet-scorching stuff. He was my first heroic romance and my first crushing heartbreak.

"I'm coming," I called out, jumping up and running for the closet. Tossing my damp clothes in the overflowing laundry basket, I grabbed a fresh shirt and pants, then darted into the bathroom to splash cool water on my face and readjust my hair into a messy bun. I tamped down the nausea rumbling in my belly and answered the front door. I wasn't exactly in the mood to see him, but I didn't want to look like a slatternly old hag either.

Damn, he looked good in a leather jacket unfit for the warm May weather, white V-neck T-shirt, and dark jeans. I immediately noticed he had lost weight since I last saw him almost a year ago.

He held out a colorful bunch of flowers wrapped in yellow gauze. "Long time no see," he said after a moment of disorienting silence. "May I come in?"

"What are you doing here?" I asked, all Italian attitude with my hand perched on my hip.

"Nice to see you too." His dark hair hung in loose curls around his face, and familiar tattoos crawled over his skin, peeking out from under his shirt collar in tribal shards. In all our years together I had never grown tired of his face— those lips that savored every inch of my body once upon a time, that cheek scrawled with scruff I still yearned to touch. Sensual. Sexy. Exciting. No matter how much I hated his brooding nature and arrogance, it was unabashedly tempered with my desire for him.

"These are for you." He handed me the flowers, then strode past me into the belly of the apartment. "What the hell? You're living like this?" He gestured to the rumpled blanket on the floor, the scattered magazines, the numerous half-empty glasses littering the table, the partly chewed toast I couldn't stomach finishing. "You ever clean, Liliana?"

I used to love the way he called me by my real name: Liliana. No one else did, but I always thought it sounded exotic and poetic as it rolled off his tongue. Now it only sounded caustic.

"I don't recall inviting you over to insult my house-keeping." I found a clean vase in the cupboard, filled it with water, and stuck the flower stems inside.

"Sorry. I needed to see you. Talk to you in person." He shrugged off his jacket and hung it on a chair. A whiff of the leather reminded me of the nights he used to take me out, arm around my shoulder, tucking me against him.

"Oh, well, the mess is because I've been sick. Still am, in fact." Unable to fake it anymore, I dropped onto the couch, nestling into the armrest. I held a beige pillow in front of me like a shield.

"Sick, huh? You're not contagious, are you?" His voice was skeptical. I couldn't tell him I was sick from withdrawal and anxiety over the tire-slashing business.

"No, don't worry your pretty little head. You can't catch it. And in case you were wondering, yes, I'm clean."

"Oh. Gotcha. I'm sure you are."

I heard the condescension, and I couldn't ignore it. Not after all we'd been through together. "Wait—back the truck up. What's that supposed to mean?"

"I don't want to fight, Liliana. Clearly you're working through some stuff, and if this is withdrawal, then good for you. I hope you stick it out this time and get sober."

"I *am* sober, Tony." I was so convincing I even believed myself. "I got my shit together and I'm doing really well, actually. Is that why you showed up unannounced—to check up on me?"

"Of course I'll always care about you. But no, I'm not checking up on you. I've moved on with my life. That's what I need to talk to you about. I met someone."

"Oh?" This time the nausea had nothing to do with the withdrawal and everything to do with a sudden panic surging through me. No matter how bad we were together, I could never imagine Tony with someone else. He was mine. Always had been, always would be. "Some skanky bar ho?"

"Stop it, Liliana. Grow up, wouldja? She's a great girl, and I want to ask her to marry me. But I can't until . . . well, you know."

"You want a divorce." My heart cracked around the edges just saying the words.

"Yes, it's time, isn't it? It's been over a year of separation now and I want to get this sorted as quickly and painlessly as possible. I've already filed the paperwork so I just need you to look over it, have your attorney check it out—whatever you need to do. I think you'll agree it's fair and pretty straight-forward. We each take what we brought into the marriage, and Workout Wonder is all yours, obviously. I'll sign over whatever I need to."

"This is what you want?"

I was sure he was being manipulated into this.

"Yes. I love her."

I couldn't let him go. I wasn't ready. I'd never be ready. We fit together, were broken when apart.

"Tony, you can't deny the chemistry between us, and I know she can't hold a candle to what we had. Why can't we try again? I swear it won't be like before. I'm clean. No more pills. I can be a better me—for you, for us."

He shook his head. Was that pity in his eyes? "We've been down this road a million times. I'm through. And I think you should move on too. Get clean for *you*. Get better. Get your life back on track. You've always been better without me, Liliana. Let's just let each other go without the drama. Please?"

No. I wouldn't accept it. I needed to know who I was dealing with.

"What's her name?"

"Why do you want to know?"

Ah, defensive. So she was a secret, was she?

"There's no need to be so guarded about her. If you're as serious as you say you are, I'll find out eventually. I'm just curious."

"Fine. Her name is Sienna."

"How old is she?"

"Does it matter? We love each other. We want to start a life together, maybe even have kids together."

"So she's young then."

"God, Liliana, get over yourself. She's twenty-three, all right? Older than when we started seeing each other."

"Wow, you're old enough to be her father. How's it feel being a sugar daddy?"

"You know, I expected your resistance, but I didn't expect you to act like a damn child. Just sign the papers and stop harassing me, okay?"

"Harassing you? What the hell are you talking about?"

"The constant texts. The voicemails. You drunk dial me all the time. It's pissing Sienna off, and me too, for that matter."

"No I don't!" At least I didn't think I did.

"Oh, really? Here, have a listen to this." Pulling his cell phone out of his pocket, he pressed a series of buttons and held it out for me to hear. "This was from two nights ago."

My voice on speakerphone, slurred and sounding like a pathetic, needy loser:

Hey, sexy thang. I miss you. Thinking of you and your hands all over my body. I want you back if you'll take me. I think about you constantly. Call me. I love you, Tony. I'll always love you. Oh, and it's me, Lily. I'm sure you figured that out already, though. I miss you. Did I say that already? I don't know, but get your ass over here. Puuhhleeeeease?

It wasn't one of my finer moments. I was definitely high when I left this message, but I had no recollection of doing so.

"This is one of a hundred, Liliana. It's gotten out of hand. *You've* gotten out of hand."

If I had been doing this while high, what else had I done that I didn't know about? The implications were frightening. I was living in a blackout.

"So you've let Sienna listen to these messages?"

"Of course. She's my girlfriend. We don't have secrets."

"And was she pissed when she heard them?"

"Wouldn't you be?"

And the puzzle pieces clicked together. It all made sense now. The threatening note. The breathy prank calls. The slashed tires. His girlfriend was after me, and I almost couldn't blame her. With my temper, I would have done the same. Tony certainly had a type—fiery and jealous.

I felt both terrible and relieved that it was Sienna. How could I have ever thought Robin or Willow were behind it? I got up and headed to the bedroom, returning with a knife in hand. I held it out to Tony. His hands flew up defensively and he stumbled back a few steps.

"I'm not going to stab you, *idiota*. You know your girl-friend is a psycho? I think this belongs to her. She left it in my tire last night."

Tony scoffed, then carefully took the knife. "You get what you give, Liliana." Was he taking the side of his girlfriend of one minute over me, who he'd known for almost twenty years? "God knows how many enemies you've made due to your poor choices. You're a liar and an addict. So before you come at my girlfriend for whatever is going on in your wasted life, how about you get your act together first? And leave me and Sienna alone."

Wordless. Helpless. Powerless. He left me like that as he stormed out of my apartment and out of my life.

But I couldn't lose him like this. Not without a fight. Italian women didn't back down. No, I would win over some skanky-ho *puttana*. I always did when it came to Tony. Mine. If I couldn't have him, no one would. Especially not some tire-slashing tramp named Sienna. If the years with Tony had taught me one thing, it was how to get him back into my bed . . . and I knew just what to do to bait him.

Chapter 30

Mackenzie

Crows are said to be a bad omen, a harbinger of death. If any bird earned that reputation I would think it would be a buzzard. After all, they appear at the first sign of death and feast on it.

Two buzzards picked at a dead squirrel in my front yard. The poor thing had been splattered by a passing car, and some animal lover, hating to see the critter so dishonored, had tossed the bloody carcass into my yard. Thanks, but no thanks.

Today I felt like that squirrel. Smashed beyond recognition. No one knew this, though. Lily mistook my avoidance for being my usual introverted self. Aria thought maybe I was just anxious. And Owen, well, he was decidedly oblivious to my emotions and moods.

I watched the world from my living room window, while Owen took his post-coital nap in our bedroom. Apparently it was exhausting degrading his wife on top of a Maytag top-loader. Aria had smothered herself in baby oil and was sunbathing in the backyard, which I warned her about. But to my fair-skinned teenage daughter who despised her pale legs in shorts, skin cancer was a fair exchange for a tan. This was what women did, hiding the sorrow behind sun-kissed smiles. I always thought of that riddle: if a tree falls in the forest and no one is around to hear it, does it make a sound? The answer is no. I was the tree, falling, crashing. Nobody listened or cared.

Shy and timid—these were words often used to describe me by those who never bothered to take more than a passing glance. When applied with such force, the words soon became tools that chipped away at me, creating who I was on the surface, shaping me with each syllable. But at my core, underneath the hardened plaster that everyone inter-preted as me, I wasn't who they thought I was.

In fact, no one knew the girl behind the mask. Even I hadn't seen her true face. Not fully, at least.

It was easy to miss the real me. The angry me. The passionate me. The indomitable me. Of course Owen would laugh at such adjectives used to describe his meek, obedient wife. Always so agreeable. Never confrontational. A wall-flower. If someone bumped into me on the sidewalk, I was the first to apologize. If another parent challenged my childrearing methods, I would humbly seek their approval. If a Facebook "friend" questioned my latest post, I would hastily delete it. Ever the people pleaser, I had lost all fight.

Until now.

Until my doorbell rang.

Until I answered it, finding Robin standing resolutely on my doorstep, her clenched jaw saying it all. Something had happened, something that would destroy our friendship for good.

"Hey, Robin."

Dark clouds heavy with rain gathered in the sky behind her, matching her angry scowl.

"How could you do that to Ryan?" Robin demanded.

I had no idea what she was talking about. I needed her to understand this. She and Lily were my only allies; I couldn't risk losing her, no matter how disappointed I was in her son. "Do what?"

"Pressing charges against him. Claiming he raped Aria. We've been friends forever, Mackenzie. How could you without talking to me first?"

"Robin, I swear it wasn't me. Owen must have . . ." Had he done it behind my back? Did Aria know?

Robin's lips began moving so fast, the words poured out quicker than my brain could translate. "Well, you can thank your husband for the detective who showed up at my house to bring Ryan in for questioning regarding the rape accusation, which Lucas had to witness! The poor kid thinks his brother is going to jail now. And why? Because of an accusation that *you* made. You put that thought into Owen's head. Ryan could go to jail over this—and you don't even know all the facts! And did you know that Owen punched Ryan in the face? I bet you'd side with your husband on that too, saying my kid deserved it."

There were too many pieces flying at me all at once. The sky cracked open with a sprinkle. "Calm down, Robin. Can you come in so we can sort this out? It's about to pour out there."

I pushed the door wider for her, but she shook her head, took a step back, her entire body trembling.

"No, I don't want to be anywhere near you right now. It's taking every ounce of self-control I have not to slap you across the face, Mackenzie. But I wouldn't want to be arrested for assault, you know, because that's what you do. Send your friends to jail and ruin their lives."

"I honestly didn't know Owen did that. I swear. I never went to the police, and I can't imagine that Aria would have without talking to me first about it. I still don't think she knows—"

I felt a presence behind me, then turned face-first into Owen's chest. "That's because Aria didn't go to the cops. I did. Because I'm protecting my daughter." His voice was thick from sleep.

Robin scoffed. "Protecting her? You're putting her private life on public display so that you can pretend your little girl is still Miss Perfect. Wake up, Owen. Your princess is growing up, making her own choices, whether you approve or not. She's not the victim here. My son is."

"Your son deserves to rot in prison, Robin. He's a rapist, and that's where rapists belong—either in jail, or dead."

"He didn't rape her, you asshole! Have you even bothered

to talk to your daughter about what happened? Or her part in it?" Spittle flicked across my face as she screamed past my shoulder where Owen stood, stoic and smug.

Always right. Always calm. Always watching and waiting for the right moment to belittle and crush his opponent. Usually that opponent was me, the emotional nag. Now it was Robin, the nag's crazy best friend. *Former* best friend.

When Owen said nothing, I turned to look at him, his eyes staring blankly back at Robin. When his gaze shifted in defeat, Robin seized her advantage.

"You haven't talked to her, have you? You probably don't have a clue about what even happened that night, other than bits and pieces you pick up in overheard conversation, because you never really listen or care. Don't act like you're protecting anyone but yourself and your self-deluded reality."

Robin pushed past me, her finger tautly aimed at Owen's chest.

"I know you, Owen." She jabbed him once, her voice a low growl. "I've known you for almost two decades. You pretend to be so holier-than-thou, acting the part of dedicated provider, but the reality is that you treat your family like garbage, you think even less of your friends, and you fight not because it's right, but because you like winning. Even if you're winning at your own lonely game. Even if winning costs my son his life. You're a narcissistic, weak little man who bulldozes over others to make yourself feel big and powerful. Well, I won't let you run over my family. I promise you, Owen, you won't win this time. I will take you down . . . to hell, if I have to."

I wanted to applaud her. But I couldn't, because I stood

in an impossible place between my husband and my best friend.

Robin glared at him for an uncomfortable moment, then turned to me.

"And you—I pity you, Mackenzie. You're dead to me. Don't call me, don't speak to me. We're done."

"Robin, please—" I begged, reaching out for her, but her back was already turned and she was halfway off the porch.

"Let her go." Owen grabbed my shoulder, pulling me back. "You don't need her."

I watched as the first person I had trusted completely blustered down my sidewalk and out of my life. We had history together—literally. It was freshman year in Humanities 101 class, and Robin Goldman picked the wobbly chair next to me. I was a Dean's List student, studious and friendless. Robin was outgoing and thoughtful, the kind of girl who befriended the unlikeables. When I wanted to hide in the library, she would drag me to social events. When we collided, everything changed.

She'd invited me to lunch after that first class together, and she wouldn't accept no for an answer. I needed a friend like her. That day we made fun of our professors. We rated hot guys. We shared our meals. We laughed, we teased, we connected. That day we didn't just become lunch buddies; that day we forged a friendship that would eventually be tested with fire. A literal fire. A fire that had destroyed my face. If we could get through that, certainly we could get through anything.

"Hey, Robin," Owen called after her. She paused mid-stride but didn't turn around. "You dare talk to me about protection? I once protected you and Ryan—at a price you'll never be able to repay. I gave you back your life when it was taken from you, so don't be so quick to judge me from your pedestal."

Robin twisted around, her scowl a strange blend of hostility and curiosity. "What the hell are you talking about? How did you *protect* us?"

I grabbed his arm in a silent reminder to shut the hell up before he landed us both in prison. It wouldn't do to orphan our daughter before she graduated high school.

Ignoring Robin's question, Owen slammed the door shut, and I slammed my hand into his chest.

"Why would you say that? If she found out, you'd go to jail, Owen! *We'd* go to jail. That was a really stupid thing to say. You're getting too big for your britches, you know. You're not untouchable."

"Don't you dare speak to me like that. You show respect when you talk to me. It's your fault we're in this mess to begin with."

"Hold your horses. *My* fault? You're the one who went to the cops about our daughter having sex with her son. Way to escalate things."

"You're the one who let Aria get out of control. You're the mother; it's your job to instill values in our child and to keep your psychotic friends in check."

"Robin's not psychotic. In fact, I think she's right about this."

"Why are you defending her after what she did to you? You look like that because of *her*."

My hand quivered under the instinct to hide the scar, but

I forced it down. I would no longer hide my face. I would no longer resent what happened. Robin made a mistake that cost me my face. But I made a mistake that was costing her son. We all fucked up royally sometimes.

All I knew was that I couldn't take it anymore, the back-and-forth blame, always coming back to me. I screamed at the top of my lungs until my throat ached and my vocal cords were raw. Years of abuse, of fights, of fingers on my neck, of bruises on my body, of manipulation and control . . . all of it flew out in one prolonged animalistic howl. I didn't care if the whole neighborhood heard me. Let them hear, let Owen cringe with embarrassment. I wasn't his mousy wife anymore. I was a lioness who'd found her roar.

"That's just it, Owen." My voice took on an unnatural growl as something grew inside me—boldness. "Aria's not a child anymore. She's growing up, and regardless of what happened with Ryan, that should be her decision to make, whether she presses charges or not. I don't know the truth about whether it was consensual or not, but you shouldn't force her into this or else you're no better than Ryan by stripping away her voice."

I already knew I had said too much when his hand swung out, swiftly gripping my throat.

"I warned you once, Mackenzie. This is your last warning."

As his hand tightened around my neck, I felt the embers of my courage come alive. I felt the phoenix rising from the ashes of a girl burned alive long ago. I wouldn't let Owen win. I wouldn't let him use Aria, or me, or Ryan, or Robin to stroke his fragile ego.

His mouth was a breath away from mine, his words hot

on my skin. Reaching up, I clawed at his right eye, raking my fingernails down his face. He screamed and let go, covering the red furrows with his palm.

"You damn bitch!" he screamed.

I laughed in his face. "Aw, did you just curse? Well, well, well, so the high and mighty Owen Fischer has finally fallen down to earth with the rest of us!"

He lunged for me, but I was quicker. I ran to the kitchen to grab my car keys and cell phone, then to the coat closet for my purse. I'd grab clothes later. I glanced out the kitchen window into the backyard where Aria flipped over on a striped beach towel, earbuds in her ears and oversized sunglasses shading her face. She'd be okay until I returned. Owen would never touch her; he never had.

"Where do you think you're going?" Owen yelled, still protecting his face with one hand while reaching for me with the other.

"Out! And don't try to stop me or those buzzards out there will be picking at your body next."

I darted past him toward the front door, swung it open, and looked back at the life I was leaving behind. Nothing but a house of horrors.

Standing on the porch, I shot a text to Aria, explaining I would be spending the night away to clear my head, but to contact me if she needed me. Owen huffed, unwilling to chase me. Owen didn't chase. He controlled from his La-Z-Boy. But not any longer. "Fine, go. But the locks will be changed before you get home, so don't bother coming back."

I didn't plan to come back. Not now, not ever again.

Chapter 31

Robin

By the time I got home my fists were no longer shaking with rage. My face was no longer flushed with fury. The hot emotions had ebbed, replaced by a placid resolve. I learned something today. Something that could clean up the mess that had been made of my life.

I once protected you and Ryan—at a price you'll never be able to repay.

Owen Fischer had a secret, and I would unearth it and then bury him with it. A costly secret that had something to do with me and Ryan. But what could it possibly be?

I wasn't some naïve waif Owen could manipulate. I wasn't

259

his doormat of a wife he could wipe his dirty feet on. I was a smart, resourceful woman; hear me roar. And I would tear Owen limb from limb for destroying my son's life.

Ryan's statement had been short, with Grant's guidance. "Just tell them what happened as you remember it. No more, no less," Grant had advised. So Ryan did. Then it was over. I had imagined the interrogation would go on for hours, but then again, I watch too many crime shows. Grant returned home with relief in his eyes, although when I pressed for details, he couldn't get a read on what the detective had been thinking.

"It's just a matter of waiting it out at this point. You did good, son," Grant said as he patted Ryan on the back like he'd just made honor roll. With a somberness that broke my heart, Ryan headed to his bedroom and I hadn't seen him since. That was hours ago.

I reached for my glass of wine that still sat untouched on the coffee table, and downed it in one long gulp, allowing the tang to course through my veins and relax me. The house was blessedly quiet—a rare commodity for any family with kids—the foreboding calm broken only by the distant sound of Grant mowing the yard and the laughter of Lucas and Willow playing on the swing set.

"Higher, higher!" I heard Lucas yell while Willow pushed him. "I want to reach heaven!"

I wondered if such a place even existed.

I considered dusting or mopping or starting dinner, none of which I felt like doing. It was either busy myself with housework or ponder Ryan's situation until my brain exploded. I was pretty sure my brain was already mush by now.

After tummy time with Collette on the floor and sorting the mail on the kitchen counter, which consisted mostly of weekend ads for can't-miss furniture deals and fast-food coupons, I put the kettle on to boil. The wine on an empty stomach wasn't sitting right. A cup of tea would help me center myself, focus on how to get the information I needed to blackmail Owen, to figure out what he was hiding. Or there was still always Grant's plan of poisoning the bastard.

When the pot whistled, I poured a cup of green tea and let the leaves—and my brain—steep. If I thought that Mackenzie would side with me, I would have gone to her with my questions. Clearly she knew about whatever Owen did, but she'd protect her jerk of a husband even at the cost of her own soul. She was gutless and guileless, a deadly combination for a woman. Her submission made her weak, and her innocence made her passive. A woman afraid to get her hands dirty was already beaten.

I paused beneath a hanging picture of Mackenzie, Lily, and me, taken on Mount Washington, the stunning Pittsburgh panorama behind us. We had just finished riding the historic Incline car to the top, our hair whipping around our flushed faces as we stood on the observation deck admiring the three rivers that snaked under massive iron bridges, coming to meet at what locals called The Point. The Mackenzie I loved was passionate and bright, full of adventure. How could a woman so full of light let a man snuff her out?

I sipped my drink, then heard a distant sobbing. At first I thought Lucas or Willow had had an accident. I checked outside; Willow was still pushing Lucas, who exhorted her to "make me fly, Will!"

The sobbing was coming from upstairs. I tiptoed to Ryan's room and pushed the door open a crack. Lying facedown on his bed, head buried into his pillow, Ryan shook with sobs and my heart broke. My boy was crumbling apart, and there was nothing I could do to save him from disappearing.

"Hey, Ry. May I come in?"

He whipped his head up in embarrassment, eyes rimmed in red and wet with tears.

"Yeah, sure." He shuffled aside, making room on his bed for me.

"Are you worried about the charges?" There was no point tiptoeing around reality. Here we were, facing the ugly head-on. My son had spent the morning at the police station being picked apart like he was already guilty.

"What if I go to jail, Mom? I'll never be able to get a decent job; I'll have a permanent criminal record. And Aria . . . I love her, Mom. I would have never hurt her on purpose. Does she hate me?"

I stroked his hair, my fingers tangling in his chestnut curls.

"Honey, you're not going to jail. We'll fight this together. And Aria's not the one who went to the police. Owen did. He's trying to ruin our lives because he's a vengeful man, but he won't win." I rested my forehead against his, then whispered, "I have a plan to stop him."

He looked at me, eyes intense. "Do you think I raped Aria?"

Ryan read my face, searching for the truth. He was the son of a rapist, so it had crossed my mind. But Ryan was nothing like Geoffrey.

"Of course not. I know you, and that's not something you would do. I wish you didn't have to worry about this. You need to put your focus on keeping your grades up, enjoying the rest of baseball season, and looking forward to college next fall. Can you do that for me?"

He shrugged. "I guess. If this all goes away and I'm not spending my freshman year of college in jail. I just wish I knew what Aria was thinking right now . . . if she thinks I raped her."

"Only you two know the truth."

"I don't know, Mom. It's all so fuzzy, like I told the cops. We were both wasted, and she was all cuddly with me. When I kissed her, she kissed me back. I thought that meant yes. I wasn't trying to force myself on her. But like I said, we were both kinda drunk, so I don't know if maybe I should have stopped . . ."

"Stop right there. Don't you blame yourself for this. You both are responsible for your choices that night. If you both were drinking, then you both made poor choices that put you in this position. It's not your fault if you didn't force yourself on her."

What did *force* actually mean, though? Manipulation? Coercion? Simply taking advantage of a drunken girl? There were too many nuances to slap a definition on what was rape and what wasn't. I'd been the victim before. I knew how it destroyed lives, but this was my son we were talking about. Was he solely responsible for both their bad choices?

A week ago I would have said yes—that drinking with an underage girl then taking advantage of her submissive nature was knowingly wrong. But now that my own son was the one doing it, that emphatic yes became a wobbly no. Protecting my family loosened my moral code.

"Do you think the cops will see it that way?"

"I don't know the answer to that. Rape is a serious offense, and it all depends on how Aria spins it. But I think that since you both were drinking, the cops will see it for what it really is—a mistake that you both agreed to at the time."

Even as I uttered the words, I wondered if I truly believed them. I could believe them now, for the sake of my son, but what about that night so long ago? If I hadn't followed a veritable stranger down that alley, if I hadn't worn that out-fit . . . Was I basically consenting because I hadn't escaped, or because of what I'd worn, or because I wasn't strong enough to fight back? And was what happened with Ryan and Aria essentially the same thing? If I hadn't been so blinded by trust, would any of that have ever happened? And if I could have stopped it but didn't, did that make it my fault—or worse, my *choice*?

These were questions I had asked myself for years, a mixture of guilt and crooked responsibility that led to self-blame and ultimately self-loathing. I couldn't imagine that the little boy I'd doted on for eighteen years could be capable of stealing the innocence of a young girl. I wondered how many parents couldn't see the monster through the bias of parental love. But my son wasn't a monster. I had to keep telling myself that.

The memory of that night gripped me, pulled me under. It swallowed me whole, like it often did when something triggered it. A movie. A novel. A #MeToo testimony on

Facebook. Right now it was the face of my own son looking up at me, the distant echo of his rapist father. I couldn't help the tears that now came.

"Mom, are you okay?" Ryan sat up and hugged me, consoling his own mother for a pain he didn't even know about. I didn't want to tell him what he came from. I didn't want to slice open my scarred-over wounds, but maybe it was time the truth came out. Maybe the truth would teach Ryan what my parenting couldn't—that he should never create a victim. If the heartbreak of discovering what happened to me saved a girl from being his prey, then my job as his mother was to break his heart.

"No, honey, I'm not okay." It trickled out. A word here, a sentence there, an entire story of suffering. "There's something you need to know about your past. Your biological father, Geoffrey Faust . . . he wasn't a boyfriend or anything. He . . . he was a casual acquaintance. And he took advantage of me. He didn't check whether I consented—and I'm telling you this because I don't want you to ever make that same mistake."

"Oh my God, Mom. I'm so . . . sorry. But I promise I'm not like that. I'd never intentionally hurt Aria . . . or anyone else."

"I know." I reached for his hand and squeezed. "You have nothing to be sorry about. From a tough situation came the most beautiful gift I could have asked for. You made my life complete, gave me hope that not every bad thing that happens defines the future. A blessing came out of that darkness, and I wouldn't trade you for anything. Not even if it meant having a do-over."

"Do you think I'm like him?" Fear trembled in his words, a fear I had wondered about many times myself. Now I knew the truth.

"No, you're nothing like him. You've got a beautiful heart, a caring soul. That's why I'm telling you all this, so that you know how much pain you're capable of causing. With one action you could destroy a woman. But also, with one act you could empower her. It's all about choices and making the right one."

My truth was louder than words. He was pensive for a long time. I didn't know what thoughts rumbled through his head, or how my revelation would impact him. Then he asked me, "Be honest. Do you see him when you look at me?"

My mind flashed back to seeing Geoffrey again for the first time since that awful night. I didn't recognize him—if he was indeed the same Geoffrey Faust—the years had changed him so much. In fact, he looked nothing like I remembered, and nothing like Ryan. But in the hazy memory of that night, when Geoffrey still had his youth, I saw Ryan's features.

I wanted to lie more than anything, but Ryan deserved honesty. After all the years of half-truths, I couldn't keep spinning the web. "Sometimes, yes. You have his eyes. Bright blue. But who I really see is your dad—Grant. You've inherited all his best qualities. His intelligence. His heart. His humor. The things that matter most. That's why I didn't want you to meet Geoffrey. I don't want you to have anything to do with him."

"Does anyone else know?"

"Auntie Mac knows everything." I wondered if Mackenzie was still their auntie, now that we weren't friends.

A thought burrowed into me, connecting scattered dots. Only Mackenzie knew about what Geoffrey did . . . and yet Owen had mentioned protecting Ryan and me. Mackenzie may have told him, which wouldn't have shocked me. Even though I had sworn her to secrecy, she'd always felt obligated to tell Owen everything, even other people's secrets. Perhaps Owen was referring to something that happened with Geoffrey. Had he gotten involved in some way?

I could always visit Geoffrey again and ask him myself, but something was suspicious. Lots of things, actually. First, his denial. I hadn't expected a confession, but it was as if he had no earthly idea who I was or what I was talking about. How could he have completely erased that night? Either he was a serial rapist who couldn't keep track of his victims, or he truly didn't remember it.

Then there was the fact that nothing about him rung a bell. Even his voice didn't sound the same. People's voices didn't change that much, did they? And a voice wasn't something you could easily fake. Although I had known so little about him back then, he had left a brand on my memory that still burned. I had expected my showing up out of the blue after all these years to shock him, at least a little. And yet he was completely unfazed.

The details didn't add up. Geoffrey swore he didn't know me, and I had to admit, he was pretty damn convincing. He didn't look like the man I remembered. The more I pieced together, the more jumbled it got. The only explanation was that Willow hadn't found the same Geoffrey Faust from my past, and Owen possibly had something to do with it.

"You said Auntie Mac knows about it," said Ryan. "Do you think she told Aria?"

"No, not Aria, but possibly Owen. I think Mac might have told him based on something he said today." I didn't add that I was starting to think it was possible—maybe even likely—Owen had something to do with the unknown fate of the real Geoffrey Faust.

"You saw Mr. Fischer?" Ryan asked. "Did you speak to him about the charges?"

"Yes, and like I said, I might have a way of convincing him to drop them."

"Mom, please don't. He could hurt you." Bruises still marred Ryan's face where Owen had pummeled him. My fingertip traced the purple ring around his eye socket. Come to think of it, the Geoffrey at the apartment had brown eyes, not the vibrant blue that Ryan had inherited. I knew it in my gut—he wasn't the Geoffrey Faust from my past, but the real one was out there somewhere, and somehow Owen knew where he was.

"That's exactly why I can't let Owen get away with it, honey. He's violent. Assault charges are just the beginning. We'll go back down to the police station to press charges against him—see how he likes having an arrest record."

"So he can get a slap on the wrist? They'll probably side with him since I'm technically an adult and he only gave me a black eye for having sex with his underage daughter when I deserved worse."

"Then what, Ryan? Unless I can dig up dirt on him, how am I supposed to stop him, short of killing him?"

The question hung in the air, stifling and heavy.

"Then that's what we do—kill him." I turned toward the doorway, where Grant now stood. Without another word, he set something on the dresser, then slid it closer to me.

A prescription bottle. I crossed the room and picked it up, thinking it must be the pain medicine for Ryan's face. As I read the drug name, I realized it was for something much more sinister.

"Grant, you shouldn't have brought this into our home," I whispered to him. I couldn't say what I wanted to say, that the thought had crossed my mind more than once. That just maybe this could save our family.

"Mom, Dad, what is that?" Ryan asked, peering over from the bed.

"Nothing." I slipped out of the room, heading for my bathroom. Shoving the bottle into my vanity, I leaned against the sink, my breath shallow, my thoughts racing.

This is the only way, the darkness echoed inside my brain. I couldn't shut it off, not until Ryan was safe and Owen was no longer a threat.

It was at that moment I realized I had lost myself to the demon clawing its way out of me, because I was willing to do anything to protect my child . . . even to the point of murder.

Chapter 32

Lily

Tony looked so serene lying next to me, asleep in the bed we had shared once upon a time. The bed that should have been *ours*. The bed that held memories of erotic foreplay, passionate screwing, and tender pillow talk. It had been so good with him. Why did I have to burn down everything I touched?

Although it was still dark outside, I knew Tony would wake up soon, groggy and confused by the drugs and alcohol. First he'd wonder *what* happened, then he'd wonder *how* it happened. But for now, I'd relish the nostalgia. I was too anxious and blissful to sleep. Contrasting emotions swirled inside me—everything but regret. I could never regret a night with Tony, no matter how much I should have felt guilt over it.

I'll admit it, what I had done was wrong. But when he had left so brusquely earlier, with such contempt for me in his eyes, I had to fix it. I had to burrow my way back into his heart. Hours after he left, I had figured it all out. I opened up with an invitation for a peace treaty. A toast to signing the divorce papers.

"Bring over all the paperwork," I had said when I called. *"I'll sign whatever you need me to sign if it'll make you happy. All I want is for you to be happy."*

A lie, of course. I didn't want him to be happy; I wanted *me* to be happy. If I couldn't have him, I'd destroy him instead. And several spiked drinks later, he was putty in my hands.

I touched Tony's face, tracing his chin. The past twelve months had distanced us, and yet I felt closer to him now more than ever. And it wasn't just the after-sex high. We had shared something real, and while I had spent our entire marriage erecting a wall he couldn't penetrate, it had merely been a wall of glass. He had seen the broken girl behind the glass and loved her anyway.

From under the covers he stirred, and I snuggled into the crook of his body. It felt so warm and safe, unlike all the other men I had dated over the past year. They had been hard bodies intended to fill a temporary gap between my sheets, but they had never been Tony. No one could compare to him.

I remembered when the accident first happened, I had been left crippled both emotionally and physically. The cuts all over my body represented the cuts all over my soul. The strong, independent woman I had been suddenly vanished into a fearful sobbing mess. I could barely function, the constant pain shredded my will to live, and the surgery to repair my back left me swollen and scarred. Yet through the opiates, the physical therapy, the slow healing process, Tony assured me of how beautiful I was, how strong I was—all that motivational shit people feed you when you want to shove a pistol in your mouth and be done with it.

He had been right, though. My body eventually healed, my scars faded . . . but the drugs . . . those I couldn't shake. Whether it was phantom pain or full-blown addiction, I don't know why I couldn't stop. Tony had begged, pleaded, threatened—and yet the pills always came first. I always chose them, or maybe they chose me. I don't know. But eventually Tony gave up, and I couldn't blame him. I certainly wouldn't want to live with someone like me, never knowing from one day, one hour to the next which version of me you were getting.

The day he left, he broke me for good. I couldn't see myself through the haze after that. I became a shattered mirror, my cracks hiding any good left inside me. My weakness became my weapon, shards of glass I'd cut myself with: Alone, slice. Depressed, slice. Ugly, slice. Until I'd bleed my heart out onto the floor, staining everything and everyone around me. Friends, family, lovers. I became unbearable to be around, so I buried the pain a little deeper.

Tony had been my only chance at redemption, and I had blown it back then. But I wouldn't lose him again, no matter what it took.

Tony and I were both naked. Wrapping him in my arms

now, I spooned him with my breasts pressed against his back. My touch stirred him awake. He stretched languorously but didn't turn over.

"Good morning, beautiful," he said, yawning.

I had missed that daily greeting. As I nuzzled his neck and wriggled against him, I realized it had also been my first full night sober in months. This moment suddenly felt like a turning point for me, like in a romantic flick when everything begins to flow back to where it's supposed to be for the happily ever after.

I fondled him and he stirred to life. "Want to go for a morning ride?"

He chuckled throatily and turned over. "You better know it—*Liliana*! What the *fuck*?" His back stiffened as realization settled in, then he jumped out of bed and pulled the corner of the sheet, wrapping it around his waist.

"What's wrong?" I asked, all innocence.

"What's *wrong*? Did we . . . what happened last night, Liliana?" His wild eyes roved around the room, as if he'd forgotten why he came here.

"We made love. Then did it again. And again. You told me you wanted to give us another try."

Okay, so he was stoned when he said it, but it was still true.

"Oh no. Oh no no no." Tony rummaged along the floor for his clothes, growing more frantic by the second.

"Calm down, Tony. You're freaking out. Take a breath."

"Calm down? I just cheated on the woman I want to marry! What did we drink last night? Did you—you drugged me, didn't you?" He was throwing words now, and the blue vein on his forehead throbbed. "Damn it, Liliana!" He slammed his fist on my bedside table, rattling the lamp and alarm clock.

I slunk out of bed and threw on a robe. "You're scaring me. Can you please slow down and relax?"

"Relax? How do you expect me to relax when I have to go home and tell my fiancée what I've done?"

"Then don't go home. Stay."

"Stay? You slammed that door shut when you chose drugs over me."

"Oh, don't pin our breakup on me. You chose to leave me. You knew I was struggling and you couldn't hold my hand through it. That is on you."

"What did you expect from me? You were constantly popping pills, always a mess . . . I couldn't live with you anymore."

"But that's what you vowed to do when you married me—for better, for worse, and all that shit. I needed you, and you walked out on me at my lowest point like our marriage certificate wasn't worth the paper it was printed on. How could you do that when I gave you every part of me?"

"I'm sorry I hurt you." His voice was mellow now, the fight gone from it. "But what you did last night was evil. I know exactly what you did. You purposely lied to me, drugged me, then seduced me. What am I supposed to tell Sienna? She's probably wondering where the hell I've been all night. I can't believe I trusted you. I should have known better. You've only ever cared about yourself."

By now he'd found all of his discarded clothes and was

mostly dressed, hopping as he pulled on his socks on the way out of my bedroom.

"That's not true. I did it for you—because I can love you better than she can. I know you, what you like, what you want, who you are. When you were a hundred pounds heavier, who loved you? Me! When you were jobless, who supported you? Me! I never judged you, never looked down on you, never resented you. I loved you for who you were, always. Can Sienna say that? If you gained that weight back, would she still lust after you? If you lost your job, would she happily support you? I don't think so, Tony, because there is no one else who would lie, drug, and seduce you just to keep you. *That*, my friend, is how much I love you. There is nothing I wouldn't do for you."

He stood at the front door, one hand resting on the door-knob, worming his foot halfway into one shoe while holding the other.

"There's nothing you wouldn't do for me, huh? Then do this one last thing: let me go."

Chapter 33

Mackenzie

It was a strange, unexpected thought as I glanced over at the man I had married, wondering how the ugliest of hearts could be wrapped in the most beautiful skin. Evil never sleeps, they say. But I was watching it sleep at this very moment, in my own bed.

My bedroom was unusually silent, devoid of the stentorian snoring that usually tortured my ears all night long. Owen slept more soundly than usual, it seemed. Maybe it was a fitting way to go. He didn't know I was here, my eyes glued to him slumbering. I imagined what dreams fluttered through his head, what fears manifested or hopes surfaced. My last dream was about Robin and I taking a beach trip together, wriggling our toes in the sand, running in the surf. We were friends again in my dream. But that wasn't last night, because last night I hadn't slept. Instead I sat in my car in an empty parking lot brooding and plotting. Then plotting and brooding some more.

Memories of Owen choking me kept me company in my car for hours. Bruises and red dashes across my skin pulsated in the darkness. His words belittling me, stripping me of all dignity, stealing all my self-worth, echoing against the walls of my mind. I came to a realization last night: I couldn't live with him anymore. And I couldn't survive without him. But with his insurance policy, I could rise again.

Now here I was, standing above my husband, my mind clear and my hatred fully formed.

How evil and love coexisted inside of me was a mystery I couldn't solve. Owen had been my first love, the one who burrowed into my heart for keeps. No matter how much he had rotted on the inside, he was a gorgeous man to look at. He'd always taken great care of himself, working out regularly at the fitness club and eating healthily—which meant I'd had to give up some of my favorite Southern fried dishes. I'd often compared him to Bradley Cooper, my personal Hollywood heartthrob, but Owen would just shrug and say that looks weren't everything. He was right. If only I had seen what was underneath the handsome façade, I wouldn't be standing here contemplating murder.

The day we first met, he had approached me in the cafeteria, buttoned-up shirt straining against his rippling muscles, his posture straight and soldierly. And like a good little soldier, he was always ready for battle.

He battled against my friends to date me and won. Then he battled my parents for my hand in marriage and won again. He battled through our twenty-plus years together to maintain control. He won again and again, until now. Now it was my turn.

In the darkness I watched him lying there on his side, gray bedspread pulled up to his chin. Gray, the color of our life together. The color of our bland marriage, full of routine predictability because God forbid we ever go on an adventure together. We shopped at the same stores, dined at the same restaurants, prepared the same meals, spent our weekends doing the same thing over and over on endless repeat, day after week after month after year. Daring to color outside the lines would certainly send our lives crashing into the abyss, as far as Owen was concerned. And so on it went in predictable banality, so much that sometimes I wanted to lash out and do something daring just to see what would happen. Would our insular little world explode? Would we survive the change?

Fear drives evil, and Owen was deeply afraid. A man controls someone else because he's afraid of losing his puppet, or more likely, himself. Just as Owen controlled me, because I let him be what he wanted to be—powerful and in charge. In the bedroom he made sure I knew this, and for those hellish minutes he had full control over my body, my voice, my will.

I loved him every other minute in the day except for those minutes when I hated him, loathed him, wished him dead. And those minutes added up night after night. He had chipped away at my self-worth until nothing remained. He had sabotaged my friendships, turning people against me. I suffered in silence, because Aria at least remained untouched. Owen was my cross to bear, but Aria . . . he wouldn't be hers.

But things changed. Owen changed. Aria changed. And now I had changed. I touched the sore spot on my neck that had already begun to purple. I hoped my concealer would be sufficient to cover it, since a turtleneck in May would raise red flags. I'd gotten used to hiding my face along with the bruises—mostly easy to cover on my upper arms or ass. But every once in a while it wasn't so easy to hide, and using the old "I ran into the door" excuse never worked. Friends saw through it. Hell, even strangers knew that line. It had become something of a twisted game keeping the secret from Aria—that her father was a boxer in the bedroom and her mother a weak punching bag.

Last night I made the decision, for real this time. I wanted Owen out of my life and no longer in a position to taint my daughter's perception of men and marriage and relationships. But if I left him, he'd still have his chokehold, because he controlled the money that controlled me. I could get a crappy job with my limited skills—a career sacrifice that all stay-at-home moms blindly made as we trusted our husbands to stand by us until death do us part. I could barely scrape by, but he'd end up with full custody of Aria, because money bought lawyers who bought custody. Real freedom was what I wanted, and I knew just how to get it.

Despite Owen's empty threat, the locks hadn't been

changed. In fact, like an idiot he had left the back door cracked open, an invitation for trouble. He was lucky it was only me slipping in through the back and not some vandal. He had no idea how much I did for this family behind the scenes, keeping us safe and fed and out of debt. What gratitude did I get? None. Well, it was time to pay up.

After eighteen cell phone messages alternating between threats and pleas for me to come home last night, each one drunker than the next, I knew I had him where I wanted him. You see, Owen was a deep sleeper to begin with, but after a couple of drinks he slept like the dead. I knew he'd turn to alcohol after I left and didn't immediately return. It was his crutch when he couldn't cope.

I didn't get home until after three in the morning. Not wanting to be seen out in public, I had parked at the empty Monroeville Mall parking lot, just sitting and thinking and conjuring up a simple plan—so simple I didn't think it would work. When I got home, it didn't take long to stage the house without waking everyone, and before the blush of dawn I had finished my ultimate masterpiece. It looked perfect, from the broken glass of the back door, to the missing wallets, and even the stolen jewelry and other small valuables. The perfect staging for the perfect crime. And Owen's precious Lexus that kept us car-rich but savings-poor was long gone, dropped off in the middle of the ghetto with the key in the ignition, where some lucky thug would be enjoying a free joyride this morning.

All that was left was to complete the mission. Maybe I was a coward for plotting it like this, for waiting until Owen was defenseless and asleep, but I knew my limitations and I knew his strengths. This was the only way.

The barking of the next-door neighbor's dog prodded me with sudden urgency. Standing over him, I gently moved the covers just enough to reveal his neck. Hot tears burned my eyes, and I swallowed the knot in my throat. I'd miss him. I'd spent half of my life with him. I'd probably never find someone who could love me again, not with the way I looked . . . But that was Owen talking, wasn't it? He was the one who told me I was too ugly to find love elsewhere. He was the one who constantly reminded me how much I needed him. He was the one who stole pieces of me until there was nothing left. Manipulating. Controlling. Gaslighting. Owen was getting what he deserved.

You think I'm ugly? I'll show you ugly. The thought was bitter but satisfying.

One . . . two . . . three, I counted in my head.

I banished the sadness and pressed the kitchen knife against his throat, my hands shaking but my resolve solid. I inhaled a draft of courage and lifted the knife. The blade glinted against the bathroom nightlight, which was casting my shadow across the floor. I closed my eyes, turned my head, and dashed the blade across his throat, using my weight to press the blade in deep. I couldn't watch myself do it, so I let the pressure guide me. Initially his skin resisted, then I felt the pop of his flesh slicing open. Another push and the cartilage and soft tissue of his larynx gave way. I waited for something to happen, for him to scream in pain, for him to fight back . . . but nothing happened. He peacefully drifted off, and I was almost glad for him.

Then he was gone.

Chapter 34

Mackenzie

Sunday Morning

It took me eight minutes to properly wipe off my fingerprints following instructions gleaned from a Google search, then dispose of the knife. A simple drop-off in the neighbor's garbage can several streets away, far enough that the police wouldn't likely search it and deep enough that the owners wouldn't notice it. As the moon hid behind a veil of clouds, I speed-walked home, avoiding streetlights as best I could. Pulling my phone from my pocket, I called Lily, desperate for the favor of a lifetime.

"Why are you calling me at the butt crack of dawn?" Lily

said after picking up on the first ring. Lily always had a way with words.

"Sorry for waking you, but it's urgent. I need a favor." I didn't know how much to say. All I knew was that my phone records would show this call when the police started investigating me, as they most surely would.

"Never mind, I was already awake. What kind of favor?"

"If anyone asks, I spent the night at your house last night. Okay? We had drinks at your place and I slept over. Then I left this morning—right around now. Then I called you to let you know I got home safely. Got it?"

"No, I don't *got it*. I can't be your alibi tonight. Wait until tomorrow."

"It's too late for that. Please."

"Mac, what's going on? Are you okay?" Uh-oh. I had triggered Lily's worried voice. And she wouldn't drop it until I answered to her satisfaction.

"I can't tell you yet. But you'll find out soon." I didn't want to drag her into it or make her an accomplice, so the less she knew, the better. I had already destroyed one friendship; I didn't need to lose the other.

"Ohhhh . . ." I heard the wheels turning. "Did you leave Owen?" Her voice lit up with pride. "Good girl!"

"It's a little more complicated than that, Lil. I need you to vouch for me . . . to the police."

"*I malano miau!* Are you serious? What kind of trouble are you in?"

"You'll find out soon enough, but please? I need you to do this. Besides, I kept my mouth shut about you and Grant. You wouldn't want Robin to find out, would you?"

I hated myself for blackmailing Lily, but my survival instincts were kicking in. I needed her guarantee.

"Listen, Mac, you know I would do anything for you, but you couldn't have spent the night because Tony was here all night. If that comes out, your whole story falls apart."

"Tony's there?" I yelped. "That's great!" Here I was, a newly minted murderess, and Lily's reconciliation with Tony seemed more important. I knew Lily still loved him, pined for him, tried every way to replace him in her heart. If I couldn't have my happy ending, at least Lily could. I was glad for her, even while I had my husband's blood on my hands, figuratively speaking. It was actually not nearly as gory as I had feared and expected.

"Yes and no. It's not exactly good news, but I'll explain later. Anyway, I'm not sure he'll be thrilled to accommodate any of my requests after today."

I calculated the odds of Tony's sleepover coming up in a police interrogation. If she buried it, I doubted they'd dig deep enough to find out. Lily was my only shot at a credible alibi.

"Look, you're the only one I can ask. If the police come asking questions, just don't mention Tony and it should be fine. They have no reason to go looking for him unless you bring him up. I wouldn't ask you to do this if my life wasn't on the line here. Please."

The silence stretched long and thin. I knew Lily, the eternal pragmatist, was wondering what exactly I had gotten myself into, and assessing her potential culpability.

"Fine, I'll vouch for you and keep Tony in the dark. Just one question: are you okay?"

I laughed a sob. I was on the verge of crying, but I needed to hold myself together for what I was about to do next. "Ha. I've never been better. But I gotta go. I'll explain everything later. I love you so much, Lily . . . and thanks."

I didn't have time to fully process the fact that Tony was back in Lily's life, but I'd mull over that later once my own skeletons stopped jangling. As I hung up, I noticed two voicemail messages I hadn't listened to when I had skipped through Owen's slew of calls. I clicked on the first one:

"Heeey, Macky-poo." It was Owen, from last night. Drunk as a skunk. And using the pet name I loathed. "Please come home. I need you. I love you. Just . . . come home. Please, baby."

My chest constricted. I couldn't breathe. With hands on my knees, I bent over, gasping while the corners of my vision darkened. Owen was gone. Dead. Forever. I couldn't pull him back. I couldn't fix what I'd done. And now, when it was too late, the reality caved in on me.

A car's headlights crested the hill behind me, scaring me. I shouldn't be seen out here on the street. I ducked into the bushes, hiding until the vehicle passed. I waited, watched . . . breathed. At least I wasn't panicking anymore.

One more message, if I could handle it.

"Strong, be strong." I'd never had any use for motivational speakers, but right now I could have really used one. "You can do this, Mac."

I held my finger over the voicemail icon, shaking violently. It was Owen again, but this time more lucid. As I listened, I realized this voicemail could cause me a lot of trouble. I considered deleting it, then wondered if the cops could retrieve it and how they would interpret it. But I didn't have time to worry about that. I had to prepare for the performance of a lifetime. Though, with the emotional overload surging through me, it wouldn't be difficult.

My dark house loomed up ahead on the sleepy street, and I briskly jogged the rest of the way home. When I entered, I headed straight upstairs, cell phone in hand, my nerves shot. I paused briefly on the landing as I glanced into Aria's room. Her door was ajar. She was sleeping soundly. The long night, the lack of rest, the anxiety, Owen's peaceful face, the knife slicing across his neck, the phone message, the staging, the regret, the extreme guilt . . . it was all sloshing over me now, drowning me. As I entered our bedroom, I knew I had to finish this, rise above it, push ahead. It was the only way out, so I dialed the number.

"9-1-1. What's your emergency?" the operator asked.

I hadn't gotten a word out before I fell into sobs. "My husband's been attacked. It's his throat—he was cut across the throat. Please hurry!" It wasn't difficult letting my voice naturally lose control, because I could feel myself slipping, my reality falling apart. It was all coming to a head.

"Ma'am, try to remain calm. Is the perpetrator still in the house?"

"No, no, I don't think so."

"Is your husband still breathing?"

"I don't know. I don't think so."

"What's the address, ma'am?"

I gave her my home address, then ran to the master bathroom and grabbed a handful of towels, pressing them against his neck to soak up any blood, since that's what a frantic wife who just found her husband's throat slit would do.

"An ambulance is on its way."

Minutes later I heard the squalling sirens of the ambulance and police vehicles speeding to the scene. The paramedics would rush into the house, the police would search for clues, the spotlight would shine on me. Was it worth it? It didn't feel like it anymore.

The curtain fell, and suddenly I felt so very alone.

Chapter 35

Robin

Ryan had woken up in tears—again—which led to Willow breaking out in hysterics over the police questioning her brother. Of course, Lucas saw all of the crying and felt the need to join in, which led to a house full of weeping children when Collette's pink little face turned purple with empathy wailing.

"I've got to get out of here or I'm going to lose my mind," I told Grant while I headed for the door. "I'll pick up some Dunkin' Donuts for everyone."

"Wait, Robin! You can't leave me here with four screaming kids," Grant whined.

"Welcome to my everyday life."

I handled it for hours each day. Grant could handle it for a few minutes. I headed out of the winding neighborhood plan, blasting Lady Gaga and Bradley Cooper's "Shallow."

The lyrics gave me chills, because exactly like they said, I too was diving in to the deep end, not knowing if I'd ever surface again. But I'd be wearing a little black dress when I took the plunge. The secret "date" was confirmed for tonight, the dress hanging in my closet, the stilettos polished and shiny, everything in place for a night of marital self-destruction. By this time tomorrow I could be short one friend *and* one husband.

I'd thought about Mackenzie a lot over the past couple days. Not just because of the Aria-Ryan drama, but because she was the one I wanted to talk to about Grant. Whenever I brought the subject up with Lily, she grew withdrawn, which wasn't like her. Lily had opinions on everything from politics to pasta. To now have nothing to say about my philandering husband? It was odd, but I tried not to over-think it. If I could count on anyone as my sounding board, it was Mackenzie. If I could count on anyone to man-bash for me, Mackenzie again.

Her house was only a couple minutes out of the way, so I decided to take a little detour. I don't know why I wanted to torture myself by driving by, not that I planned to actually stop. We weren't on speaking terms, and it broke my heart. But something about seeing her house, where I imagined her sipping coffee in her silky pajamas, brought her closer to me.

As I arrived, I realized why my gut had insisted on passing by. An ambulance was parked in the driveway, and two cop cars squatted crookedly along the street out front. *Oh, God, no . . . please let my friend be okay.*

I pulled in behind one of the police vehicles, parked, and jumped out of my car. As I ran up the walkway, two EMTs wheeled a black body bag out of the house, down the sidewalk, and past me. No no no.

"Excuse me!" I yelled. "What happened? Is someone—dead?"

"I'm sorry, ma'am, but I'm not at liberty to say," the tech at the rear of the stretcher replied.

I needed answers. I needed to know Mackenzie was okay. My vision grew disoriented with the flashing lights, the milling police, the burgeoning crowd of people collecting on the sidewalks. My heart thrummed wildly, deafening me against the din of speculating onlookers. And then I saw her through the parting bodies—Mackenzie, plodding behind a policeman with Aria tucked under her arm.

I ran up to her, crying happy tears. "Mackenzie, you're okay! I thought . . . I thought that was you on the gurney." Tears streaked down my face as I grabbed her in a hug. I had never felt so relieved in all my life.

Mackenzie stood stiff in my arms, but I couldn't let go. I would never let go again. As I held her, her body loosened, relaxed, then she hugged me back halfheartedly.

"Owen . . . he died." Her face was flushed and blotchy. Aria wilted next to her, sobbing, and for a brief moment I absorbed all of their sadness, all of their pain as if it was my own. I wanted to reach into the raging waters that Mackenzie was drowning in and pull her out.

"Oh, Mac, I don't even know what to say." I didn't care

about the damn fight, or the charges, or anything else in that moment. All I cared about was my friend who was hurting.

I nestled her head on my shoulder like a child, and she limply let me.

Then she looked up at me with watery eyes and said the strangest thing: "I don't feel anything anymore. I think I'm broken for good."

"No, honey, you're not. We'll piece you back together, I promise."

Mac wiped away a streak of tears and I helped clean off a black smudge under her eyes.

"Whatever you need, I'm here for you," I vowed.

I had left her to die once before, but I'd be damned if I did it again.

2001, BEAVER FALLS, PENNSYLVANIA

Mac and I had skipped all our classes together in a day of no regrets. We were more than just girls in a dorm, arranged together by some administrative coincidence. We were destined to be friends. Destined for greatness together.

If Mackenzie was solid ground, I was rushing water. She was steady and reliable while I was always moving, always flowing. But we worked, chaotically beautiful like a Wassily Kandinsky painting.

Our dorm was cluttered with clothes, makeup, papers, books. Somehow our shared closet had exploded all over the sofa and two chairs that furnished our living room. I could lie and say that we were too busy studying to make time for cleaning up after ourselves, but the reality was that without parents dictating chores, we did what we wanted. And tidying up hadn't made the list.

It should have, though. Maybe if it had, the accident wouldn't have happened.

"You want some mac 'n' cheese?" I offered while Mackenzie fell onto her bottom bunk. Her blond hair splayed around her head like a halo, and her arms flung open like an angel. Quite fitting, actually.

"Sure, I'll eat some," she replied. "I'm going to take a quick nap, though. I'm exhausted and my feet are killing me. *Someone* dragged me all over Pittsburgh today without telling me I should wear more comfortable walking shoes."

"I didn't expect to hit every store in the South Side! You have only yourself to blame for that."

"Whatever. Wake me when the food's ready."

I shuffled to the kitchenette and grabbed the last box of Kraft mac 'n' cheese in the cupboard. The countertop was littered with papers, so I moved them aside and grabbed the only pot we owned. After setting the water to boil, I opened the fridge to discover we were out of milk. I was pretty sure Sharon one floor down always had milk and butter on hand; the girl was a tireless baker and I loved her for it. Especially when she came around delivering homemade chocolate chip cookies to our dorms.

Slipping into flip-flops, I headed downstairs to see Sharon about the milk. Twenty minutes into bitching about our professors, the smoke alarm started screeching throughout the building.

It took a minute for my brain to process the events. Then I remembered.

"The stove!" I ran up the stairs just as the sprinklers activated throughout the dorm. I had forgotten all about the pot of boiling water that was likely now bone dry, the papers sitting next to it. Girls fled the building in hysterics and the shrill wail of a fire truck's siren grew closer as I reached my suite.

"Mackenzie!" I yelled, choking on the smoke pouring out of the kitchen. I glimpsed her through the fumes, arms covering her face.

"Help!" she cried. "Robin, help!"

By now the fire had spread into the hallway, blocking Mackenzie in and me out. The heat was intense; I couldn't get close enough to help her. Suddenly a flame burst high, licking the ceiling, and Mackenzie screamed.

The next few minutes blurred as the smoke suffocated and blinded me. A firefighter barked at me to get to safety, but I couldn't leave my friend. The next thing I knew, a pair of strong arms dragged me away as I watched Mackenzie disappear behind the blaze.

SUNDAY EVENING

The silk of my black dress felt like a cool, rich second skin. I'd picked this dress for the irony. I'd worn it on our honeymoon, and Grant could barely keep his hands off me when he saw me in it. Three times—we had made love three times that night all because of this dress.

What with the extra poundage I'd gained after *birthin' four young 'uns*, as Mac used to quip, it was a miracle the dress still fit fifteen years later. Maybe it was a miracle if the nuts and bolts of any marriage still fit together fifteen years later.

Couples got restless, complacent, needy, didn't they? To give it all up now, after all we'd been through, seemed a waste—our early years of financial struggle, surviving on ramen noodles, building a medical practice from the ground up and all the pain that went with it, raising four kids, Willow's lacrosse games, Ryan's baseball games, pool parties, vacations with six people squeezed into two bedrooms, sporadic date nights, sexless months, births, deaths, love, loss . . . we'd gone through it all together. I couldn't imagine not having Grant to go through it with.

Life could be taken away at any moment, I had learned today. After empty consolations while Mac grieved Owen's death, I had nothing left to offer other than my company. She turned it down, wanting to be alone. I knew she needed space to mourn, just as I needed confrontation to find truth.

I arrived at Boot Scooters fifteen minutes before our scheduled rendezvous. I had intentionally picked an out-of-the-way place—no chance of running into anyone we knew and blowing my cover. The bar was a real dive, like one of those seedy joints you see in the movies but doubt really exists. There were tacky neon sculptures of cowboy hats, motorcycles, and naked women on the dark paneled walls. Country music—not rockin' contemporary, but old-school "tear in your beer" stuff—blared from a battered old Wurlitzer jukebox. I stood out like a nun in a whorehouse—another funny Mac-ism. But I looked damned sexy in that dress, if I did say so myself. Making my way to the bar, every male head turned.

"I'm meeting somebody," I said to the barkeeper, "and I want to surprise him."

Pamela Crane

"Got a booth in the back yonder," he said, gesturing languidly.

I looked. It was in a dark, private corner, away from the noisy jukebox and the main crowd, which was thin at this early hour.

"My date will be coming in any minute now. He'll ask for me."

While pouring two beers from the tap, it was a full five seconds before he answered. "What name?"

I told him.

The bartender studied me, his eyes flashing with sudden interest. "Seems like I've heard that name before."

I chuckled softly. "Yeah, maybe you have. Here's a fiver for your trouble."

As I walked away, I made a point of swaying my hips. I felt the bartender's eyes glued to my ass the whole time. I have to say, it felt nice to be ogled, even by a sleazy barkeep. I settled into the booth with a good view of the full room. The only light was a tea light in a small frosted vase on the tabletop. If I leaned back, my face was hidden in shadow. Perfect.

A few minutes later Grant entered, his dark brown hair neatly combed but curling at the ends. He wore a nice jacket over a collared polo, and it looked good. He always looked good, even if I didn't tell him often enough. He didn't fit in here either. He walked up to the bar and spoke to the bartender. Grant seemed confused by the man's big grin then walked toward me.

"Anastasia?" he asked as he neared my dark corner.

"Good evening, Grant." I spoke in the husky voice I'd been practicing and fancied I sounded something like Demi Moore.

"Dark in here," he said as he reached to shake my hand.

"I like the dark," I said, rising from my seat. "Fun things happen in the dark."

That was the moment he saw my face. I had to bite my tongue to keep from laughing. "Like what you see, you cheating bastard?"

"Holy crap! Robin! Honey, I can expl—"

"Save it, Grant. You know, you really shouldn't use your real name on dating sites. It makes it too easy to find you."

The bartender came over with the drinks Grant must have ordered, a White Russian—my favorite—for me, a pint of Guinness for him.

"You two gettin' acquainted? Good. Now, don't be doin' any kinky bondage crap." Chuckling, he headed back to the bar.

Grant slapped his forehead with his palm. "Anastasia Steele! Now I get it. No wonder the bartender looked at me so weird when I asked if you'd come in yet. God, I'm such an idiot!"

"No argument there."

It was hilarious that he hadn't recognized the name of the main character from *Fifty Shades of Grey* that I'd adopted for my alias. We had watched the movie together, and made fun of it, a couple months ago. I didn't admit it then, but I was jealous that we could barely get a passionate kiss in, while Anastasia and Christian were at it like rabbits.

As we settled into the booth, I felt unusually calm, given the circumstances. I drove here prepping for a fight. I had imagined myself beet-faced, screaming, crying. Nope. Instead I adopted a calm, centered veneer. We could talk this through, figure it out, because I had laid my rage to rest. I just wanted answers so that I knew how to move forward. No matter what, I'd be okay. I was a survivor . . . hell, I was a thriver. I conquered my past, raised four great kids, helped build Grant's medical practice . . . if I could do all that, I could do anything with or without a man.

I lifted my glass up in a mock salute. "Why'd you order *my* drink for your ho?"

"I don't know. Habit, I guess." He waited for me to speak, but when I didn't, he said, "I'm not sure what I'm supposed to say here, Robin."

"The truth would be a good starting point." I gulped half the drink because I had a feeling I'd need it to endure this.

"You want the truth? Okay, here it is. I'm miserable. You haven't touched me in months. You realize it's been several months since we last had sex—before Collette was born. I have needs, and sometimes my hand just isn't enough. I need physical contact. With another human. So am I sorry about hurting you? Yes. But I'm not sorry for wanting more from you."

More from me, huh? As if I wasn't giving every part of me away already.

"Why didn't you talk to me? I had no idea you felt this way. But going outside our marriage, Grant—that's unfor-givable."

"Is it as unforgivable as hiding almost fifty grand in debt from your husband?" He stared at me, his gaze hard and calculating.

"How long have you known?"

"Long enough. You've been lying to me, Robin. Just like

I lied to you. That's when this all started. The first time I saw the credit card statement about a month ago. When our mortgage payment got declined, I began looking into our checking and savings accounts. Empty, Robin. You spent every damn cent we had. And on what? Stuff we don't need. So naturally I checked the credit card. Maxed out at over forty thousand dollars. I was so angry I didn't know what to do, so I talked to a female friend about my stress. I didn't bring up the debt, just bullshitted about how I was feeling inside—inadequate, unattractive, feminine shit like that. Then it led to flirting . . . and . . ."

I waved the rest of his excuses away. "I've got it, I've got it. You don't need to go into detail."

"There hasn't been a slew of women, by the way. Only one time with one person. That's it. This dating app thing—I only just opened a profile. I was feeling . . . lonely, I guess. I needed a release after everything going on with Ryan and the debt. But you—or *Anastasia*—were the first person I connected with, and as you can see, I'm not very good at it."

One time with one person. Was that worth divorcing over? Was it any worse than my spending problem?

My thoughts wandered to the home-wrecker. I wondered who she was. Was she prettier than me? Younger than me? Better in bed than me? Was it just sex or was there a meaningful emotional connection? Once I knew, I couldn't unknow it. I wasn't sure I wanted to carry that burden.

"So if it wasn't me who showed up tonight, would you have slept with her?"

He shook his head. "I don't know. I was tempted by the idea of it, only because I've just been a mess, totally inside my head all the time, stressed out over the money and everything going on. I just wanted to bang it out, you know? But you're really the only person I want to bang it out with."

I laughed. Not because anything about this was funny, but because the tension was so high I needed to loosen it. "That's the most romantic thing you've said to me in months."

He chuckled, but it held the regret of a guilty man.

"You have every right to be furious, Robin, to leave me. But I want to fix us, if you'll forgive me. I want to try again, do better. But I need you to put us first just like I need to put us first. We need to connect physically, emotionally. And you need to stop going crazy with the spending. Are you willing to try again? To forgive me?"

He searched me with soulful eyes that had seen so much over the years. They had lusted after me in our youth. They had adored each baby I'd birthed for him. They took pride in me when I did something grand. They gave me comfort when I needed it. They sought wisdom from me during life's big decisions. Was life worth living if Grant wasn't watching?

I tossed back the rest of my drink, letting the smooth liquor run down my throat. Could I really forgive him for sleeping with another woman? Maybe I could forgive. But I could never forget.

Chapter 36

Mackenzie

Detective Bill Rossi could smell the fear in me. I saw it in the way he aimed his beady eyes at me and lobbed question after question, trying to trip me up.

I shivered in my seat as the vent poured cold air over my bare arms. The air-conditioning was set too low for Western Pennsylvania balmy May weather as it blasted through the interview room. That's what Detective Rossi called it, as if I was interviewing for a job, but I knew it for what it was: an interrogation room. The room where they would pull apart my statement, searching for holes and inconsistencies and any trace of a lie.

I hugged my arms, rubbing my hands up and down until the goose bumps settled back into my skin. The lukewarm black coffee—they were out of creamer and sugar, he said, as he placed the Styrofoam cup in front of me—did little to warm me. Beside me sat Aria, zombified with grief, and Detective Rossi sat opposite us holding a pen and pad of paper. I asked if I needed an attorney, to which he replied, "Not if you don't have anything to hide."

I did, of course, but I couldn't let him know that. So I answered his questions one by one, crying real tears between the script. I wasn't a coldhearted bitch who didn't love her husband, after all. Owen had been my world. But when your world begins to turn dark and dangerous, you have to ask yourself if that's really where you want to live. And I knew the only way out was until death do us part . . . his death, unfortunately. It had to be done, no matter how much I loved him or how much the act blackened my soul.

This is what I told myself to feel better. To justify what I had done. So far it wasn't working.

The detective glanced at his notepad, then looked up at my daughter. "Aria, you say you were home all evening last night and didn't hear anything or see anything?"

I hated that my innocent daughter had been dragged into this.

She dabbed her eyes with a tissue the detective had handed her. "I was in my room most of the night, since Dad was drinking. A lot. I could hear him watching television and fuming about Mom being out, but that's all I heard. I had earbuds in most of the night, listening to music. The first thing I heard this morning was Mom screaming and crying that she found Dad with his throat . . ." She didn't finish. She didn't have to.

Detective Rossi vigorously chewed his gum, then he shifted to me. I smelled the mint on his breath. "One more time, Mrs. Fischer, please explain for me exactly what happened, starting with last night. Every detail you can think of, big or small."

I had already given the same story twice now. But I knew better than to sound defensive and annoyed; that was a sure giveaway of guilt. I calmly told the story again. "We had gotten in a tiff yesterday afternoon and I needed some fresh air and went to visit my friend Lily. We ended up drinking, so I spent the night at her place, since I don't drink and drive. You can check my voicemail messages from Owen—he called me over a dozen times asking where I was."

I knew they would stumble across the messages eventually, so my plan was to offer as much truth as possible—the fight, me leaving, his messages—to appear fully transparent. I could control how the story was told, but not how it was interpreted.

"Why didn't you return his calls?"

"I was upset. Haven't you ever gotten in a fight with your spouse? Sometimes you just want some peace. That's all I wanted."

He nodded. What did that mean?

"What time did you leave Lily's?"

I pretended to think it over. "Um, I ended up heading home pretty early in the morning—it was still dark out. I couldn't sleep and I felt okay to drive, so that's why I left."

He made a check mark next to something I'd previously said. Good, I wasn't deviating from my story. "What happened when you got home?"

"When I got home this morning, I noticed the back door glass was smashed in, so I ran upstairs to check on Aria and Owen. Aria was asleep, but I found Owen . . ."

I stopped, the image of his lifeless body lying there overwhelming me. By my own hand. His face a dull gray as morning sunlight rose over him. A sob slipped out, then another as it hit me that I would never see that face again.

"Take your time, Mrs. Fischer. I know this is hard."

"Sorry." I closed my eyes and inhaled a calming breath. "I'm okay."

"You're doing great. Now think back on the fight yesterday. Try to remember what you two were fighting about. It might be important." Although his words were intended to sound compassionate, they came out cold, calculating. He didn't care about my grief; he only cared about solving a murder.

A tissue box sat on the table. I grabbed one and wiped my nose to buy time. This was the third time he'd asked about the fight since we'd gotten here, and it wasn't for no reason. He was fishing for information he already knew. "Oh, I remember now. We had been fighting about something he did behind my back—to a friend of ours."

"Did that fight have anything to do with the recent charges your husband pressed against . . ." He read from the page in front of him. "Ryan Thompson?"

"Why yes, that was exactly what we had been fighting about. He pressed rape charges on behalf of Aria without talking to us first. We're close friends with that family. I just didn't understand why he would do that."

"Dad did what?" Aria's attention swung to me.

"Your father went to the police about what happened between you and Ryan. He formally filed rape charges. I wanted to tell you yesterday when I found out, but everything happened so fast."

"Why didn't he ask *me* what happened? Or if I wanted to press charges? Shouldn't that be my decision?"

The detective stepped in. "In many cases parents file on behalf of their child, especially in a case where we're dealing with an adult and a minor, even if it's consensual. It's illegal, which is why your father came forward."

"But we go to school together. Ryan's not even much older than me."

"Yes, but he's eighteen, an adult in the eyes of the law, which makes it statutory rape. Your father was right to report it." The detective turned back to me. "How did you come to find out what your husband did, Mrs. Fischer? Did he tell you?"

"No, Ryan's mom—a friend of mine since college—showed up at our house yesterday yelling at Owen about it. I overheard."

"So that gives her motive to kill him, doesn't it? Her son facing jail time. His whole life ruined before he's even out of high school. It's a pretty strong reason to hate Owen Fischer. To want him dead."

Oh God, I didn't like where this was heading.

"No, absolutely not. Robin wouldn't hurt a fly. She was upset, but not enough to kill him."

"What about Ryan? Certainly he must be pretty angry to be looking at a possible jail sentence, thanks to your husband."

I couldn't let Detective Rossi pin two innocent people to his list of suspects. I would rather take the blame than let that happen. "No, I don't think so. They're well off, and it was clearly a robbery. Stuff was missing, the police said—cash, my husband's car, jewelry. Why would they steal stuff if they only wanted to kill him?"

"To stage it. Make it look like a robbery when in fact it was a murder all along."

"No, I really don't think so. If you knew the family, you'd know it's not possible."

"That's what they said about Jeffrey Dahmer and Ted Bundy," Detective Rossi said with a deadpan expression. "You really never know someone until you slip into their skin."

That's exactly what the detective was trying to do—get under my skin, rove inside my mind, discover my secrets. It was impossible to tell from his inscrutable face if he was having any luck as he watched me, like I was a zoo animal behind glass. He wanted to break through that glass, and if I had to, to protect Robin I just might let him.

Things were quickly spiraling out of control, sorrow and regret fogging up my judgment, and there was no way to put Humpty Dumpty together again. But no matter how much I lied or killed or ran to protect myself, I would never send my friends to hell in my place.

Chapter 37

Lily

It was officially the worst day of my life.

Up until now, the day of the car accident had been, when my body was broken along with my dreams, but back then at least I had Tony to hold my hand through it. And my two best friends to bring me casseroles and cake. Today I had no one. I was bound to Mackenzie by a lie, estranged from Robin because of an affair, and torn from Tony, the only love of my life, by addiction. What else was here for me? Nothing but mistakes, regret, and anguish.

As I sat in my car in front of Robin's house, it was a last-ditch effort to fix the damage I'd done. There was just so much damage.

Detective Bill Rossi had left my apartment after an hour and a half of questioning that I lied my way through. I hated lying almost as much as I hated being a drug addict, but they somehow went hand in hand and their grip was tight.

"Was Mackenzie Fischer here with you last night?" he had asked point-blank.

"Yes, sir. She slept over after we'd had a few drinks." Lie.

"Around what time did she leave?"

"It was early this morning, sometime around three thirty, I think." Another lie.

"Did you speak with her after she left?" This was the only question I could answer truthfully.

"She called me when she got home, then again after she found Owen . . . dead." For a moment I had relived the conversation in my head, Mac calling me frantically. *He's dead, Lily. Owen's dead.*

She never explained how he died, but I had a dark feeling Mackenzie knew more than she was letting on. In the moment I had told her how sorry I was, but that was a lie too. I didn't feel bad for Owen; Mac was the one I was worried about. Even through the phone I could hear her unraveling as the deafening sound of sirens cut her off.

"And how did she seem when she spoke with you?" the detective asked coolly.

"How do you expect a woman who just found her dead husband to sound? She was a mess. I could barely understand what she was saying."

I wasn't sure if I had aced my little interrogation, or what all of this meant for Mackenzie. Was she in trouble? Every call I made went straight to voicemail. All I wanted to do was open a bottle of vodka, pop a pill, and tuck today away forever.

It had been a shit-show of a day, with Tony leaving this morning in an angry huff after I confessed to spiking his drink—only a little bit, I tried to explain, just enough to loosen him up. I had a right to him, if you ask me. I was still technically his wife, after all, so I felt I was due. He disagreed completely, but I didn't give a shit. The man had torn my heart in half when he refused to give me another chance, instead professing his love for a chick he hardly knew.

On top of lying to an officer of the law and pissing my soon-to-be ex-husband off, I fell into another Workout Wonder scheduling nightmare, courtesy of Robin. She had managed to find time to schedule Ricky's workout on the day I already had Samantha's session booked, so I had to call both clients and straighten it out because God knows what further damage Robin would do if I left it up to her. As I shut the car door behind me and headed up her walkway, I had already decided I wouldn't tell her any of this. The poor woman had enough burdens to carry.

Didn't we all, though?

My breaking point was another email threat from Asshole Irving, this time via his lawyer. Add to all this the withdrawal ravaging my body, giving me spasms and headaches and chills and nausea, and I felt like I was in the ninth circle of hell. God only knows what the detective thought when he saw me—a sweaty, shaky, paranoid slob. I guaranteed he'd be investigating me further . . . most likely on drug charges.

I had been stuck on this merry-go-round too long, seeing the same sights pass by in a blur. Round and round I went, never going anywhere, never feeling anything but sick. It was time to hop off the ride. My life as I recognized it would officially be over today. But I had forged my own fate. Dug my own grave. My bad choices had led me here, to Robin's front door, and it was time to spring-clean my attic of secrets.

An owl hooted forlornly from a sycamore tree in the next-door neighbor's side yard as I stood on the front porch, nervously pacing. A glow shone from Robin's living room window, but inside it was quiet. I imagined Grant watching television in their bedroom, the two little ones tucked soundly in bed, while Willow sat at the kitchen table cramming for a Monday-morning test at school tomorrow and Ryan played video games in the basement. Robin would be cleaning the kitchen, which she always did at night when no one could mess it up again. Through college she had been the night owl among us three friends, always busiest while everyone else slumbered. I didn't know if that was what their evenings looked like in reality, but it was a pretty picture to draw. Maybe a picture I even wanted for myself. Without all the kids, of course. Though I could tolerate one. Maybe.

I sighed heavily, then knocked. I knew better than to ring the doorbell with a sleeping baby inside.

The rumble of footsteps drew nearer, then the door cracked open. Robin peered through the sliver, looking at me curiously as if she didn't recognize me.

"Lily?"

"Hey, Robin. Can we talk for a minute?"

I couldn't imagine the thoughts steamrolling through her head right now at my unannounced late-night visit. Especially with everything going on with Mackenzie at the moment.

"Sure. Is everything okay?"

"Um, let's sit down first."

It was a brisk night, a sweater kind of night, but still comfortable. A walnut-stained Amish swing hung at one end of the porch, filled with fluffy pillows. I walked toward it. "How about out here?" I figured it'd be best to keep the conversation away from prying ears.

"Okaaaay." I heard the worry. I felt it too.

Although masked in night, we exchanged a knowing look. Our oldest friend's husband had died under mysterious circumstances, yet our silence vowed to never speak of it out loud. The murder was too harrowing to give voice to. Even if Mac had something to do with it, we'd never tell, because we all knew what Owen was capable of.

"Is this about me dropping the ball on the admin stuff for your company?" Robin asked. "I know I've messed a few things up, but I can do better, Lil. I'm still learning the ropes, but I really need this job." She was pleading with me now, and I felt horrible that she felt such guilt over something so trivial in the grand scheme of things.

"No, it's about something else. You know I love you, right?"

She sat down beside me, pushing pillows around until she was comfortably propped up.

"Of course. We're like sisters . . . only without the drama and competition." She smiled. Oh, how I would miss that smile.

"I have something to tell you, and I know you're going to be angry, hate me, probably never want to see or speak to me again, and I don't blame you. But I have something else to say before I drop this bomb, since afterward I don't think we'll be on speaking terms."

Her eyes narrowed, the crank turning slowly. "You're scaring me." Her words came out a whisper, and I wouldn't blame her imagination for jumping to worst-case scenarios. This was definitely worst-case territory.

"You've been the one person who I could turn to for anything, Robin. You've never judged me for my pill addiction and never made me feel like I was unfixable. No matter how many times I screwed up, you were always there to help me stand back up. I owe you my life, because without you I would probably be dead by now."

Her hand reached for mine, resting on it with comforting softness. "I'll always be there for you, Lil. That's what best friends are for."

"Which is why I'm moving to California."

Her hand flew to her mouth. Cold, empty air replaced the spot where she had touched. "What? That's ridiculous. Everything that matters to you is here in Pennsylvania. Your whole life is here."

"*Was*. Everything that mattered *was* here. But not anymore."

"I don't understand."

"Tony and I are making the divorce official. He's marrying someone else, and he deserves happiness. Being married to an addict isn't easy, and it's time he moved forward and found something better. As for Workout Wonder, I'm going to take the company with me and rebuild. It won't be hard—you know how bullheaded I am about making things happen. But you, Robin, you're the hardest for me to leave behind because you're, well, family."

Her lips opened to speak, to protest where we both knew this was heading—it was good-bye. I held up a silencing palm.

"I did something unforgivable."

I hesitated. Once I said it, it was out there forever, words spinning in space, crashing into her life. "I slept with Grant—once. It was selfish and mostly my fault, because I was lonely and messed up and needy. So please forgive him. Please work things out. I'm leaving because you two need to fix things, and you can't do that with me here. I know you two can work it out because he's crazy about you, Robin. It was never love for us. I filled a temporary need that you didn't. I'm not justifying it, but that's the truth. So there—you have the truth. I'm sorry, and I hope you two will do what's best for your beautiful family; a life that I wish I could have, a life worth fighting for."

Robin's wordless gaze hit harder than any emotional shit-storm I could imagine. I stood up and the swing rocked behind me. I was ready to be screamed at, slapped, kicked off her property. Yet Robin sat there in shocked silence. Her eyes watered, a tear slid down her cheek, falling from the edge of her jaw. She felt so distant from me, then the elastic snap of full comprehension brought her back. When she spoke, her voice was choked and raspy.

"So you were the girl—the one he told me about. Wow. I didn't see that coming."

"He told you?"

She nodded, barely visible in the shadow. She sniffled. I had made my friend cry on the inside—the worst kind of grief. The grief you couldn't show.

"Are you guys fixable?"

"We'll see. I want to be. I feel like I should be hating Grant . . . hating *you*. But I'm just . . . numb."

"I'm so sorry." Now I was crying, sobs from my belly shaking my whole body. "I'll miss you so much, you have no idea."

The hole in my heart widened, so much I thought I'd be swallowed up inside it. I hated good-byes, and this would be the last time I'd see Robin. Gazing out upon the black night, a reel of memories unfurled. The time we went skinny-dipping at Myrtle Beach during spring break. The ski trip to Seven Springs where Mackenzie accidentally went down a black diamond slope and nearly killed herself. The San Luis orphanage where we built a playground for the kids one summer after sophomore year. The first time Robin got drunk—which was the last time Robin got drunk. Mercilessly teasing Mac by humming "Dueling Banjos" on the road trip to meet her family in the sticks of North Carolina. Each bachelorette party. Each wedding. Each pregnancy announcement and each pregnancy scare. Each baby shower. Each child's birth. Each and every major event, we shared. And the little ones too. All filed away in the cabinet of my mind, cracked open when I needed a smile. There would be no more new memories. And I wondered if the old ones would ever taste so good again.

We'd been through so much together over the years. But

I was doing the right thing, and that's all that mattered. I'd grieve the loss of my friendship, let the guilt of what I'd done make me a better person, then move on. I had spent too long mourning what I didn't have; it was time to start living instead. I just hoped that Robin and Grant could do the same.

Robin stood up to hug me good-bye. "I'll miss you too." She pulled away, fixing those intense brown eyes on mine. "At least it was you. I know it's a weird thing to say, but I'm glad he ran into the arms of someone who loved us both. Had it been anyone else, she would have tried to take him away from me. At least you're giving him back."

"Robin, he was never mine to give back. He has always been yours, and he always will be."

Chapter 38

Owen

Owen Fischer had grown up around guns. By the age of five, he was already spending weekends target practicing with his dad at the local sportsman's club, and he was a decent shot too. By seven he could hit a beer can at twenty-five yards. When he was thirteen, his dad bought him his first pistol, a 9mm. And by eighteen he was a marksman, frequently competing in and winning competitive shooting tournaments, and a proud card-carrying member of the National Rifle Association. Owen's dad made sure he knew the foundation of responsible gun ownership: how to properly clean, handle, carry, and store his weapons. How to treat a gun was instilled deep; how to treat others, not so much.

"If you can handle the responsibility of a weapon, you can handle anything," his dad had taught him.

Except when Owen got angry. When Owen got angry, he couldn't handle himself, let alone a deadly weapon. His father's rules flew out the window, and recklessness flew in. And right now, Owen was angry. "*Righteously angry*," he called it when Mackenzie begged him to calm down.

It started with a fight. And it ended with a murder.

Owen didn't personally know Geoffrey Faust. As far as he was concerned, he would have never crossed paths with the degenerate if it wasn't for Mackenzie Kirkland's soft heart. Everyone on campus had noticed and gossiped about Robin Goldman's growing belly. She was a flirt, which automatically made her a whore, according to most of the students at their small college. Yet when Robin refused to drop out and instead have the baby, that was more shocking than her pregnancy.

Like every other classmate, Owen had assumed a one-night stand had caught up to Robin. That's when Mackenzie set him straight. After she'd told him what Geoffrey had done—a secret Mackenzie had vowed to keep for Robin, then slipped up and shared with him after one too many vodka Jell-O shots one night—Owen's moral indignation was triggered and his vigilante impulse kicked in.

His father would have killed him for sneaking the gun out of the gun safe. He would have killed him a second time for concealing it and taking it to a college campus. But when it came to justice, Owen didn't see in shades of gray. Raping and impregnating a girl and then leaving her high and dry was crossing a line punishable by death.

Geoffrey Faust would deserve what he got. Hopped up on testosterone and self-righteousness, Owen wanted to play judge, jury, and executioner.

Nico Bartelli wasn't Owen's usual fare when it came to friends. But when you've grown up with someone since first grade, you know if you can trust them or not. Owen trusted Nico with his life . . . and the biggest secret he would ever have.

Although Owen, for the most part, had trodden a straight and narrow path, Nico wasn't as lucky. His grades had always been subpar, and his parents didn't care enough to notice when he started hanging around with a high school gang. Drug deals and car thefts and run-ins with the law had been his initiation to a life on the streets.

When Owen now reconnected with Nico, he discovered his old friend was a shell of the guy he'd known. He'd done jail time for petty crimes, dabbled in drugs and illegal gambling, and occasionally made extra dough as a police snitch. The small-time hustler was all too happy to accompany Owen on his "mission" this brisk spring night, figuring he'd at least get his rocks off with a little excitement. Owen didn't mention to Nico that he'd packed a Glock 19 in the pocket of his Tommy Hilfiger jacket.

It wasn't hard to track Geoffrey Faust down. One call to Pizza Joe's, where Robin had first met him, and the teen who answered gave up an address where Geoffrey usually crashed. Geoffrey turned out to be an easy target.

They found his beat-up Toyota Corolla pulled to the side

of an unused road that led to a forgotten park's overgrown entrance. Beyond the gate was a dirt path that now only saw the footprints of drug dealers and secret lovers. Honeysuckle vines snaked along the walkway to a small clearing where the carcass of a merry-go-round rusted in a rank sea of nimbleweed and quackgrass. The skeleton of a swing set remained, but the swings had long ago dry-rotted away. From the dusky edge of the tree line, Owen and Nico watched as Geoffrey sold a skittish-looking teen a dime bag of weed.

The kid dashed off into the trees as Geoffrey pocketed the ten-spot in his Eckō brand cargo jeans, then headed back toward his car. Stepping out of the shadows onto the moonlit path, Owen and Nico cut him off.

Geoffrey curtly lifted his chin in acknowledgment, playing with the rim of his Von Dutch trucker hat. "'Sup."

"'Sup. You Geoffrey?" Nico asked.

"Who's asking?"

"We wanna score some weed. We heard you could hook us up, man."

Geoffrey looked from Nico to Owen and back again. "Sorry, dude. Just sold my last bag. Besides, your Ken doll buddy here looks like a cop to me."

"I'm not a cop," Owen said evenly.

"Then who the hell are you?"

"Never mind who I am."

"I don't have time for this cloak-and-dagger shit," said Geoffrey. He tried to walk around them on the path, but Owen grabbed his shoulder.

"Get out of my way, motherfucker!" said Geoffrey, shrugging himself loose.

Owen backhanded him across the mouth. Geoffrey reeled, then looked quizzically at Nico.

Nico laughed nervously. "I'd watch my language if I was you, G."

"He's right, *G*," said Owen. "I ought to kill you just for your foul mouth."

Geoffrey laughed and spat on the ground. "With what? Your bare hands?"

"I could." Owen drew his weapon and brandished it in the moonlight. "But I'd rather use this."

Geoffrey took a step back. "Easy, man. You don't want weed. What *do* you want?"

"I have a friend who says you're her baby's daddy. What about it?"

"Naw, man, bitches be crazy. I ain't never got a girl pregnant."

"Robin Goldman begs to differ." Owen leveled the Glock, aiming it at Geoffrey's heart.

"Yo, I swear, I didn't get your girl pregnant!" Geoffrey screamed, throwing his hands up in surrender. "I don't know any Robin, dude."

"Well, that's even worse if you don't remember the girl you raped, Geoffrey."

"Shit, man, I don't know what you're talkin' about. If your girl got herself raped, she probably wanted it. Have you seen these college girls around here? These bitches are beggin' for it."

"That's the only admission of guilt I need," said Owen.

"There's a special corner of hell for scumbags like you. And that's where you're going—*now*."

Owen didn't hesitate. Geoffrey was just a 3D version of the targets he had shot at all his life. A *pop* broke the silence of the still night air, then Geoffrey hit the ground with a soft thud.

Right in the heart. Dead on impact.

"Holy shit, Owen! I thought you were just bluffing." Nico's eyes goggled in horror, his mouth frozen in an O. He was a common criminal, not a murderer, and he'd never seen this much blood before.

"Come on, we gotta get rid of the body," Owen ordered, but Nico couldn't move. His feet were dead weight.

"Nico! Get it together, man!" Nico jolted, snapping out of his trance. "We gotta hide the evidence."

With chilling detachment, Owen picked up Geoffrey's limp arms. "Grab his legs. We'll bury him in the woods where there's not a lot of foot traffic."

Spooked, Nico numbly obeyed. Together they carried the body deeper into the woods until they found a remote spot where the ground was soft and there were plenty of leaves at hand to disguise the grave. Owen had brought shovels; they fetched these, along with rags and flashlights, from his vehicle, then blistered their palms as they dug a hole big enough to drop the body in. But first Nico cleaned out Geoffrey's pockets, taking his car keys and wallet, then unlaced his Timberland boots.

"Dude, his shoes?" Owen scoffed.

"What? They're a hundred bucks a pair! Besides, it's one less piece of evidence to leave behind," Nico reasoned.

"Good idea. Nobody'll be able to ID him, if the body's ever found," Owen remarked. "Which it won't be."

"You sound pretty sure of yourself," said Nico as he rifled through the billfold's contents.

Owen was matter-of-fact. "I'm not worried. Trust me, nobody's going to miss a lowlife like Geoffrey Faust." He kicked the corpse.

"Especially if Geoffrey Faust is alive and well," Nico said.

"What are you talking about?" Owen asked.

"Dude has a clean record, a bank account, employment history . . . how hard would it be to just take his place?"

"You're serious? Why would you want a dead guy's identity?"

"I already got an arrest record and nothing to live for. But Geoffrey's a clean slate. His death could be my second chance, man." Nico traced the edge of Geoffrey's driver's license.

"Look, do what you want to do. But it'll be getting light in a few hours. We've gotta hurry."

Hours of sweat-stained shirts and bloody hands later, they filled in the grave and covered it with a bed of leaves and pine straw. Over this, they arranged small logs and heavy stones in a natural-looking pattern. They used a pine limb, dense with stiff needles, to brush away their footprints. The trail of blood from the execution site to the grave they sprinkled with gravel and dirt.

Together they buried the one secret that would hold Owen captive for life. But Owen was good at hiding things. He swore Nico to secrecy, and the punk readily agreed. He had seen what his trigger-happy friend was capable of.

The sun was just rising as they headed back to the road.

Nico took off in Geoffrey's Corolla. Owen, carrying both shovels, walked to where his car was parked.

And there, standing next to the trunk, was Mackenzie with her arms folded across her chest. Owen halted mid-stride. Her hooded eyes said it all; she'd seen too much.

"Mackenzie—"

"Dammit, Owen, what have you done?"

Chapter 39

Mackenzie

"Hey, honey. You okay?"

Aria was spread out on a full-sized bed separated from mine by a small, cheap nightstand. She glanced up at me, ears plugged with music, then returned to flipping through an old *Vanity Fair* magazine the previous tenant had left behind.

She hadn't spoken to me since yesterday. When I looked at her, I didn't see the little girl who had decorated her hair with yellow dandelions or who clung to my leg when a stranger said hi. In a single week Aria had grown into an adult, with adult problems. I missed my little girl.

With the sunrise I felt dread rise with it. I was a home-maker without a home, a mother without a child, a wife without a husband. I hadn't anticipated the perpetual state of panic I'd be stuck in when I slashed my husband's neck. Little more than twenty-four hours ago it had been a tiny thought that crept in, then it fully formed in my mind. *Take his life like he took yours.*

When I picked up the knife, I hadn't anticipated the but-terfly effect that would ripple out from there. The years of anger, pain, and injustice had taken the wheel; my body was just along for the ride. Now here I was, gazing out the win-dow at the Extended Stay hotel parking lot below, waiting for everything to come crashing down. Eventually the police would show up, slap on the handcuffs, and haul me off to prison. The fear had kept me awake all night, buzzing in my skull.

We hadn't been allowed to return to the house yet as it was still being investigated and analyzed as the crime scene, so Aria and I checked into the only long-term hotel in town, since I wasn't sure when we'd get to go home. Every phone call made me jump, and the patter of feet in the hallway outside our door made my heart skip a beat. It was a waiting game at this point: waiting for Detective Rossi to figure out I was a cold-blooded murderess.

It was shortly after ten o'clock when I recognized the detective's black sedan pull into the parking lot. The temp-tation to run was strong, but I held my ground. He wasn't accompanied by other policemen, so I figured I was safe . . . so far. I imagined when the day came that I was officially under arrest they would arrive with guns drawn and sirens blaring—just like on TV.

"Detective Rossi is here," I said to Aria.

She closed the magazine and popped her earbuds out. "Then I'm going for a walk. Text me when he leaves."

"Be safe, honey," I reminded her ironically. The monster wasn't out there on the streets; it was living with her.

Aria swept past me out the door, leaving me alone with my anxiety. It was better this way; I had wanted to avoid forcing Aria to endure these "interview" sessions, especially without an attorney representing us. I had barely had a day to figure things out, let alone pack some meager belongings and find a place to sleep, as everything was moving so quickly with the investigation. How did anyone throw together a defense team on such short notice? Milk, bread, and a criminal defense team weren't exactly part of our family budget. Anyway, if I had immediately lawyered up, that would only make me look guilty, or at least suspicious.

I hurriedly brushed my hair and splashed water on my face to make myself somewhat presentable, but I didn't have time to hide the dark rings under my eyes or the pimples splotching my temples from stress.

A knock on the door, a detached greeting, a declined offer for a cup of burned coffee. Whoever had stayed here before me had cooked a crisp black residue to the bottom of the carafe, which no amount of scrubbing could clean. After pouring myself a cup—cheap coffee being the only sustenance I'd had in twenty-four hours—Detective Rossi directed me to the cheap round dining room table that accommodated four, if squished knee to knee.

"I'm going to cut to the chase," he began, setting his briefcase on the table. "The preliminary autopsy report came back. I have some news."

I swallowed a mixture of anticipation and fear, waiting for him to continue. He passed a folder to me, opened it up, and pointed to the top piece of paper with the heading *Autopsy Report*.

"According to the medical examiner, your husband didn't die from the stabbing, Mrs. Fischer. He was already dead from lethal cardiac arrhythmia before his throat was cut."

I ran my finger down the long line of medical jargon that I didn't fully understand.

"Wait—what does that mean?" I couldn't make sense of the words. Something about Owen already being dead . . . that couldn't be possible.

"Lethal cardiac arrhythmia is a heart attack. Your husband was already dead from a heart attack before the perp cut his throat."

I looked up at the detective, who chomped on a piece of gum. The man sure loved his spearmint.

"How were they able to determine this?"

He ran his finger under a line of text. "It explains it here, but you may have noticed when you found your husband that there wasn't much blood coming from his neck."

"Honestly, I was in such a panic when I found him, I didn't really notice anything but the big gash."

"Well, he didn't bleed out because he was already dead.

The ME is determining the approximate time and cause of death, but we think it was poisoning or a drug overdose, based on the preliminary toxicology report. As you can see, this leaves us with a lot of questions."

"What kinds of questions?" I didn't want to know, but I needed to be prepared. My hands trembled, so I tucked them under my legs.

"Like who would have poisoned him. And why. And with what. Somehow the postmortem wounds play into all that, which we're looking into. As you can appreciate, when a man is first poisoned and then coincidentally has his throat slit on the same day, well, it arouses a lot of suspicion."

"So you think it's the same person."

"Most likely. And most likely a female. Poisoning is more common among women than men." His eyes assessed me like I was a lab specimen, not a grieving widow. "Maybe they poisoned him, then wanted to make sure the job was finished. Or staged the break-in to hide the poisoning. It's not an uncommon spousal tactic."

And there it was. Sweat trickled down my armpits. I was suspect number one, not that I had expected it to go any other way. It was always the husband . . . or the wife. At least on those lurid *20/20* murder mysteries Owen and I had watched faithfully every Friday night.

"Are you suggesting I murdered my husband? Because I've told you my alibi and it was confirmed."

"I'm not suggesting anything, Mrs. Fischer. Yes, we confirmed your alibi, but poison could have been administered at any point. Depending on what was used, it could have taken effect at any time. The crime scene investigators should be able to piece everything together once they're done working the scene and compiling the facts. We'll be subpoenaing all phone calls and messages, see if anything turns up."

I swallowed the lump in my throat. Owen's last voicemail. Shit.

"Plus we're interviewing witnesses and possible suspects, so we'll get to the bottom of it soon. We'll find your husband's killer, I promise."

I could taste the threat beneath his fake courtesy.

"You have witnesses?" It had been dark out, so early. Who would have seen anything at that hour?

He grinned. I shivered. "You'd be surprised how early some elderly people wake up. And there are lots of elderly people in your neighborhood; they might have seen something useful. You know as well as I do, Mrs. Fischer, that in today's society there's always someone watching. Someone who might have seen who took your husband's car, or if any unfamiliar vehicles were parked on the street. All it takes is one pair of eyes to glance out the window at just the right moment to see what happened."

"So you *do* have witnesses then."

"I'm not at liberty to divulge those details, but let's just say no one is ruled out yet. However, if you cooperate and continue to be open and honest with me, it'll make things a lot easier for you."

He stood up and rapped on the table.

"I do need to warn you, though. We'll be keeping tabs on both you and your daughter, so don't leave town."

"I won't."

As he left, I knew it was time to lawyer up, although I had no idea how to go about finding the right one. After an online search, I discovered we wouldn't qualify for a public defender because we made too much money, yet our savings were meager. How the hell would I find the money to afford decent legal aid? By the time I found a job—I had already started looking weeks ago without telling Owen, but the pickings were slim—and had a paycheck coming in, it'd be too late. And the insurance company wouldn't pay out until the investigation was completed.

But the bigger question was, who had gotten to Owen first? Lily had access to drugs, but they were prescription drugs. Could those even cause a heart attack? I had no idea, but I suppose too much of anything could do lethal damage. Not to mention, Lily had never approved of Owen, found him controlling and abusive. But enough that she would kill him? It didn't ring true.

Robin was the only one I could imagine who would want Owen dead. In fact, the whole family had motive. As a doctor, Grant had access to any number of drugs and I bet Robin was angry enough to kill. Or maybe Ryan wanted vengeance after Owen attacked him. As my mind began to arrange all the pieces in various patterns, the door rattled as someone knocked. I nearly jumped out of my skin.

I opened the door and found Detective Rossi. Again. "Everything okay?"

"Mrs. Fischer, I was just heading to my car when I got a call. I'm going to need you to come down to the station with me."

My heart stopped. I barely got the words out. "What about?"

"We found something that could break the case open. Meet me in the parking lot—and bring your daughter."

I could feel it in my bones that it was over. Somehow I was going to be incriminated for a crime I didn't end up committing after all. *Irony* didn't begin to cover it.

I texted Aria to meet me out front, then headed outside to meet Detective Rossi. He was waiting at his car for me, coolly leaning against the hood, arms folded across his chest, sunglasses hiding his judgmental eyes. When Aria arrived, she had questions that I couldn't answer and the detective refused to.

"We'll discuss it at the station," he answered simply.

"Can I drive myself?" I asked. Something about sitting in the back of a police cruiser seemed awfully fated.

"It's probably best that you both ride with me. Don't worry—I don't mind bringing you back." His finality gave me no choice.

He escorted us to the police station in silence. I held Aria's hand the whole way, and she clutched mine like it was a lifeline. When he asked us to sit down, we weren't offered coffee or soda this time, which told me it was worse than I thought.

The detective held a picture out as he sat down.

"Know what this is?" he asked.

I did, but I didn't want to say. It was Aria's bag of pot. I warned her with a look not to speak.

"No."

"We found it in Aria's drawer. Aria, I'm sure you know what this is, right?"

She shifted rigidly, picking at the chipped red paint on her fingernails. "A friend asked me to hold it for him." *Liar.* The giveaway was all over her face.

"It's foxglove, a poisonous herb that when ingested can cause irregular heart function. Even death. Any idea why your *friend* would ask you to hold on to a poisonous herb?"

"No, sir," she answered. Still peeling tiny red curls of nail polish. Still lying.

So it wasn't marijuana. I couldn't believe what I was hearing. Had my sweet, innocent girl poisoned her father? And who had given it to her?

"Detective, I'm sure this is a misunderstanding." I was shocked. I didn't know what to say, but I needed to say something. "Aria would never hurt her father. It can't be what it looks like."

"We've put a rush on the toxicology report, Mrs. Fischer," he growled, then turned to Aria. "And *you* better have a damn good explanation for why this was in your drawer."

Chapter 40

Robin

I sucked at apologies. It might have been due to a bad combination of my father's pride with my mother's feistiness, but
when it came to saying those two simple words, it was like
pulling teeth to push them past my lips: *I'm sorry*.

Today was the first time it came easily. Friends had a
way of taking a wrecking ball to those walls we fashioned
brick by brick. Especially friends who were hurting more
than you. I thought my mire was deep, until I waded in
hers and sank.

Mackenzie answered the door of her hotel room looking
like death warmed over. Her hair was limp and unwashed,

and a sweatshirt and sweatpants hung on her bony frame. I'd never seen her look so disheveled . . . and skinny. Depression and death—the latest weight-loss fad.

"You finally decided to go dirty blond." Humor had always been our icebreaker, but it landed awkwardly today. She barely cracked a smile. "I'm so sorry, Mac. I'm sorry for everything." I shifted my weight, unsure if I was welcome to hug her. Oh how I wanted to hug her.

"How'd you find me?" she asked curtly.

"Through Lily. I've been trying to reach you. I stopped by the house but there's crime scene tape blocking the entrance. Are you okay?"

"No, I'm not okay, Robin. Nothing's okay."

I heard the pain in her voice. More than anything I wanted to reach across the gaping divide. I stretched out my hand to touch her, but she moved away.

"Can I come in? You need someone looking out for you." She sniffled, then wiped her nose on her sleeve. "No, I don't think that's a good idea. Everyone around me is a suspect in Owen's murder, and I don't want to drag you into this."

"I don't care about being dragged into it, Mac. That's what friends are for—to wade through the muck together. You shouldn't be alone right now."

"I don't know . . ." Her voice wavered. That was enough of a yes for me.

"That's it—I'm not giving you a choice about it. I'll go pick up something to eat. Grant called off work today and is watching Collette for me, so I'm all yours."

I pushed my way past her, entering the modest living

room—bedroom combo. The only thing "living room" about it was a love seat nestled into a corner across from two double beds. The suite stank of body odor and something I couldn't identify. Rotting food, perhaps? Depression? I knew the scent of despair because I had done my share of wallowing in it.

I desperately wanted to clean for her, but I knew she didn't need that right now. What she needed was a shoulder. The cushions on the scratchy plaid love seat hung halfway out, so I pushed them back in with my knee and sat down. I imagined Mackenzie was spending too much time curled up on this sofa and so wondered if a walk outside might be a better idea.

"What are you hungry for?" I asked, pulling out my phone. "I'll find someplace close and we can go together. Get you out of this dank apartment."

"I couldn't eat even if I wanted to. I'm a mess right now . . . and they think Aria might have done it." She joined me on the love seat. Up close her bedraggled state and reek of misery hit home.

"Aria? No way. I don't understand. What does Aria have to do with what happened?"

"They said he had a heart attack . . . and they think it's from either drugs or poison."

"I thought . . . the news said something different." I didn't think Mackenzie wanted to rehash the gory details sensationalized by the local news.

"That his neck was sliced open? Yeah, that apparently happened after he was already dead—from a drug-induced heart attack."

"How would Aria even have access to a drug like that?"

"I don't know, Robin. I don't know. But look, I've been meaning to talk to you about everything with Ryan. Honestly, I can't think or talk about Owen right now. I'm worn slap out. I need to shift gears to something else before I lose my mind."

"Sure, honey. We can talk about whatever you want." I patted her knee reassuringly.

"Thanks," she muttered. "As you know, Owen was the one who filed the charges. I'm going to ask the cops to drop them. I never thought things would get so out of hand over that."

"Hey, let's not think about that right now."

"No, it's important. Owen filed the charges and he's not here anymore, is he? So let's just move on, right?"

I hadn't been sleeping much, which gave me time for thinking instead. Thinking about my marriage, my friends, my choices. As much as I wanted Ryan's life to move on, I knew what it felt like to lose your soul, to grieve over that missing piece of who you are when a man thinks he can steal your body as if it was his own. I had never gotten justice with Geoffrey, but I'd be damned if I'd let Aria become a victim like I was. Even if that meant putting my own son on the stand.

"Mac, I want Aria to make that decision, no one else. I want her to think about it and decide if it's something she should do. She's the one who was wronged here, not any of us. If Ryan did something to hurt her, he needs to take responsibility for it. He needs to make amends for it. I don't know what really happened that night—only those two kids do. So we should let Aria decide. Are you okay with that?"

She watched me with a curiosity I had never seen in her

before. Like she was trying to interpret something beyond my words. "Are you sure you want to put that risk on Ryan?"

"I have two girls, Mac. I would never want Willow or Collette to be forced into silence or not given the chance to speak up. Women have been regarded as collateral damage in the so-called man's world for too long, threatened or shamed into hiding their wounds. It's time for that to change. It's time for us to speak up and protect one another, and the first step toward doing that is to raise honorable men. If my son screws up, he has to fix it. He can't get away with it. I would do anything to protect my girls. The same goes with Aria. You're family, Mac. I only want what's right. I've talked to Ryan and he's okay with it."

Tears trickled from my eyes as I articulated a conviction that had been repressed for too long. I wished I could have rectified my own injustice long ago, but the wound had eventually scarred over. I didn't want to pick at it and make it bleed. Mackenzie's arms wrapped around me, and soon we were crying together so hard I thought my chest would crack open.

"Oh, Robin, I'm so proud to be your friend and so sorry that you had to go through that. But I promise, you'll get your justice. I swear on my life."

"It's okay, Mac. We don't always get it. I just have to mourn that loss and move on. I can't let it devour me, but I can become stronger and raise better men from it. My past has given me a voice to fight for a cause. And it's given me Ryan, so I guess something good can come out of something so evil."

Amidst her pain, Mac managed a wry chuckle. "Why do I feel like I should be singing 'I Will Survive'?"

I laughed too. "Yeah, I guess I need to step down off my soapbox, huh?"

"Maybe, but what you said—you're absolutely right." After a long pause, she added: "Do you think you'll ever feel whole again?"

I knew she was asking the same question of herself, and for her daughter too. I shrugged and picked at a loose thread hanging from the arm of the couch. I couldn't answer that today. Maybe tomorrow, or the day after that.

"One can hope. But it takes time. Give Aria time. Give *yourself* time."

Mackenzie grabbed my hand, holding it to her chest. That's when I saw it—the bruise on her neck.

"What happened there?" I asked, gingerly grazing the mark. It looked like a long blue and yellow finger.

Her palm reflexively covered the bruise.

"Nothing worth mentioning."

"Haven't we gotten past the point of superficial nothings? I'm pouring my heart out to you, Mac. You can trust me."

She glanced away. There was something between the lines she was holding back.

For a long moment I didn't think she would end up telling me, but when she finally turned to me, I saw a fierceness in her eyes that I always knew she had but until now had never tapped into. "Robin," she began, "I've done something horrible . . ."

I didn't speak, and I didn't judge, while she dropped her darkest sin at my feet so that I could help her pick up the pieces.

* * *

By the time I got home, Grant was already cooking dinner and the house was unusually quiet, except for the sizzle of mesquite sauce bubbling on the stove. The scent of barbecue chicken and roasted potatoes wafted across the house, making my mouth water. Wearing oven mitts, he glanced up at me and smiled. For once it felt good to be home.

"Dinner will be ready in a couple of minutes. And Collette's been fed and is playing with Lucas in his room. So far no one's crying or fighting, so I'm guessing they're entertaining themselves okay."

"Wow, look at you, Mr. Mom. Home all day with the kids—is your sanity still intact?"

He erupted in a belly laugh. "I don't know how you do it every day, but I love you for it. You're tougher than I ever gave you credit for, babe."

Even that tiny acknowledgment felt like huge praise. I never expected or sought gratitude for what I did as a mother, as a wife, as a homemaker, but sometimes a person simply needed to be appreciated. Finally Grant understood that.

"Did you hear that Lily is moving away?" I watched for his reaction. Nothing but a surprised raise of his eyebrows.

"Really? Good for her." He seemed unmoved by the news.

Our gazes locked in a shared understanding that with Lily gone, we could distance ourselves from the mistakes. Leave the past in the past.

I grabbed my Burberry bag and brought it to the kitchen. "I have something I need to show you." It was silly, I knew, but it was monumental for me. Everyone had their own vices; now I was facing and defeating mine. It would be hard, probably one of the hardest acts of discipline I'd do in my adult life, but it needed to be done. No one would really understand the power of my impulse unless they had walked in my shoes—my overpriced Gucci impulse-buy shoes. But I was going to rectify it, smother that urge, starting tonight.

I found my wallet, slipped the credit card out, and held it up for Grant to see. Opening the junk drawer, I grabbed a pair of scissors and placed the card between the blades.

"Drumroll, please!"

Grant obliged, making a trilling sound with his tongue and rapping his fingers on the countertop.

With a grand flourish I guillotined the evil plastic and let the halves fall to the floor.

"Ta-da! First step in licking my spending problem accomplished! Next I'm going to start selling some of my stuff online to pay this thing off—on my own. I even found a job I'd love to do that's perfect for me. It's mostly nights, so we won't need childcare for Collette. I'll just need you to help out more in the evenings. What do you think?"

Winding his way around the island counter, he stepped in front of me, held my face with his oven-mitted hands, and kissed me. Kissed me long and deep and lovingly, a passionate *Hello, I'm back* between long-lost lovers.

When at last Grant broke the kiss, he said, "Robin, I think you're amazing and brave, and I'll do anything to support you, to love you, and to fulfill you."

I knew in that moment that we were going to be okay. Better than okay. Already we were changed, better than we'd been for months. It didn't mean it'd be a smooth, easy road, but it meant we were willing to try. Trying was the first step toward succeeding.

As the oven timer beeped, I slipped out of his arms and grabbed my cell phone. Pulling up the number I had saved, I dialed and the receptionist answered after the second ring:

"Hello, this is the Women's Rape Crisis Center. How can I help you?"

I took a breath, flashed Grant a nervous grin, and replied, "Hi, I'm calling about the job posting you have online. I'd like to submit my application . . ."

Chapter 41

Mackenzie

Everything felt so wrong, so twisted, so upside-down. I hadn't expected Aria to become a suspect. I had already decided that if they pinned Owen's death on her, I would take the blame, but I hoped and prayed it didn't come to that. But what if she had done it? The thought curdled in my stomach—my little girl, a killer? Like mother, like daughter . . .

I had spent the afternoon cooped up in four hundred square feet of compact hotel living, searching online for a defense attorney, all requiring retainers I could never afford. How did any average-income family ever afford a criminal defense team? I kicked myself for losing Owen's Lexus, because that would have been the first thing I sold to finance my defense. The excessive car payments alone had already used up half of our monthly budget, and the mortgage took up the other half. Now without Owen's income I was screwed. I needed a solid attorney and cash to pay the bills, and Owen's life insurance was proving worthless. If the cops ruled his death a suicide, there went the money. If the cops ruled Aria or I killed him, there went the money. The only shot I had of survival was a flimsy house of cards that didn't tie me or Aria to Owen's death . . . which seemed unlikely, since I *had* tried to kill him. They'd find out. They always found out.

It was right before Aria got home from school—she had insisted on going, if only for a respite from crying on the sofa all day—shortly after three o'clock when my cell phone rang. I recognized the number immediately and hesitated to answer.

"Hi, Detective Rossi." My voice was shaky. At this point every call brought more bad news, and I dreaded what today's would be.

He was curt. "I need you and Aria to come down to the station. As soon as possible."

At this point we had been there so much it was starting to feel like a second home.

"Can you tell me what you want to speak about?"

"We'll discuss it when you get here." He hung up, and I wondered if that was code for *be prepared to get officially arrested.*

The detective knew exactly what he was doing. Making me sweat, leaving me wondering, hoping one of us would confess so he could get his A-plus gold star for a job well done. I wouldn't make it easier on him. I'd show up prepared for anything.

When Aria walked through the door and dropped her book bag on the table, I patted the unmade bed for her to join me. She pushed aside a heap of rumpled sheets and clothes and sat.

"Aria, the police want us to come back for more questioning, but we need to be prepared for whatever they ask. Do you understand?"

She nodded wordlessly.

"I need to know what that 'pot'"—I air-quoted the word, because now we both knew the truth—"in your drawer was all about. Why did you have foxglove, and what did you use it for?" I didn't want to jump to the conclusion that she had used it to kill her father, but what other conclusion was there? I needed to get ahead of this, and the only way I could do that was if I knew the truth—every awful, heartbreaking piece of it.

"It was for an experiment." Aria picked at her cuticle, avoiding my eyes.

"You expect me to believe that? Where did you get it?"

"Ryan gave it to me." Oh, things sure had a way of coming full circle. "But I swear I didn't use it on Dad."

I would have let her lie her way through it if her life wasn't hanging in the balance.

"Honey, I need you to be honest with me. That's the only way I can save you. They think you killed your dad with it. Did you? Because if you did, I'll say it was me. I'll take the blame. I just need to know the truth." I picked up her hands, cupped them between my own. I needed a connection to her before I lost her.

"No, Mom, I swear! I thought about it—that's why I got

it in the first place, but I couldn't go through with it. I was just so mad at what Dad was doing to you. The bruises. The control. I know he loved you in his own weird way—and he loved me too, I guess—but I saw what he was doing to you. He was destroying you, Mom. I wanted to stop him."

"You saw? Why didn't you say anything to me?"

"I could ask you the same thing. You think I've been oblivious all these years? That I don't see how he hurt you day after day? Besides, what could I say that would change anything? You wouldn't stand up for yourself, and I'm just a kid. I can't stand up for you. That's why I wanted him gone, but I knew you would never do anything about it." She pulled her hands free and shifted away from me to the other side of the bed. "But I didn't end up doing anything about it either. I guess that makes us both cowards."

"No, Aria, we're not cowards. We were never weak. It's just that when you love someone, you hope they'll change. Every morning you think maybe today they'll be better. Maybe today they'll be the person you know they can be. Your father wasn't always the way you remember. He used to be a good man—a little rough around the edges, but he always wanted to protect others. Even if his version of protection was distorted."

I glanced down at my fingernails, chewed and chipped. I remember what changed Owen. How could I ever forget? The night he took a man's life was the night he gave away his own.

"Then one day, long ago, he did something that changed him . . . hardened him. It ate away at him and stole who he was. Controlling me was his way of reining that in, of feeling in charge of his life again. But it doesn't work that way. The more you pull someone closer, the more you push them away."

By the time we reached the station I was utterly exhausted. I collapsed into the metal chair from both mental fatigue and physical malnourishment. I needed to eat something, but my stomach tightened at the thought of food. At least if I ended up in jail I wouldn't be in there long before I starved to death.

My mind hadn't stopped running for three straight days, and I had barely eaten or slept since Saturday afternoon after the fight. I now understood the effectiveness of sleep deprivation interrogation techniques, because I would have said anything just to put my brain at ease and take a long, restful nap.

Detective Rossi sat down across from us, his glare unreadable. I could never tell if he was pissed off or pleased, or something in between. I imagined his face would crack if he smiled.

He slapped his usual folder on the table, and the overhead light blinked and buzzed. "So, we got the toxicology report back along with a new development in the case."

My heart sank like a rock to the ocean floor.

Chapter 42

Mackenzie

Detective Rossi slowly opened the folder like it was a performance. I wasn't ready for the verdict. I needed more time. More time with Aria. More time with my friends. More time for my life. But I had a feeling my time was up.

"It turns out it wasn't foxglove that killed your husband, Mrs. Fischer. It was cocaine."

"Cocaine?"

I actually laughed out loud, because the idea of Owen using cocaine—or any drug for that matter—was truly laughable. He was the most outspoken anti-drug person I had ever met. He'd even done presentations at Aria's elementary school when

351

she was in second grade. She'd been mortified and got teased for two days straight after Owen performed his little skit dressed like a thug offering drugs to the kids.

"That's crazy. Owen would never use drugs in a million years. Not even marijuana. He called it a gateway drug and was convinced people became addicts after one hit."

The detective leaned back in his chair and its joints squeaked. "That's actually why it killed him—he had no tolerance whatsoever. We believe someone sneaked into the house and spiked his whiskey with it—enough to kill a horse. That amount of cocaine to someone with no tolerance can easily cause a heart attack. I'm shocked he didn't taste it going down, but he might have already been two sheets to the wind when he was drugged."

I wasn't sure if it was the shocking news or the lack of sustenance, but everything in the room spun around me like a Tilt-A-Whirl. I leaned over, pressing my forehead to my knees as the nausea swilled and heaved.

"Are you okay, Mom?" Aria's arm draped across my back, her face next to mine. If I'd had anything in my stomach I'd have projectile vomited.

"I'm okay, honey." The lies we tell our children to make them feel safe. "I'm just feeling a little overwhelmed right now. I need to catch my breath." I sat back up, pushing the queasiness back down in my gut. "Do you have any leads on who might have drugged him?"

"We lifted fingerprints from the whiskey bottle as well as from the back door. We think the killer broke into the house while you were out, then spiked Owen's liquor." He fanned several photographs across the table, each one numbered in the corner. One showing sooty fingerprints on the bottle of whiskey Owen usually kept in the liquor cabinet. A picture of the back door where a mess of fingerprints collided. A close-up of the broken windowpane. And various other images from my house.

"And we got a match in the system. A drug addict who's been arrested quite a few times for possession. Do you know someone by the name of Susan Faust?"

Faust.

"Oh my God." I hadn't meant for the recognition to slip out so obviously, but there it was.

"So you do know Susan. Who is she?"

I scrambled for an explanation—one that didn't include Owen's secret sin, the darkest one of all. No matter how much I wanted out of my marriage, I still loved him. I didn't want to tarnish his memory. And it certainly wouldn't look good for me to have been hiding the murder all these years. I wondered if I would go to jail if they found out what I knew. Was I an accomplice? It wasn't a risk I could take.

"I knew a guy named Geoffrey Faust back in college. Well, *knew* is an exaggeration. He was more of an acquaintance. Worked at the local pizza shop. But I don't know a Susan."

"Susan is Geoffrey's mother. Any idea why she would want Owen dead?"

Oh. My. God. I knew exactly why. Time had caught up with Owen. Susan must have figured it out—that her son was dead, that Owen fired the shot that killed him. But how? Only Owen and I knew what he had done . . . and one other person. A friend of Owen's whose name I never got. I remembered seeing a man leave in Geoffrey's car.

Oh what a tangled web we weave when first we practice to deceive. My wise grandmother had often quoted that saying, and how right she was. I was the fly stuck in the web that Owen had spun.

I didn't know how to talk my way out of this other than with sheer ignorance. I had promised Owen long ago that I would bury him with that secret. I didn't want to go back on it now . . . not after everything I'd done. Not unless it was the only way out.

"No, sir, I don't know why she would target my husband."

"One of your neighbors saw a woman fitting her description at your house last Tuesday. Do you recall this?"

The woman I had seen running from my house and who nearly plowed me over—that must have been Susan.

"Yes, I actually do remember that. I had just gotten home when she was leaving. I thought she might have been selling something or maybe had the wrong house."

"So you don't know what your husband and Susan talked about? Because we have her in custody, and she seems to think Owen killed her son. She claims she's been watching Owen for some time . . . waiting to confront him about it. That's why she was there that night."

"Sir, I have no idea what you're talking about. I have no idea about any of this. I wasn't there when they spoke."

Detective Rossi collected the pictures, stuffing them into a messy pile. "Well, if you think of anything, please let me know. We'd like to close this case as quickly as possible so that your family can have closure and move on."

Move on. It sounded unrealistic. I wanted it more than anything—not so much for my sake, but for Aria's. The poor girl deserved some normalcy after the turbulent week she'd had. The drama with Ryan. The loss of her father. Not to mention the years of watching Owen's abuse, silenced by fear. How much more could one girl take? Though if she was anything like me, we had thick skin that calloused easily.

It was time to save my daughter. Owen and I both owed it to her. I had one last ace up my sleeve, a confession that could end this whole investigation, wrapping it with a bloody red bow. Owen's voicemail, which I hadn't gotten around to deleting.

I turned to my daughter. She couldn't hear this. It was just too much. "Aria, could you wait for me in the hallway? I need to talk with the detective privately for a minute."

"Mom, no. We stick together—we always have. I'm not leaving you."

"Aria—" I began, before Detective Rossi cut me off.

"Do you trust your mom, Aria?" She nodded. "Then give us a minute. She'll be okay." The detective pulled out his wallet and handed her a dollar bill. "Grab a snack from the vending machine. We'll be done by the time you get back."

Aria hesitantly accepted the cash, then closed the door behind her.

"Go on, Mrs. Fischer."

"I might have something that will help you. I didn't know what he was talking about when I first heard it, but it's all starting to make sense now." I placed my phone in the center of the table, clicked on the voicemail icon, put it on speaker, and waited. Owen's voice from beyond the grave filled the austere room.

"Hey, Macky-poo." I still hated that nickname. Even dead,

Owen managed to push my buttons. "I know you're upset, but I wish you'd come home. I owe you an apology for earlier. And another apology for lying to you. I figure I should just come clean now so that we can get everything out in the open. Then you can decide if you still want to come home or leave me forever."

His message was interrupted with a sob, and I faintly heard him crying before he found the words again.

"Remember last week when you asked me about that woman leaving the house? She was Geoffrey's mom. She knows about . . . what I did. I guess she had been looking for him—found Nico instead, using his identity. Nico told her everything about that night. I guess the guilt was too much for him. I told her that her son was a sick rapist and that's why I killed him, to protect every other woman from him. But the truth is I'm no better. I treat you like a whore, not the woman I love. I'm so sorry, Mac. I love you, and I promise to change . . . if I get that chance. I don't know if the cops'll be coming for me, probably Nico too, poor bastard, but I'll face it like a man. Hell, I'll face it like *you* would, because you're the bravest person I know. And you've raised Aria the same. Until my last breath I'll try to be a better man for you. I'd die for you."

Poor Owen. He had no idea how prescient that vow would prove to be.

Chapter 43

Aria

It had been six days since Aria lost her father, her home, and her identity. She had never been the daughter of a typically dysfunctional family like she thought she was. All along she had been the offspring of a cold-blooded killer.

The house had finally been cleared by the crime scene unit for them to move back in, so at least things were given the appearance of normalcy again. But it wasn't home anymore, because home is where the heart is, and there was no heartbeat in this loveless structure.

Aria lay on her own bed in her own bedroom, as her mother washed dishes downstairs and her friends texted her to see how she was "hanging in there." It only took six days for the surviving Fischers' world to move on like nothing had happened.

Dinner conversation had been stiff tonight as they picked at their chicken teriyaki. Her mom mentioned selling the house, if anyone would buy a murder house, and chatted about getting a job, creating a career for herself. Aria knew the truth—her mother had tasted freedom for the first time and it was delicious.

Sprawled out on her bedspread, she kept a book propped open with her elbows as the story took her captive. Anything was better than being in the present, two doors down the hallway from where her father's dead body had been found.

A tap on her window startled her, then another tap. The press had hounded her and her mom for days, yelling questions at them from the curb while video cameras recorded their every move. But by now the media had all trickled away, their bloodhound sense sniffing for a new lead in someone's devastation.

Stepping over piles of clothes and shoes on the floor, she made her way to the windowpane, raised the blinds, and glanced out. She pushed open the window with a grunt, though the screen stopped her from leaning out.

"Ryan?" she called into the darkness. It was the first time she had seen him since *that night*. The porch light barely illuminated his face enough to identify him, but the Iron Man sweatshirt gave him away. "Do you want me to come down?"

He stepped directly below her window, close enough that

he didn't need to yell up to her. "No, this'll be quick. My mom told me you guys dropped the charges."

"Yeah, well, I didn't think it was right to ruin your life over one night. We were both drinking, so . . . My dad was the one who had filed them actually, not me."

He averted his gaze, staring at something far away down the street, then back up at her. "Look, I think you should go through with it."

"What? Are you kidding?"

"No, this isn't reverse psychology or anything. I just wanted to tell you I'm sorry. I know maybe this isn't a good time after all you've been through this week, but I wanted you to know I never meant to hurt you. I . . . I've always loved you, Aria, and I want you to do what you feel is right."

"It doesn't feel right putting you in jail, Ry."

He didn't speak for a moment, and seeing his face glistening in the light, she realized he was crying. "I was wrong. I probably did take advantage of you, and I should take responsibility for that. My mom's been lecturing me about how men exploit and abuse women. I resisted at first, because I didn't want to think I had done that to you, but she's right. Don't let me off the hook just because you're afraid. I won't resent you for it, I swear. I love you, Aria, and I know you'll do what's right for you."

Aria opened her mouth to protest, but he was gone. He slipped back into the shadows and drifted off down the darkened street. Aria considered his words, his maturity, his willingness to change a world where women were victimized, where her own mother had been emotionally and physically abused, and where Aria had lost her voice in the babel of judgment and shame and fear. The time was ripe to remind the world that women deserved more, that women should never be silenced.

And the time for men to get away with stealing women's souls was over.

Chapter 44

Mackenzie

My hands trembled as I held the letter postmarked from the Allegheny County Jail. It was from Susan Faust, the woman who had murdered my husband—at least before I had attempted to. We had that in common, I guess.

I opened the envelope and unfolded the white college-ruled paper covered in hasty scribble:

Dear Mackenzie Fischer,

I can't say I'm sorry for what I did, because that would be a lie. We both lost people we loved, but when you think about it, we all got what we deserved. Your husband was a killer, my son was a rapist, I was a thief and an addict and a negligent mother. Karma's a bitch, huh?

The only victim here is you. And for that, I'm sorry. I'm sorry to have made you a widow and made your daughter fatherless. But it was never Owen's call to play judge, jury, and executioner with my son. And it wasn't my call to do the same with Owen. But we did what we did because at the time we thought it was righting a wrong of some sort, even through the act of committing wrongs ourselves.

I always thought I was a victim too. Addict boyfriend who pulled me down. Never able to get clean or on my feet. Always lingering on the outside of my own life, unable to step in fully. But don't be a victim. Be a victor. I took from you when I shouldn't have. But as the trial will be coming up, and I know I'm going to have to look into your and your daughter's faces, see the pain in your eyes, I want you to know why I did what I did. They'll spin things the way they want them spun, but I want you to hear my truth.

You might think you know what motivated me. Avenge my son and all that. But it wasn't just about vengeance. Your husband took a life, just like my son took a woman's soul. They can't hide who they truly are—the worst kind of thieves. When I got sober almost a year ago, the first thing I did was go looking for my son. I hadn't seen or spoken with him in over twenty years. Why? Because all I cared about was my high. My son stole that from me every time he'd flush my drugs down the drain, so I threw him out. Mom of the Year, right?

I looked for him because I wanted to show him I

changed, that I was back for good—clean and sober. Word got around that I was searching for my son. I found him—well, a stranger living in his shoes. He told me my son was dead, and that if I kept our conversation a secret, he'd point me to the man who took my son's life.

That led me to Owen. And it led me to you.

When I first confronted your husband that night you saw me, he told me to leave, told me my baby was a rapist piece of garbage. To find out that the son you bore became the thing you hate, well, it hurt. Bad. And to find out someone else took away my only chance at redemption, well, you obviously now know how I felt about it.

I came back full of vengeance that night you left. If I'd known your daughter was still home I probably wouldn't have done it. But I thought Owen was home alone. Even more convenient that he had been drinking, left the open bottle of whiskey on the kitchen counter. So I broke in—I've become adept at it over the years—gave him enough cocaine to kill him, and left feeling avenged.

Now all I feel is emptiness.

May my son and your husband rest in peace. It's the only thing I can hope for such damaged individuals who obviously suffered in their lifetime to become the monsters they did—a monster I've now hosted. Maybe that monster lives in you too. Kill it while you still can.

Susan Faust

DOC 9852435

I folded the letter back up and slipped it into the envelope. I wasn't sure what to make of it, whether I was even legally allowed to write back with the trial coming up. But I figured from one mother to another, from one hurting heart to another, I would reach out after the trial. Maybe write her a letter, visit her in person, show her what forgiveness looks like. I'd let the idea marinate and see where it took me when the time was right.

In the meantime, the question of my culpability continued to haunt me. Shortly after Susan Faust was implicated in Owen's death, I had Googled *can you murder someone who is already dead?* The search led me to numerous references to "impossible crime," a legal term I'd never heard of, defined in legalese a layperson like me couldn't decipher: It shall not be a defense . . . something about misapprehension of the circumstances . . . yada yada . . . impossible for the accused to commit the crime attempted.

What the heck did I read? With further digging, I stumbled across an article on one site that gave an account chillingly similar to my personal circumstances:

After making sure he's in a deep sleep, a woman stabs her husband multiple times to ensure he is dead. But unbeknownst to the wife, her husband suffered a massive heart attack after going to bed before she stabbed him, and thus he was already dead. Therefore, it is impossible for the wife to have killed her husband. However, the wife could still be charged with attempted murder, because she acted upon the presumption he was alive. There was an attempt to commit murder. The impossibility of "killing" a dead person would be indefensible in court.

So there it was, in black and white. I tried to rationalize the situation. Most people, knowing all the circumstances, would agree Owen "deserved" to die, for being an emotionally and sexually abusive husband, and for murdering Geoffrey Faust. Yes, Susan Faust and I each had very good reasons for killing Owen. Susan had just beaten me to it, and now she was looking at life in prison. And I had gotten off scot-free.

Was I a horrible person for letting Susan Faust take the rap? Should I turn myself in? If I did, what earthly good would it do anybody? It would destroy Aria's life. The kid had suffered enough. And so had I.

The more I thought about it, the harder it was to wrap my mind around it. I knew if I didn't get help, I'd go out of my mind.

I came from a long line of Southern Baptists. Growing up, the church had been an important part of my life, and I had often relied on my faith to sustain me in times of trouble. Over the years I had backslid, as Mamma and Daddy would say. I couldn't remember the last time I had attended church. In his arrogance Owen had denounced religion in general—and Southern Baptists in particular—as a crutch for the stupid and the weak.

Maybe I was weak, but weren't we all at one point or another?

I found the Bible my parents had given me following my baptism when I was ten years old, tucked away in a box of childhood mementos, dusty and forgotten. Settling into a comfortable chair, I said a prayer to God, and started reading at the beginning.

* * *

Aria's footsteps descended the stairwell, and I glanced over at her. So much had happened in the last three weeks that I wasn't sure how she was even still standing. Everything with Ryan, her father's death, and then the big decision on what to do about Ryan. In the end she chose not to press charges, although I'll never understand why. Part of me wanted her to take up the fight, but she admitted that she loved Ryan and part of her had wanted that night to happen. In the end, it was a big enough part to accept what they did together.

My first thought turned to Owen—what he had done to me for years, which I endured simply because I loved him with a damnable loyalty. It was a stupid emotional form of logic, freedom to keep hurting me because his love was bigger than the bruises. He saw past my disfigured face and still wanted me, and back then that was enough. What a fool I was.

We're trained from an early age to value beauty. *What a handsome little boy*, we say. Or *What a pretty little princess*. So we grow up believing that if we're not beautiful enough, we won't be loved. Then someone comes along and loves you anyway, and you make him God over you. Even when he is in fact the devil.

Over time, abuse eats away at logic and love, and all that remains is an empty bitterness. I didn't want that for Aria, but if I had learned anything, it was that one should never take away or take on the voice of others. It was Aria's right to decide what she wanted to do, and for her it was easier to move on this way. Her experience was hers; mine was mine. I'd support whatever she decided, because she had earned that choice. My young daughter had more courage than I ever had, and I'd watched it blossom over the past two weeks along with the crab apple tree out front. In a single spring my daughter had grown up.

At my feet Lily's cat Stormy wound around my legs, meowing for attention. Lily rarely cried, but parting with her beloved kitty had brought on the tears. I vowed to give him the love he deserved and told her to visit him anytime. By him I meant *me*. God, I would miss her.

"Want some coffee, honey?"

Aria had decided she was adult enough to start drinking coffee, and lately we'd bonded over the variety of creamer choices. Her favorite was peppermint mocha; mine was coconut cream.

"I'll give you the rest of the creamer," I said with a lilt of temptation as I shook the near-empty creamer bottle.

She held something out to me—a folded card. There it was, plain as the blue words against a white backdrop:

To the beautiful Aria Fischer,
Will you be my date to prom?
Yours truly, Ryan

"He's asked you to his prom?" The question came out more as an excited yelp. Aria jumped back. I wasn't sure if I should laugh or cry. "What are you thinking?"

"I'd really like to go with him." She searched my face for a reaction. "Are you angry?"

"Angry? Of course not, honey. If you care about him and he cares about you, why not go? Just no drinking this time."

"Mom!" Aria chided. "I'm a little scared, to be honest. I'll be the only sophomore there. What if he leaves me to hang out with his friends?"

I pulled her into my arms, hugging her tightly and planting kisses on her head. Any other parent might have told her what to do, but I learned that character was built one choice at a time.

"You can't control other people's actions, but you can control your reaction. Decide to have fun no matter what. And I do know one thing—only an idiot would leave a girl as beautiful as you alone at prom."

Aria pulled away just enough to look up at me and smiled. "I never really thanked you, Mom."

"For what?"

"For giving me my voice back."

I shook my head. "No, Aria, you've always had your voice. You're just now learning how to use it. And so am I."

I had learned a lot in the past few days. For a long time I had lived in the company of demons—demons of my own making. Owen's death wasn't the answer. The answer had always been buried under the lies I sold myself—that I wasn't good enough, pretty enough . . . or enough. Embracing who I was and who I wanted to be, that was the answer. Loving myself enough to fight for myself. I wish I would have learned it sooner, but it wasn't too late. It was never too late.

Robin and Lily had always seen my worth; if only I would have too, maybe Owen would still be alive. Maybe, maybe, maybe. I didn't live in a world of maybes, but I did live in a world of endless possibilities that started with today.

Epilogue

One year later

BODY OF ACCUSED RAPIST FOUND
May 12
Beaver County, Pennsylvania

The body of Geoffrey Faust, the suspect in a string of college rapes in the early 2000s, was found in an abandoned park in Beaver Falls on Monday morning when police acted on a tip about the location of the body. In the murder conviction of Susan Faust in July last year, mother of the deceased, details were made public regarding the disappearance of her son. While no evidence had surfaced regarding Mr. Faust's whereabouts, Susan Faust

369

alleged that Owen Fischer, 42, had been responsible for her son's murder.

After murdering Mr. Fischer with a cocaine over-dose last May, Mrs. Faust was found guilty and sentenced to life in prison. At that time, Mr. Faust's disappearance was still under investigation.

The Beaver Falls Police Department recovered Mr. Faust's remains in a wooded area. The body was identified using dental records. The cause of death was a single gunshot wound to the chest.

As a result of publicity surrounding Mrs. Faust's trial, three women have come forward with rape allegations against her late son, who recognized him from photographs.

There was more in the *Beaver County Times* article Robin read online on the sofa in her downsized living room in a house half the size but full of twice the love, yet she stopped reading. This was Robin's past, her ghost visiting her. No one felt his presence but her and the other girls he haunted. She had gotten the job at the Rape Crisis Center and fielded a call from one of Geoffrey Faust's victims herself, encouraging her to go to the police. Twenty years ago women had been ashamed to report their assaults for the usual reasons: self-blame, fear of being stigmatized, dread of having to testify in open court, reluctance to ruin the lives of their assailants, and so many other self-defeating reasons. But a new age was dawning. More women were realizing that in a rape, the only victim was the woman, never the man. Helping these women felt good. Damn good. Robin had found her mission in life.

Grant swept into the living room carrying the mail, then dropped an envelope on Robin's lap.

"Something came for you," he said.

She immediately recognized the significance of the thick white baronial envelope. She slit it open with her finger, and pulled out a lovely card framed in wildflowers.

Liliana Maria Santoro and Luca Fontana joyfully invite you to celebrate their wedding . . .

Jumping up from the sofa, she darted across the living room to the kitchen where her phone was charging. Ripping out the charger, she speed-dialed Mackenzie.

"Let me guess," Mackenzie said before Robin had a chance to speak. "You got Lily's wedding invitation too?"

Robin huffed. "When did you get yours?"

"Yesterday. Lily told me she was going to invite you. Are you going to go?"

"To my best friend's wedding? Of course. It's been over a year since I've seen her and I still love the bitch." She chuckled. "So yeah, I'll be there."

A wet cooing sound paused the conversation as the line rustled. "Sorry," Mac said. "Raina's trying to eat the phone."

"And I bet you're loving every slobbery minute of it, aren't you?"

Mackenzie laughed. "What can I say? Fostering suits me. Raina's even inspired me to write another children's book. Because the first one sold so well, my publisher wants to release a whole series."

"That's great, Mac! You always were the creative one

among us. I'm glad everything is working out with your writing—and with the baby. Getting any sleep?"

"Nah, but sleeping's overrated. Will you be up for a visit this week?" Mackenzie asked. "Have ourselves a playdate?"

"Sounds great. Collette needs a distraction from the teething," Robin grumbled. "I didn't expect to be dealing with this in my forties, but at least now I have you to go through it with me."

"Well, don't get too down on yourself. I was thinking about you and me hitting Los Angeles and throwing Lily a proper bachelorette party."

Robin chuckled. "You, me, and Lily going wild in the City of Angels? What could possibly go wrong?"

Oh, if only they knew . . .

Acknowledgments

Being a writer is like being a mother. You funnel all of your passion and energy into this beautiful little thing you created, then one day you let it go off into the world and you just pray it thrives without your constant hovering. Except if your books were your babies, they'd starve to death, because your real-life kids don't give you a moment alone to write. Thus is the life of a writing mother.

Much like being a mother, I can't take all the credit. This book is about friendship—and friends are the roots of life. They keep us grounded, and I am lucky enough to have several of them to help me stay motivated when I wonder if I should put writing on pause until my kids are older. Emily Sutton, your voracious love of books—*my* books—inspired me from the very beginning when you read draft after draft, reminding me of my strengths and lifting me up from the mire of exhaustion. I'll always thank Gwen

Stefani for bringing us together all those years ago in high school. And every writer needs a sidekick to tell complete strangers about your books, because we writers are too shy to do it ourselves. Jessica Young, that's you—the perfect sidekick who makes me feel like a celebrity. Love and Learn Daycare should put our faces on its brochure.

The real dream-maker is my editor extraordinaire, Katie Loughnane. She saw my gift, my potential, and turned it into a career. Thank you for taking a chance on me, Katie, and for embracing my words. With every step, the fabulous editors at HarperCollins (Bethany, Tessa—sending you love and gratitude!) guided my characters and my story into something I'm proud of. May your red pens never grow weary. My editor at Proofed to Perfection Editing Services, Kevin, always gets first look at my work, so thank you for your witty comments and extensive edits that perfected my craft. You are God's gift to editors.

There are many behind-the-scenes staff at HarperCollins who carry the heavy load of design and publicity, and while I don't know your faces, I know your handiwork and you're each amazing. Thank you for creating art and beauty in this world—even when that beauty is a "murder book."

My family and friends are of course always at the top of the thank-you list as you support my writing, buy my books, spread social media love, and do so much more. Then there are the four that made me the Mental Mommy I tap into when creating characters—my beautiful kids. Talia, Kainen, Kiara, and Ariana, your enthusiasm for Mommy's writing fills me up when I'm empty. Your insights on moms going crazy always give me a laugh, and I promise to pay for your therapy bills someday. Craig, the man who gives me writing retreats and forces me to take breaks so I don't burn out, you're the hero who rescued me. Thank you for reading each of my books when I know you'd rather read Stephen King, and for telling me I'm one of the greats and meaning it. Your faith in me is as endless as my love for you. Thank you for being the kind of husband I don't want to murder (most of the time).

How could I conclude without acknowledging my fans—*you*, dear reader? Thank you for buying this book, for reading my words, for reviewing it online, for loving books as much as I love writing them, for celebrating imagination and thrills that authors work so hard to create. Although my stories may be dark, my heart is happy because of you. I hope I always deliver the twists and drama you're looking for.

Pamela Crane is a *USA Today* bestselling author of almost a dozen novels. She loves writing about flawed and fascinating heroines. When she's not cleaning horse stalls or changing diapers, she's psychoanalyzing others.

Sign up for her newsletter at pamelacrane.com where you can find free books, fun giveaways, and sneak peeks at her future releases.